Last Orders, Please!

McGuffin

IRISH RESISTANCE BOOKS

First published in November 2000 by
Irish Resistance Books
4 Craft Village
Derry, BT48 6AR
Tel./ Fax: (028) 71 262 879
irb@mcguffin.freeserve.co.uk

© McGuffin/ IRB
All rights reserved

Front Cover: Turf Lodge, Belfast 1981
Photograph by Jürgen Schneider

ISBN 0-9539482-0-X

Printed in the Republic of Ireland by ColourBooks, Dublin

All rights reserved. No part of this publication may be reproduced or transmitted in any form or by any means digital, electronic or mechanical, including photocopy, recording, or any information storage or retrieval system, without permission in writing from the publisher. The book is sold subject to the condition that it shall not, by way of trade or otherwise, be lent, re-sold or otherwise circulated without the publisher's prior consent in any form of binding or cover other than that in which it is published and without a similar condition including this condition being imposed on the subsequent purchaser.

Contents

Introduction	7
Revenge For Skibbereen	9
The Pedagogue	15
Last Orders, Please!	27
Judas' Carry-Out	33
The Stag Night	41
Spiderman v. The Big Doc	47
May The Farce Be With You	55
Stevie	69
Blues For Allah	73
I Danced With The Man Who Danced With Chuck Berry	79
Norman I	85
Who The Fuck Is Demis Roussos?	91
Paxo	105
Hi-Jack In The Hong Kong Horror Hotel	115
But He Never Coveted His Neighbour's Ox	127
The Badger	133
Hoover aka JEHoova	139
His Way	145
The Depth Charge Man	151
The Baten Docket	157
The Pilgrimage	165
The Grapes Of Wrath	173
The Man Who Shot D.I. Swanzey	182
Norman II	185
Glossary	195

"He Who Laughs Last Has Not Been Told The Terrible Truth"

INTRODUCTION

These tasteless tales were written between 1975 and 2000. Some of them have been published in several German editions, principally *'Der Mann, der mit Chuck Berry getanzt hat'* (Edition Nautilus, Hamburg, 1993). Others have been published thanks to John McNally in a greatly abridged English language edition (*'Tales From The Barricades'*, McNally&Loftin, Santa Barbara, California 1990).

The author, as usual, takes no responsibility for all allegations, rumours, and malevolent scéal. In some cases names have been changed to protect the guilty; in some cases not. For the horrible truth is that these stories, with only two exceptions, are true. This reflects very badly on humanity and indeed, the author, but surely only the truth shall set us free.

The author wishes to thank the production staff of Christiane Kühn and Adrian Kerr. Thanks are also due to Joe McAllister, Jürgen Schneider, Brian Artur Grimshaw and especially to Jack McKinney.

As always, thanks to Cormac for his splendid artwork. Thanks also to Latuff and McLachlan.

In memory of:

Sean McDermott, Mickey Hughes,
Robin Dunwoody and Jackie Crawford

Dedicated to Christiane

Revenge For Skibbereen

Brian Artur Grimshaw sat up in his hospital bed and fixed me with a reproachful eye. Although I was engaged in a work of corporeal mercy, viz. visiting the sick, in Grimshaw's eyes that didn't cut the mustard. I'd neglected to smuggle in a bottle of Bushmills. Propped up on his pillows, his head swathed in bandages, the big man sulked. I tried to propitiate him as I absent-mindedly ate his grapes.

"Hilda been by today?"

He brightened immediately. "No, thanks be to Christ." He was a religious man at heart, was Brian Artur, his father having been a priest, or so local legend had it.

"There were these two Orangemen," he said. I sighed. Although my respected sage and mentor had a great mind, his jokes were usually lousy. Ignoring my wince Grimshaw continued. "And they were lost in the Sahara. Miles from anywhere and the heat is murderous, and they can't stand any longer and they're dying of thirst and crawling across the sand and Sammy looks up and he turns to Billy and he says, 'Billy, d'ye know what day it is?' And Billy summons up his last bit of saliva and turns his head and says, 'No, Sammy, what day is it?' And Sammy gives him a withering stare and says, 'Shame on you, Billy, don't you know it's the Twelfth of July?' and Sammy looks up at the sun beating out of the Himmel and he says, 'Well, at least the lads got a good day for it this year.'"

I groaned. "What brought this on?" I asked, "Apart from it being that time of the year." Brian Artur smiled. "You never did meet the Uncle did you? ..."

The Uncle, it transpired, was a Sarnie man. Amongst other things, of course. This was in 1935, you understand, long before the Welfare State and the unemployment money that saved many a Paddy from leaving home in search of exploration and exploitation.

Anyway, Brian's Uncle Tony was, apart from anything else, and, it must be said, he'd do anything else if there were a few shillings to be made, primarily a Sarnie man. There are not too many of them about these days in the old Emerald Isle.

Oh sure, there's mobile fish and chip vans, serving recycled grease and what the locals tastefully refer to as 'guanoburgers', and Mr. Whippys and Mr. Softies with their jingling chimes and their synthetic ice cream. There's licensed bandits with their Big Macs and their Wimpeyburgers, both equally soggy and plastic. But it was all different back in the hungry thirties. Then if you were out for a 'dander' or a stroll and felt peckish you had to rely on the man who sold chocolate and 'Yankee apples' or on Sarnie men like Uncle Tony or his mate Luigi: the men who pushed the handcarts around selling sandwiches, for that's all 'Sarnies' are.

The Uncle came from the Markets, a Catholic ghetto in South Belfast. Every weekend he and his lifelong friend Luigi would go into the wholesalers and buy a load of bread, processed meat, cheese and assorted salad, take the lot home, make up sandwiches and sell them from their barrow to whichever sporting, religious or political crowd they could find. If all else failed, they could always hawk the stuff to the cinema queues. They had been doing it for years. As they used to say, "No sweat." Sectarianism, the bane of the North of Ireland, was at a low ebb then, no thanks to the craw-thumping 'men of God', and one of the high spots on their calendar was the 'Twalf', the 12th of July when, every year, the Loyal Orange Protestant defenders, up to 100,000 of them, would march, sweating in their three-piece suits and their bowler hats, eight miles out of town to the field at Finaghy where they could spend their time cursing the Pope and damning all Teagues to the fiery furnace.

Tony and Luigi were true Catholics of course, but business was business, and when the Orangemen arrived at the field and took off their shoes to ease their bunions in preparation to listening to the usual sectarian ranting they were tired, hungry and easy meat for the Sarnie men.

1935 was different however. The Outdoor Relief riots of the previous year, when unemployed Catholics and Protestants had joined together for the first time in eons to demand more money for the unemployed and an end to the Dickensian Workhouse system had terrified the landed Protestant gentry, and they had resorted to the usual tactic of 'beating the Orange Drum', as Winston Churchill put it. The inevitable result had been sectarian rioting and five people dead.

Consequently, two days before the Twelfth, the Uncle and Luigi were not too surprised to get a knock on their door at ten o'clock, just after the bars got out. It was a couple of local Orange heavies from nearby Donegal Pass. "Tony Kelly?" "Yeah?" "You thinking of doing the field again this year?" "Yeah." (The Uncle was a man of few words, most of them unprintable, apparently.) "No chance, Sunshine; no Teagues allowed."

The Uncle protested, using some of his limited but interesting vocabulary, but deep down, he knew it was 'no go'. He did his best to haggle, but, in the end, as the thugs knew, he had to settle for the best terms he could get. He and Luigi would make up the sarnies as usual, the Orange heroes would come round and collect them and the handcart on the 11th night, sell the food at the field, return the handcart and give a derisory amount of money, if they felt so inclined, to the Uncle for his trouble. It was Hobson's choice. So what's new? As they say in Belfast, "What do you expect from a pig but a grunt?"

But it rankled. It may have been a fact of life, but it was a galling one nonetheless. When a man has very little but his pride, it may become very important to him. The next morning the Uncle was round at Luigi's house early. "Ya coming for a gargle." It wasn't a question. Together they walked down Cromac Street, their boots clattering on the paving stones. Although it was only 8 a.m. there were many familiar faces at the street corners: men with the look of unemployment etched deeply into them. Those lucky enough to have a job had been at work for an hour already; those without had nothing else to do but mooch around, looking for something to fall off the back of a lorry.

Tony and Luigi started on the 'circuit'. Although the pubs didn't officially open until 10 a.m., there were still plenty of 'shebeens', illicit drinking dens where men with a few pennies could go to slake their thirst and brood upon the injustices of life. They were not quick drinkers. Nor were they the kind of happy drinkers that you find at parties, marriages or funerals. They were what is termed in Belfast 'serious drinkers', in both senses of the word. They didn't talk much as they sipped their pints of black porter, but then, they didn't have to. They were both brooding upon the injustice that had been done to them, and, by extension, to all who adhered to 'the faith of our fathers'.

By 5 p.m., three shebeens and five pubs later, they were 'well oiled'. This, despite appearances, is a fairly precise phrase. It indicates that although they had passed the stage when they could be said to 'have had a few', they were not as yet 'stocious', 'steaming' or falling down drunk. By now they were in Madden's notorious bar in Smithfield

Market. Outside the traders went about their daily task of selling second hand junk; inside the serious drinkers and thinkers sat in the gloom. It was Luigi who spoke first.

"Revenge," he said. "Revenge for Skibbereen." Luigi had, of course, never been in Skibbereen, a deserted village in the deep southwest of Ireland, in his life. Few had. The village had been deserted since the famine in 1845 which had killed off the occupants or forced the lucky few survivors to take the coffin ship to America. But Luigi knew the mournful ballad of the same name by heart. All 47 verses of it. It was his party piece at both marriages and wakes. For Luigi, although his family had forsaken the blue skies of Naples for the grey mists of industrial Belfast to open an ice cream parlor when he was eight years old, was at heart an Irish patriot. A bar room Republican.

Sometimes he was almost able to convince the more credulous or drunken amongst his bar room companions that Wolfe Tone, the father of Irish Republicans, had been an Italian like himself. 'Wolfie Toni', he used to say, and like all converts Luigi studied 'his country's history and the sacrifices made' and had to try harder.

"What the – expletive deleted – has Skibbereen to do with it?" asked the Uncle. "It's them bloody bigots turning us out of the field on the one day when we can make enough money to take the wife and weans to the seaside for a holiday that I'm thinking about." "I know," said Luigi, "but it's symbolical." The Uncle snorted. Luigi was his best friend, but give some of these eejits a bit of education and next minute they'd be spouting these big words at you. That was the trouble these days. Too much bloody education.

"All right," said the Uncle, glancing at the pub clock. "Time we got these sarnies together. Have you any money left?" Luigi nodded, unhappily. "Look, Tony, why don't we give it a miss this year. Let the Orangies whistle for the sarnies. These things flare up and die down. We'll be back working the field next year, you know that."

The Uncle snorted. "Bloody typical!" These pint patriots would chicken out when it came to striking a blow for Irish freedom at the first sight of a collector for the Republican prisoners welfare fund. For, when Luigi had excused himself and gone to tap some money from an acquaintance, a great idea had come to the uncle. He had been staring out of the fly-blown window across the street at the pet shop.

The Uncle started tunelessly whistling 'Four Green Fields' to himself. Then he rose. "Come on, Luigi, me old segocia, there's work to be done. Kathleen ni Houlihan has need of the sons of Ireland tonight." Luigi stared at him bewildered. Had the old fool taken leave of his senses or had he just a drop too much taken? But he knew better than to argue. Shaking his head he followed the Uncle out the door and across the street.

The Aunt was away looking after a sick sister in the country that night, which was just as well, for I doubt that she would have been her usual tolerant self had she seen the pair of them that night fumbling for the latch key. The Uncle had a sack slung over his back, which twitched and jerked spasmodically in the moonlight, while Luigi was laden down with loaves which he had scrounged from the night shift at the local bakery, after much haggling.

Once inside the tiny back parlor the Uncle dumped the sack on the floor. The monkeys inside yelped. "Start buttering the bread, Luigi, ould hand, and have you got a shilling for the meter," was all he said.

Nowadays I suppose you'd have a squad from the Royal Society for the Prevention of Cruelty to Animals battering down the door before you could even take a poker to a wriggling wee ape and toss it into the oven, and I suppose that's a good thing, but in those days folks weren't so squeamish. All the same, the dawn it was breaking o'er Belfast before the Uncle straightened up, opened the window to try and take away some of the smell and awoke Luigi. He was asleep, slumped over the table with a huge pile of tastefully buttered monkey sarnies in front of him.

Grunting with satisfaction, the Uncle loaded up the handcart which stood, as always, in front of the fire, which by now burnt low. "Monkey sarnies," he muttered to himself. "Good enough for them!"

All went according to plan. He dumped the skins out on the rubbish tip out back, managed two hours sleep and was up when the Orangemen from the Pass arrived, grinning broadly, at 8 a.m. "All right, Paddy," the first one said, handing over half of what he had promised, and taking the handcart. "What sort of sarnies did you do?" "Meat ones," mumbled the Uncle, while Luigi snored on. "We'll leave the ould cart back tonight, if you're lucky," jeered the second heavy. "Pleasure to do business with you." "Yeah," replied the Uncle.

The 'Twalf' that year was a scorcher. The sun beat down on the big parade as they lashed their Lambeg drums and themselves into a frenzy of righteousness. The loyal little old ladies in their Union Jack dresses twirled and danced and showed their wrinkled stockings. The grizzled war veterans, the survivors of the Somme and Mons, marched, ramrod stiff, and the small children waved their flags and ran in and out of the parade. His Majesty, off decimating grouse (or is it grice?)

on his estates in Scotland would doubtless have been proud of them, as they trudged up the Lisburn Road to the Field, there to reaffirm their sacred pledge to keep the 'croppies' in their place.

The Uncle and Luigi were not, of course, at the field that year. They got a 'lie in'. But they were, about 5 p.m., in Shaftesbury Square to watch the marchers as they returned, spiritually refueled for yet another year. The sun had obviously taken its toll. So too had the drink, but the Uncle swears to this very day that that year there was a certain definable pallor about many of the sons of William of Orange. As one veteran stopped, removed his bowler hat and threw up in the gutter, Luigi turned to the Uncle, his eyes sparkling.

"Revenge!" he said. "Revenge for Skibbereen!"

The Pedagogue

Being a sad episode in the brief teaching career of Brian Artur Grimshaw, BA. (Failed)

The third time that he stumbled, the notion flickered across Brian Artur's mind that he might be pissed out of his gourd. The class took it very well. The Pox did not

It had been an exhausting morning. Accompanied with dogged determination by a hangover which would have corroded aluminium, a legacy of the previous night's farewell party for Eamonn McCann who had just been rusticated from the hallowed halls of academe for dissipation, he had stumbled into school prayers at 9 a.m. An unwashed sea of boredom greeted him.

"Ohgodhelpustofollowthypreceptsinourdailyroundthecommontask amenhymn99allthingsbrightandbeautiful – dismiss ..."

9.10 – 2D The medieval monastery – expurgated of all references to sex, sin, sodomy and simony – why bother? 2D could teach those decrepit old monks a thing or two about the inequities that lurked in the human heart.

9.55 – 3E for Religious Instruction. "I don't care if you are a pagan, Grimshaw, Mrs. Withers is out with food poisoning and since we do have to have you in the school for teaching practice, the least you can do is help out. And none of your damnable atheism, young man! Remember, I have to make out a report for the Ministry about your four weeks here."

"Right class. The Good Shepherd."

"Please Sir, how DO you shag sheep?" (Well, to start with, you wear a kilt, not trousers. Sheep can hear a zip fastener from one hundred yards.)

This from young Harold McCusker, the eczema kid, who looked as if he were quite at home in a pair of wellies and had been there before. It was going to be one of those days.

10.25 – Lukewarm tea, the color of the Orinocco on an off day, and a stale cheese roll which looked as if it were a refugee from the great bread strike of 1947. Brian Artur sat down amidst the senior citizenry. What burning topic of intellectual stimulation was on the agenda today, he wondered idly. What had they read in the Belfast *Newsletter* or (for those who took their prejudices seriously) the *Daily Telegraph*. Did it really matter? It would inevitably end up with 'longhaired hooligans', 'filthy Communists/strikers' and the weather soon enough anyway. Here we go. Oh, nice one, "High time we brought back National Service." That from ex-corporal Riddlesdell of the National Front. Such a nice man really, though it was a pity about those boils. "Get their hair cut." Quite good, Mrs. Chadwick, although just the tiniest bit predictable. Why did he bother? He should invest in a pair of earplugs. O shit! Here comes the Headmaster, Eric 'the Rat' McBratney, the born again bigot.

"Ah Grimshaw, young man, just the chap I've been looking for. As you may know, dear Mrs. Ruddock is retiring at the end of the month and we're collecting for a going away present for her. Since you've only been here a few weeks I've put you down for a mere 5 shillings. I'll collect it now if that's convenient."

"Fraid not, old man, can't bring myself to contribute, even to such a worthy cause as this. Can't quite see myself as an integral part of this great educational establishment, d'ye know. Anyway I hear on the old grapevine that the present is to be a Comfiwarm electric blanket and an interesting article in the consumers magazine last month was saying that that particular model had an unfortunate habit of shorting every now and then. What are you trying to do, fry the old trout?"

"Mr. McBratney to you, young man."

The rant began. Brian Artur tried to turn off but was still forced to submit to the repetitive diatribe about the low calibre of trainee teachers these days. Their rudeness, their lack of respect, their foulmouthed speech patterns and the bad end to which they all, and Brian Artur in particular, would undoubtedly come. As the Rat's wrath mounted and a coronary became more probable, Brian Artur glanced at his watch, swore, and abruptly left the room. He was late for the next class and this was inspection week.

Down the steps to 3C, with feelings of dread. "That was rash, me ould son," he muttered to himself. "Only three more days left and you have to go and screw it up. And the Pox is odds on to visit this afternoon." And at the thought of the Pox, aka Professor James Paul Knox, the blustering, buffoonish tyrant in charge of the Department of Education, Brian Artur's dire forebodings turned to acute anxiety as he quickened his pace and pushed open the classroom door.

The malaise was well justified. The first thing to greet him was the unnatural silence. Normally, arriving five minutes late he would have expected a babel of banter and a hail of missiles. Today all was quiet. Subdued giggles and titters, but all were seated. Positively demure. 'What ails you dear children? Nothing contagious, I trust', thought Brian Artur. Shit! The wee hure's melts! Not a word of warning! For there, seated at the back of the class in his ubiquitous shiny black suit, his halitosis wafting around him like steam off a dog's turd and his spectacles glinting like the moonlight off a coffin's handles, sat the Pox himself. And the bastard had indicated that he would be visiting that afternoon for Brian Artur's only half-decent class.

"Ah, Grimshaw, good of you to join us. We'd almost given up hope." Appreciative sniggers from the juvenile sadists. That's right, you swine, divide and rule! "Just fixing up to take some extra periods to help the Headmaster out, Professor. Lot of sickness about, you know. Poor Mrs. Ruddock's down with bubonic plague or something."

"Come on, Grimshaw, enough time's been wasted already. Now, what were you going to do with the class today?"

'Bugger all', thought Brian Artur to himself. He'd intended to let them scribble away while he cobbled up a 'model' lesson for the Pox's supposed afternoon visit. "Revision test, Professor," he replied brightly. A dangerous enough move as he well knew, since the class were unlikely to recall too much of his talk the previous week about King John and the barons. Still, they all watched the Robin Hood rubbish on the tube, surely they should at least have some idea about it.

"Well, class, just a few questions to remind us about Magna Carta." "Please Sir?" "Yes, Marion?" "You told us all about that last week, Sir. Don't you remember, you told us how King John was a tyrant and oppressed the people and you told us how the headmaster was a tyrant and how it would be a good idea if someone acted like Robin Hood and burnt down the school. And I asked if you were joking and you just laughed and offered me a box of matches ..." "Thank you, Marion! My, what an imagination the child has. Well now, Walker? Walker?" Jesus wept! The smartest kid in the class and chooses to mitch today!

If the class had started badly, it soon turned into a fiasco as child after child stood up and disingenuously shopped Brian Artur, with tales of intemperate remarks or opprobrious comments upon the prominent in the educational environment and the city in general. The remaining 25 minutes dragged from one ignominious faux pas to another.

With three minutes remaining it was left to young Marion, who, if she ever was allowed to grow up was shit-hot material to become a Supergrass, to deliver her own 'coup de grass'.

"Please Sir, could you explain to us one more time why you grow your hair long?"

Brian Artur rubbed his head. What was this one all about? He didn't remember talking to the brats about tonsorial affairs. Frantically, he looked around. Young Bell, one of the better kids, was shaking his head in warning but it was too late. What the hell had he said? It must have been that morning after he'd got stoned with Peter O'Neill.

Too late. The Pox, sensing blood, homed in. "What's this about long hair, Marion?" His eyes had the compassion of a shark approaching a raft of American teenagers off Stinson Beach. Young Bell, God Bless him, tried to dissuade her from the gross act of betrayal by kicking her from behind, but the dear child would not be silenced.

"It was a very interesting story, Mr. Knox. Mr. Grimshaw was telling us that according to the Bible we should all wear our hair long because if we didn't birds could get in our ears and make us pregnant. Please Sir? What's pregnant mean?"

"What??" The Pox was apoplectic. But the young tout was not to be sidetracked. "Yes Sir, Mr. Grimshaw said that that was what happened to the Virgin Mary, a pigeon got up her earhole and little baby Jesus was born, and that's why all the people in the Bible wore their hair long because they didn't want pigeons infringing with their personal liberty or putting them up the spout. He said the pigeon was called a Paraclete. Please Sir? What's 'up the spout' mean? I didn't understand that bit Sir, but the rest of it was very interesting. Mr. Grimshaw's such a wonderful teacher, Sir, you never know what he's going to say next."

'Neither do I', thought Brian Artur, as the bell rang, not to herald his salvation but merely to signal the onset of the Inquisition.

As the class shuffled out and he awaited the wrath of the Pox he caught a glimpse of little Marion's face, suffused with hideous glee. 'That'll teach me to reject the dear child's offer of a visit to the cycle sheds', he thought. The overwhelming miasma of the Pox's halitosis brought him out of his rueful reverie.

"This won't look good on your record, Grimshaw. Not good at all." His piggy little eyes glinted malevolently as he warmed to his sanctimonious sermon. "Sorry I can't stay for a little chat, Professor, but I must dash to my next class. Can't keep the kiddies waiting."

Glancing at his watch the Pox reluctantly admitted that he too was late for another appointment, and, threatening 'to have a long talk with Brian Artur after the next tutorial' he produced his bicycle clips, fastened them to his plump ankles and waddled off down the hall, leaving Brian Artur with five minutes to kill in the toilets seeking new graffiti. 'You're never alone with schizophrenia.' Thoughtfully Brian Artur added 'or paranoia' beneath the scrawl, pulled the chain and exited out the side door onto the playground, for, in fact, he had not been quite truthful with the Pox and had two glorious free periods before lunch, and had no intention of spending them at the Dotheboys Hall canteen.

Across the tarmacadamed playground, which was marked out menacingly for various forms of organized torture, ranging from basketball to grievous bodily harm, his brain seething with thoughts of revenge, not only against the Pox but the whole plethora of academic authorities, strode the would-be pedagogue. Through the side gate, a quick sprint and a leap onto the platform of a passing 69 bus.

The conductor was startled, no doubt fearing that he had been subjected to a sneak visit from a 'jumper', come to curtail his petty pilfering. "Fear not, comrade, your sins are safe with me," beamed Brian Artur, "for I am of the fraternity, a former dinger, custodian of the swaying platform and sworn enemy of all jumpers, may they rot in Hell."

"What the fuck do you mean by jumping on when the bus was moving?"

Brian Artur's feelings of camaraderie for this oppressed member of the proletariat evaporated. "It's my life, matey. Sod off!" He sat down on the vandalized plastic seat and gazed out of the rain-flecked window at the passing sights of Belfast, once heralded as 'the Athens of the North' and now noted only for its stultifying tedium (for we are in 1964, dear reader, and 'the troubles' have not yet resurrected themselves).

What secret vices were being practised behind those tattered lace curtains? he mused. How many were engaged in solitary pleasures of an onanistic nature? How many were writing yet another splenetic letter to the Belfast *Newsletter*, deploring the fact that children might be permitted to play on the park swings on a Sunday? How many had put the Protestant *Telegraph* under the door and tried to turn on the gas, only to discover that they lacked a shilling for the meter?

His reverie was interrupted as the bus trundled down Corporation Street and past the dole. "See you soon, comrades," he muttered, for he had little optimism that the State would offer him gainful pedagogic employment after the Pox and his Department were through.

Hop off at the traffic lights. Smile nicely at the custodian. "Thank you, my good fellow, a splendidly smooth ride for fourpence if I may say so, my compliments to the driver."

"Fuck off!"

Quite so. Down the alley, its paving stones worn smooth by the feet of countless winos, cadgers and head-the-balls over the centuries, and into the darkness of McMurtry's Wine and Spirit Lodge.

"Good morning, John." This to the wizened proprietor who lurked behind the wooden counter. Jesus! You'd think by now that he could afford more than a sixty watt bulb to light the place. Still, supposed Brian Artur, it made it easier to short change. "Two of your delicious ninepenny pies and a pint of Single X."

Brian Artur glanced round at his fellow morning drinkers, spotted Frank the Cadger and hastily moved over to a private snug before the bugger noticed him and put the hammer on him for a quid. Unrivaled in the entire Emerald Isle for his thick skin and persistent cadging, Frank had been known to cause grown men to dive out of windows when, miles from Belfast and secure, as they thought, in some public house in the wilds of Tirconnel, they had felt his clammy touch on their shoulder and heard his whining request for 'half a crown until the weekend'.

Frank was too busy trying to steal the pint of porter from old Tom who had dozed off at the counter to notice Brian Artur, however, and Grimshaw achieved the sanctuary of the snug and closed the door. Putting down his glass he pulled out his copy of *Pravda* (better known as the *Irish News*, an estimable Catholic paper which used to run such ecumenical headlines as 'Pope saved by son of Mayo policeman' and 'Catholic dog wins at Dunmore Park'. To be fair, its rival the *Belfast Telegraph* did have a magnificent headline, 'One million die in Bangladesh great floods, two Ulstermen saved') and turned to the racing page. A pint, a pie and a punt. What else was there left for the poor scholar these days, he thought to himself, as he selected 'Son of Zarathustra' in the 12.45 at Ally Pally. A sure thing, and reckoned to start at 5/1 against. Now all he needed was a gullible acquaintance whom he could hammer for a few shillings.

The door opened. God is good. Paddy O'Mynchey, nature's answer to a *deus ex machina*, entered, his moon face glowing in the gloom and a pint clutched in his hand.

"Thought I'd find you here, Grimshaw, what are you having?" And, wonder of wonders, O'Mynchey appears to have a large blue note of the realm in his hand. "A ball of malt, Patrick my friend, for 'tis many a day since last we met," waxed Brian Artur.

"We were drunk together only two weeks ago, you lying sot, and it's too early for malt, you'll have a pint of porter and like it."

"I bow to your superior wisdom and purchasing power, Patrick, of course, but what brings you back to our fair shores? Only last week you were reported skiving on a building site in London and being forced to drink the abominable mild and bitter of the Brits with the rest of Cricklewood's immigrants. How come this welcome return?"

O'Mynchey grimaced. "Alas, Grimshaw, a slight altercation with a large foreman from the County Cavan forced me to curtail my pick and shoveling activities, and the attentions of the bulky men of the Metropolitan constabulary towards certain pieces of worthless paper bearing my name necessitated my speedy return to the ould sod."

"Welcome home, my son. And have you any more of those attractive blue banknotes?"

The afternoon passed rather quickly. O'Mynchey did indeed have money and was prepared not only to buy Guinness and Bushmills but lend some to Grimshaw to invest on Son of Zarathustra, a noble stallion who obliged at the encouraging odds of 11/2. Brian Artur was in funds again and obviously had to repay O'Mynchey's hospitality. The rounds became doubles.

"Jesus, Padraig, is that the time!" Brian Artur started up. "I'll see you tonight, I have to get back to 4B, the little buggers will have destroyed the place."

"Aw screw it for today Brian, I'll phone in and say that you've been hit by a bus and can't make it back or have come down with an attack of piles or something."

Brian Artur hesitated. It was tempting, but visions of the Solomon Islands, the last refuge for failed teachers loomed and he opted for responsibility. (He and O'Mynchey had long decided that one of the reasons for drinking in McMurtry's was that if you didn't get food poisoning from the pies you could be presumed already immunized against beriberi, typhoid and dengue fever, or whatever other exotic diseases with which the tropics could attack a poor Irish immigrant.)

"Sorry, Paddy, hang on here and I'll be back to help you drink your ill-gotten gains as soon as I've dealt with the future generation of vipers."

And out into the drizzle of another Belfast afternoon, a dash across the street and another death-defying leap onto the ever faithful 69 bus. It was the same conductor.

"Serve you right if you broke your bleedin' neck."

"Get stuffed." Congratulating himself on this witty rejoinder, Brian Artur retired upstairs there to plot his classroom strategy. Could he get away with giving them yet another essay?

"Academy," the conductor's dulcet tones rang out from below, as he dinged the bell and the bus pulled out from his stop. "Shit," howled Brian Artur, awaking from his postprandial slumbers and scuttling down the stairs to hurl himself out onto the road. Picking himself up, he brushed himself down, shook his fist after the departing bus and attempted to sidle in through the side gate of the school. But nothing missed the rheumy and bloodshot eye of old Matt, the Headmaster's stoolpigeon.

"Late again, Grimshaw," he cackled.

Brian Artur quickened his pace and sprinted up the steps. A bad mistake. 'Should have stopped for a slash', he thought to himself as he flung open the classroom door. Too late now. Have to get them settled down before taking a break.

"Good afternoon 4B. Well, as it happens I haven't got quite all your essays of last week corrected (in fact Brian Artur had left them on the train when he'd gone down to Dublin for the weekend, but, what the hell, he figured he'd only another three more days of this tedium to endure) so for the first part of the lesson we'll talk about the Peasant's Revolt of 1381 and the splendid and progressive role played by Watt Tyler and Jack Straw when they burnt down the Archbishop of London's palace. Then I'll give you some private study to do."

Ignoring the groans, Brian Artur plowed on. "Desiree, (Desiree! Jesus, after what Hollywood epic was this child conceived!) can you tell us ..." His gruelling Inquisition was interrupted by a knock on the door. "Enter."

A nondescript little man wearing a bowler hat and carrying an attaché case sidled in. Brian Artur attempted a quizzical eyebrow. Failed. The man ignored this grimace and moved forward, hand outstretched. "Smiley," he remarked. Brian Artur's bewilderment showed. "From the Ministry," the little man amplified, addressing Brian Artur as if he were an ESN (educationally sub-normal) child. There was still not what could, in any sense, be described as 'rapport'.

The little man tried again. "I found I could fit the school in today after all." He essayed a tight-lipped smile, betraying a badly-fitting set of dentures. Brian Artur shied away, and then it hit him. Of course, the man from the sanitation department!

Three weeks earlier, under the guise of conducting a civics class, he'd had a discussion with 4B about what was wrong with the school and had encouraged them to put their complaints in writing. Apart from badmouthing all the teachers, from Wackford Squeers down to Brian himself, several of the pupils had revealed that the school was infested with rats of the four-legged variety, which inhabited the wainscotting of this very classroom.

As a result Brian Artur had had an easy skive while the pupils laboriously, at his command, composed protest letters to the Corporation about the rodent problem. A deputation to the Headmaster had only resulted in denials and threats concerning slander so the students, encouraged by Brian Artur, social reformer, had sent the letters off to City Hall. Brian Artur had obviously expected that there they would be consigned to the nearest wastepaper basket but he had clearly misjudged the municipal officialdom. Mr. Smiley's presence being the tangible proof of their concern.

Brian Artur beamed. Jovially he wheeled round and walked straight into a desk which seemed to have deliberately obstructed him. Had the last pint been a mistake? Never mind. Flushed with victory, he prepared for his finest hour, reaching out and shaking Mr. Smiley's hand. Vindicated after all these years. And in front of the class, too. The rights of the individual asserted, bureaucracy confronted and forced in the face of his inexorable logic to act. It was a model lesson in civics and self-help. Dale Carnegie would have been proud of him.

The class, ever ready for a break from the tedium, stopped their internecine warfare and prepared to pay attention. This promised to be a laugh.

"The row to the right, stand up and move your desks away from the wall. Hurry up! And keep the noise down." General Brian Artur took control. Beckoning to Smiley he strolled nonchalantly and somewhat unsteadily across to the wall and bent down to look for the telltale gnawholes. 'At least this breaks up the class', he thought. Maybe the funny little man has a gas gun in his briefcase. That'd give 4B something to talk about. Oops! Bending down had definitely not been a good idea. Picking himself up he upbraided the class. "Stop sniggering, you snotty nosed brats." Steady, he thought. Don't antagonize them. Christ! Down again. Which of the little monsters had tripped him!

Never mind. Once down on the floor he might as well make a job out of it and locate these damn ratholes. Not a bloody one! Joke's wearing a bit thin. Getting up he adopted his most threatening manner. "All right, stop messing about, where exactly are these bloody holes?"

There was a quiet cough. Discreet. 'Ignore the swine', thought Brian Artur. "Come on Jimmy, where are the holes?" A hand on his shoulder. Damn the fellow's impudence! He spun round. Too hurriedly. Rash. Get up quickly. "Just a minute, Smiley, I'm doing my best, damn you." Shouting. Must calm down. Creating a bad impression.

"Mr. Grimshaw, I'd like a word with you. Outside." Bloody cheek! Who does the fellow think he is. He's only a jumped-up turd collector. And in front of the class, too! There they are, smirking all over their pimply faces. How does he know my name? The office must have told him. Unless ... A bell started to ring in Brian Artur's fuddled brain. Smiley? Where had he heard that name before? Oh sweet Jesus! It can't be. But it was.

A glance at those beady eyes, the neat pinstripe trousers, and, as Mr. Smiley held the door open for him Brian Artur realized with a sobering shock that he was facing Aloysius H. Smiley, MA (Cantab), B.Ed., Justice of the Peace, pillar of the community and senior history inspector at the Ministry of Education.

Feverishly Brian Artur attempted to marshal his faculties and pull something out of the conflagration. Appeal to his sense of fair play? "You know how it is, old man, under a lot of stress lately, may have had just one too many at lunchtime, I mean to say, we all do now and again, eh what?" The Pioneer Total Abstinence Society pin on Smiley's lapel winked back at Brian Artur, as if to say, 'forget that one, me old son'.

As Smiley flagellated himself into a froth of self righteousness Brian Artur cudgeled his enfeebled wits. He also recalled, to his horrified chagrin, that the ratholes had been in 4D, not 4B, and that he desperately needed to go to the toilet. Finally the tirade ground to a halt. The teachers along the corridor who had been eagerly eavesdropping whipped their heads back into their respective classrooms. The giggling from 4B subsided. Brian Artur hadn't heard any of Smiley's rant after the fourth platitude, but this was it. His last chance to snatch the irons from the fire. A Clarence Darrow type performance, redolent of tolerance, sincerity and understanding? Portia and the very strained quality of mercy bit? Or defiance? A *cri de cœur*, heroically representing all the downtrodden and abused young teachers out here in Wackford Squeers land?

Ah screw it! He'd just restrict himself to a devastating retort, full of black humor and social comment. Something to go down in the volume of 'The Wit and Wisdom of Brian Artur Grimshaw' which, no doubt, some faithful scribe was already preparing to unleash upon an amazed world in case Brian Artur ever left this vale of tears.

Drawing himself up to his full 5 foot 8 inches and towering over the apoplectic Smiley, Brian Artur let him have the full benefit of his wit, wisdom and erudition.

"Fuck off, you pigeon-chested wee cunt."

Last Orders, Please !

It wasn't actually a club, and, officially, it was called the 'Angler's Arms', but, to the good and the not so good people of Lurgan, N. Ireland, it was known as the 'Kneecappers'. Respectable people didn't go there. There were frequent fights and many paramilitaries or suspected paramilitaries, along with the flotsam and jetsam of the lumpenproletariat, used to hang out there, mainly for the cheap drink which had 'fallen off the back of a lorry'.

Brian Artur didn't often drink there, mostly because it was too close to his home, and some nosy bugger might see him entering or leaving and tell 'the wife'. This, as far as Brian Artur Grimshaw was concerned, would not have been a good thing. His head was furrowed and scarred, like a First World War battlefield, as a result of incurring the displeasure of this formidable lady. To her comrades in the Father Murphy Total Temperance Cumann, Hilda Grimshaw, with her unwavering opposition to all things alcoholic, was an inspiration. To Brian Artur she was, literally, a pain in the head.

The good ladies of the Cumann had a simple motto. "Someone, somewhere, is having a good time and it's high time we put a stop to it." Hilda was their Führer, but, on this particular night in question she was off at a 'Victory to Mary Whitehouse' rally with her troops, there to view the latest collection of pornographic and smutty material which the good ladies had acquired in the past month. Brian Artur reckoned that after the meeting Hilda would be so excited and morally disgusted from watching the blue movies that she wouldn't even notice the smell of Polo mints on his breath. He could relax in front of the television and watch the late night soccer while she could rant and rave about the deplorable scenes of debauchery which, in the interests of the impressionable in the community, she had forced herself to watch. Brian Artur didn't mind. He didn't even own a pornograph.

And so, sitting over his eighth pint of Guinness, Brian Artur was relatively at peace with the world. He may not have been gruntled, but he certainly wasn't disgruntled. Things could be better. He might win the Irish sweepstake, or touch for the big lady who had just moved into number 37, or the wife might decide to visit her sister in Australia, but, on the other hand, he could be much worse off.

(There were those who had taken an interest in Brian Artur's marital status and sought to give him advice, but, as he said himself, expecting his marriage to improve was as futile as leaving the night light on for Lord Lucan, Shergar or Captain Nairac.)

So, by and large, he was feeling no pain. He'd had a fair skinfull of drink. He still had a couple of pounds in his pocket, and it was only 9.30 p.m. The young hoods in the corner, obviously underage, did annoy him with their drunken chatter, but not to the extent that he considered moving across the room and into the maximum decibel range of the jukebox.

Jarlath came in and sat down beside him. They hadn't seen each other for almost a week, and so had to have another few pints to celebrate this fortuitous reunion and discuss the relative merits of Wintergreen rub and Valium when it came to doping greyhounds. Grimshaw was an old Wintergreen man, but Jarlath, being younger, sang the praises of these new wonderdrugs and was even known to talk at times of Anna Bollicky Steroids. The craic was good, and time and pints flew.

They had just turned the conversation to the forthcoming Gaelic football match next Sunday when the door flew open and in strode two masked men. One of them stayed at the door, covering the bar with one of those newfangled foreign rifles that you saw on the television or, occasionally, in the hands of the odd Fianna teenager on manoeuvres up in the park while mitching from school. "Which one's Tonto?" muttered Grimshaw. "Shut up, he might hear you," whispered Jarlath. No fool Jarlath. Indeed it looked for an instant as if the second gunman had overheard Grimshaw's foolish attempt at a witticism as he crossed the floor in their direction, pointing a Walther P-38 pistol, formerly the property of the late Constable William McFettridge, Royal Ulster Constabulary, RIP.

As Brian Artur prepared to hastily grovel an apology, the hooded man passed right by him and Jarlath and stopped at the table where two of the young punk hoods were still sitting, the rest of their company having departed some half an hour ago, in a haze of cheap wine. "Joseph Haughey," the gunman said, staring down at his drink sodden victim-to-be. "You have been found guilty of crimes of an antisocial nature against the people of this neighbourhood. You have ignored previous warnings and are now, accordingly, to be shot in the right knee." "Fuck this for a game of darts," said Haughey, trying to stagger to his feet. The hooded man didn't wait, but calmly put the gun behind the fleshy part of Haughey's thigh and pulled the trigger. Haughey howled and fell to the floor, as the gunman made for the door, still being covered by his companion.

"Tonight's punishment shooting, which was done in your interests, was brought to you by the Larry O'Toole Commando of the Victorious Peoples Popular Front for the Liberation of Our Wee Ulster. Nobody move for five minutes. Thank you, good night, and Venceremos." They vanished as quickly as they had come.

Most of the punters returned quietly to their drinks. The barman reached, leisurely, for the phone to call for an ambulance. It wasn't the first time such a thing had happened in his bar and he doubted that it would be the last. On the floor young Haughey was still squealing like a stuck pig as the blood flowed from his thigh.

It wasn't the first time he'd been kneecapped either, but this time he was wearing his good suit. His mother would molucate him!

Beside him his friend Seany fussed and puttered around ineffectively. The situation called for a man of action, not one of his strong points. Now, give him an old age pensioner to mug or a gas meter to rob, and he was your man. But first aid? Forget it!

Crises have a way of producing their own great men. The French Revolution produced Napoleon; the Battle of Britain, Churchill; America had George Washington in their hour of need; Russia had its Lenin. And in his hour of need, at this almost existential moment, young Haughey had Brian Artur Grimshaw.

One must hasten to add that this is not in any way to imply that Brian Artur was in the same league as these great men. He hadn't enslaved half the known world, sent thousands to their deaths, or engaged in any particular feats of megalomania, but, many years ago, he had been a member of the Knights of Malta, the voluntary first aid outfit. True, he had been expelled from that august body after being caught nipping at the medicinal alcohol stocks, but, in his present exuberant state such matters paled into insignificance and he saw himself as a veritable Florence Nightingale.

"Thon wee bugger needs a Turn-knee-Kay." The Angel with the lamp couldn't have put it better. "Here, Jarlath, give us your knife." Jarlath, who never went anywhere without his 46-blade Swiss Army issue knife, handed it over wordlessly. He was in a state of mild shock.

Young Haughey wasn't feeling too great either. His mood was not exactly enhanced when, as he looked up, all he could see was a drunken Brian Artur bearing down upon him with a multi-bladed knife. "Aaaaarrrgh," he cried, or words to that effect. It is true that, even at the best of times, Brian Artur is not what one would describe as 'a pretty sight'. This is even more true when he is, as we say, full as a sheugh.

Nonetheless, he had some reason to resent this response to what he regarded as an errand of mercy. He doubted if Florence had had to put up with such hostility in the Crimea.

"Listen, you stupid wee bleeder," he slurred, "I'm only trying to bandage you up until the ambulance gets here. Otherwise, you'll leak to death." Haughey could only groan. It wasn't his night. Brian Artur's eyes were, it must be confessed, slightly blurred, but even he could see that there was a lot of blood. 'No bother to Doctor Kildare', he thought to himself.

It was a pity that there wasn't some big nurse or even yer woman from up at number 37 to swab his brow and hand him the magic scalpel, but this was, after all, an emergency.

Swiftly the man of action reached down and ripped Haughey's trouser leg with the knife, tearing off a strip. Haughey screamed. "Seany, get this madman off me." Seany reacted, snapping out of his semi-trance, and jumping onto Grimshaw's back, trying to pull him off, but the Angel of Mercy, once started, was not so easily deterred. Shrugging his shoulder, he threw the off-balance Seany onto the table, spilling the drinks and breaking the bottles. Jarlath, spurring to the defense of his friend, joined in, clinically splitting open Seany's left cheek with a judiciously aimed boot, and the rest of the punters entered the fray, under the misapprehension that 'The Duke' Wayne was about to join in and that John Ford was secretly filming the whole shebang.

Meanwhile Brian Artur was hacking away with verve, vigor and panache. He had managed to get a strip of the trouser leg off and was attempting to apply a tourniquet, using a chair leg that had become detached in the melee. "You fuckin' maniac, you've ruined my suit," Haughey was screaming. "I'll kill you, you old fool." "I may just have saved your life, you ungrateful wee get," countered Grimshaw as he strove to tighten the cloth.

Haughey screamed again, but Grimshaw wasn't able to make out exactly what he was saying, which was rather a pity. Had he been able to decipher the hapless hood's screams he might have realized that he was trying to bind up the wrong leg.

It was the ambulance men, summoned by the 999 call, who eventually saved Haughey. They had had to stretcher out seven other punters before they could get over to the corner where Haughey writhed. Grimshaw, satisfied with his work, had finished his pint and left with Jarlath. "Don't bother to thank me, son, anytime!" were his parting words, as they swayed deftly between two drunks who were intent upon doing Grievous Bodily Harm upon each other.

In his alcoholic state he was feeling rather proud of himself and was therefore off his guard as the wife felled him from behind with the frying pan as he stumbled through the front door. As he lay there semi-conscious he murmured to himself, "that's the last time I have a gargle in there. They put something evil in your drink."

JUDAS'S CARRY-OUT

Judas's Carry-Out. That's what we called him, although his given name was Judas Iscariot O'Toole. The nomenclature may seem unusual, but then, he came from a long line of touts.

The family history has proven difficult to trace, since in Ireland informers are not noted for their longevity. Whole branches of the family have died off (overnight, in some cases), and, for obvious reasons there have been frequent name changes, to say nothing of 'moonlight flits'. However, it is known that his father, Carey O'Toole, himself named after the infamous tout who shopped the 'Invincibles' back in 1882, had wanted to name the child 'Vikdun', after the Scandinavian Quisling (he was a 'war baby'), but the grandfather, the patriarch of the family, had insisted on 'Judas Iscariot'. It had more class, he felt.

The grandfather was a man of many strong convictions (and the odd acquittal), chief of which was that he wouldn't get caught. In this belief he proved overly sanguine. Shortly after young Judas's birth he was dredged up out of the River Lagan. Local people put it down to 'misadventure', as did the coroner, although the latter did query the block of cement that encased the grandda's left foot, which gave rise to the Belfast superstition that digging with the wrong foot could be injurious to one's health.

The grandda had been an interesting character. In later years young Judas was wont to boast how the 'ould one' had been in Sackville Street in Dublin at Easter in 1916 (Easter was always his favourite time of year), and had reported to a policeman that a 'Mr. James Connolly was knocking off the Post Office'. He also tried to finger Padraic Pearse for 'illegally parking' for eight days, and always liked to think that, in his own quiet way, he had been instrumental in assisting the British courtmartial officers in reaching their death verdict on the Proclamation Signatories.

(Incidentally, research has shown that Grandda O'Toole was himself actually present in the GPO during those momentous days, as a close scanning of the famous lithograph will show. He's the one trying to pick Connolly's pocket as he lies wounded on the stretcher.)

But, as usual, I digress. It is true that the Patriarch's insistence on naming his grandson Judas did occasion the odd bit of Catholic bigotry on the Falls Road in Belfast where he was brought up, but his father, a keen reader of the Bible, and in particular St. Mark where he relates how JC was shopped to the Sanhedrin, explained it as follows:

"Judas was one of yer disciples. The best one. If he hadn't touted on the Big Lad, sure he'd never have got himself crucified and died for all yer sins. And then where would we all be? We'd all be bloody pagans, that's what we'd be. Sure Jesus knew it was coming, didn't he! The rest of those Jackeen apostles didn't have the balls to do the necessary to help him implement his Da's plan, did they? Sure old Judas got a bad press, but that was just sour grapes. Besides, they didn't have press agents in them days."

This was generally said just prior to being forcibly evicted by the drunken and the righteous from some shebeen, at which he was normally as welcome as Klaus Barbie at a Jewish Defense League meeting, but, even when picking himself out of the gutter, the old man retained his dignity, with his parting shot of "Read yer Bibles, ye fuckin' heathens."

Be that as it may, young Judas grew up in Belfast reared on tales of his infamous ancestors by his devoted mother Jezebel. His father Carey had had to leave the city rather hurriedly after the police had seized a poitín still from the pigeon fancier's club and half the male residents of Sebastopol Street had been arrested. He died a few years later in Chicago of overweight. He hadn't put on much weight. Only an ounce, in fact, but when it comes in the form of a lead object in one's right earhole, it has frequently been known to prove fatal, despite the wonders of modern medicine.

When I interviewed Jezebel recently, somewhere in the fleshpots of San Francisco, she still manifested a mother's quiet loyalty and devotion, producing a tattered scrapbook which sketchily detailed her pride and joy's career.

"There's a picture of him, aged six, after he got beat up in school for snitching. There he is, he was only twelve, I think, standing with me outside the court house in Chichester Street where he turned Queens Evidence for the first time. That was a happy day, I can tell you. Oh, and look, there's him in the wheelchair after he'd been kneecapped for the third time for touting. Look at the caption, 'Squeals on Wheels'. It's a great likeness, isn't it?"

"Did you always want him to be a tout?" I asked, disingenuously. "Oh yes, there was never any doubt. Some of the family suggested that he should be a child molester or a policeman or even," she shuddered, "a politician like Gerry Fitt, but his heart was set on following the family tradition. He got promoted recently, you know, he's a Supergrass now."

I nodded. I had followed his recent exploits from afar with interest, as the saga of thirty innocent people being fitted up by Judas and the Royal Ulster Constabulary unfolded inexorably.

It had set my mind back to the last time I'd run across, but alas, not over him. It had been back in Belfast in August, 1980, I think. I'd been covering a story about the RUC's sporting events and had gone up to the Royal Victoria Hospital to interview Doc McFadden about the plastic bullets the police heroes use to kill kids with. We'd adjourned to the staff club for a few drinks and were watching the hijackers from the club window when I idly asked him if he had any more interesting stories, preferably of a sensational nature, since I knew my Editor preferred his subscribers to read between the loins. He stared at me long and hard. I got the message and another round of drinks.

"Weeeeel," he said finally, "I should nae be telling you this, since ahm doing an article for the 'Lancet' about it, but we've recently been plagued by a rash of young, and not so young, ladies coming into the hospital with only half an arm."

"What?"

"Ah dinna fash yersel' son, they're 'armless'," quipped the elderly quack as I reached for my notebook.

"Come on. Doc, give! What's this all about?"

"Just as I say. In the past five weeks I've had four cases. Ladies, ranging from 20 to 50 years of age have come into casualty in the morning with only half an arm. They refuse to give any details. Won't prefer charges against anyone and discharge themselves as soon as we've stitched them up. All give obviously fake names. Frankly, we're baffled, but at least it'll get me into the Lancet."

The investigative journalist's pulse raced. This one would be even better than my last scoop – 'Andytown budgie speaks only Irish', one of my better exposés of late.

"Any other common denominators about them, Doc?"

"Nae, except that they all suffered from myopia and were very hungover."

Suddenly it hit me! A blinding flash of satori. Like when your Zen master hits you over the head with his Kendo stick or Luigi bottles you out of the Prisoners Defense Club for winning too much on the fruit machine. Whatever. It is an existential moment that old Kierkegaard himself would be proud of. Insight. I just KNEW that Judas was somehow involved.

"Doc," I asked, "do you have any of these women's addresses?" No, he didn't. As he'd said, they'd obviously given fake IDs. I wasn't satisfied. I knew he was holding something back. I was right, after a few more Bushmills he broke down and confessed. He'd recognized one of the 'ladies' as 'Big Aggie', a local lady of leisure and pleasure who had graduated from college with a degree in advanced moaning and simulated orgasmic techniques. More importantly, she could generally be found most evenings in the Gravediggers Arms, a quaint shebeen just by Milltown cemetery. It was my breakthrough.

As I wove my way through the throng of bored teenagers who were idly burning a British Saracen tank outside Dunville Park and stumbled into a black hack I was more and more convinced. Judas was involved and Big Aggie was the key.

The rain was lashing down as I was ejected from the taxi with a cheerful oath, but this was the 'old sod', so wasn't it 'a soft rain'.

I squelched my way up to the pock-marked counter of the Gravediggers and asked for some wine. Bingo poured me a Mundies. Ah well, any port in a storm.

She was sitting at a table in a darkened corner but she wasn't too hard to miss. Most of the other customers had two arms.

"Can I buy you a drink, Aggie?" I asked rhetorically, as I risked my spinal column by sitting down on what was euphemistically called a chair in those parts.

"I'm saying nothing about it, nothing, do you hear," she muttered, as she reached with her one good arm for the bottle of Mundies. Her speech was slurred. Sometimes it's hard to tell talk from mutter.

"It was Judas, wasn't it?" I whispered.

A look of terror flickered across her bloodshot features.

"Jesus, Mister! How did you know?"

"We journalists have a nose for this kind of thing."

"Yer not going to print a word of this, are you?" she asked pathetically.

"Not a word, Aggie," I lied. "Tell us what happened." She took a slug from the bottle and wiped her mouth. "It was the old 'coyote syndrome'," she whispered. I nodded, sagely, still mystified.

"Was it the same with the other women?"

"Aye. You know the score, Mister, you're a man of the world." I nodded, smugly. Couldn't complain about that one. "Remind me, Aggie," I cajoled.

"It was dark, Mister. You know how it is. And I was well jarred. I mean steaming. And there's no light worth talking about in the White Fort. It's easier to shortchange that way." I nodded. I'd been there too.

"And he was pouring Drambuies into me. He'd just got his bloodmoney from the peelers, but I didn't know that. I swear it, Mister, it was dark. I didn't recognize him."

"I believe you, Aggie. And then?"

"You know the rest. Like I said, the old 'coyote syndrome'. You wake up in some strange bed in the morning. Your head feels as if some céili band's been practising in it all night. Your tongue feels like some Japanese wrestler's jockstrap cooked in chip fat. Your eyeballs are like two fried eggs cooked in placenta."

I shuddered. I'd been there. Go on, admit it, so have you. "And?" I prompted.

"You know the rest. Some stranger's lying there naked beside you with his head on your shoulder, and you take one look at him and you say, 'Jesus Christ! I slept with THAT!' And you know that if you make the slightest movement it'll wake up and you'll have to talk to it, and so you do the only thing possible. You bite your own arm off and crawl out of bed without disturbing it."

"The old coyote syndrome!" Of course! Why had I been so blind? What else could a decent woman do?

"Thanks, Aggie," I murmured, ordering her another bottle of wine as I slid out of the bar.

"Not a word to anyone, Mister? You promise?"

"I promise, Aggie. You can trust me."

The hunt was on. I had to find Judas. The Editor would definitely go for this one. Sex, violence, treachery, mutilation and drunken Paddies. How could the Brit bastard resist it! I splashed up the road towards the PDF club. I had to see Brian Artur. He would know where I could find Judas. Brian Artur knew everything. Not a sparrow could fart in West Belfast but that Brian Artur knew the what thereof.

Crossing the wasteground opposite the Club I tripped over a Brit soldier who was earning his meagre pittance protecting Margaret Thatcher by lying in the mud pointing his SLR at the cardboard walls of my home away from home. I've always found the squaddies to be clumsy fellows. Must come from walking backwards with a gun in their hand for four months at a time. It's enough to disorientate anyone I suppose. They've no sense of humor, either, I've noticed.

Picking myself up and wiping the blood off my teeth and the mud off my leather coat, rented for the occasion from Paramil Funeral Service, Inc., I entered the mystic and braved the gloom.

Malachy was behind the bar.

"The usual?"

"Yeah."

Who says television's killed conversation. Clutching my pint I made my way through the ranks of the unemployed, pausing only to overhear new epithets which were being hurled at Bampot Lowe as he miscued over the pool table. 'Original,' I thought. 'Physically impossible, totally unprintable, but original!' I moved on. Time was awasting and I had to talk to Brian Artur.

He was at his usual seat. I sat down uninvited. He glanced across, saw with that lightning brain of his that I'd forgotten to buy him a drink and continued his conversation with his acolytes. I summoned a waitress and hurriedly made amends. Fool that I was I'd got off on the wrong foot, but, gentleman and scholar that he was, a double Bushmills in hand, he graciously deigned to speak to me.

"Yes, Scoop?"

I came right to the point before it cost another round.

"Judas O'Toole, where can I find him?"

An appreciative titter of laughter rick o'shayed (the wellknown Irish sniper) off the walls. I prepared to grovel. A faux pas had obviously been made. I had made it. This was going to cost a few drinks I could see. The merriment subsided. Brian Artur leaned back in his chair and surveyed me with disdain.

"Did you hear that, lads, Scoop here wants to know where he can find Judas."

More laughter. Brian Artur took pity on me.

"Malachy, give our not so young friend here a drink." It appeared like magic. I gulped it down. The bastards! It was Mundies! At least I've something in common with the late Lord Mountbatten. I too hate Mondays!

Brian Artur swivelled his chair. No mean feat. The PDF doesn't run to swivel chairs. Some days it doesn't run to chairs.

"Why don't you try the Kesh."

"Long Kesh prison camp?" Always the fall guy, I stumbled on.

"Judas in the Kesh? Jesus! How come? With all the police

protection he's got, how could he end up there?"

Brian Artur looked at me, his obvious contempt mingled with pity. He decided to put me out of my mercy.

"Scoop, he touted on himself. He's going to be doing twenty long hard ones for something he didn't do. But what else was there for it? He's touted on everyone else. It's like old Jean Paul (Brian Artur never let one forget that once, while on a package tour of Paris he'd met a man whom he claimed was Sartre), bless his little Gallic soul, used to say – 'Huis Clos'. Closed Circle. Inevitably he had to make the supreme existentialist sacrifice. After all, if you're a wanker, what else can you do?"

EPILOGUE

So here I am, an exile in Babylon by the Bay. Down in the Tenderloin of San Francisco, talking to 'the Ma'.

"Well, Jezebel, how's Judas these days?" "Scoop," she says, snuffling as she cadges another hot port, "he's contracted leprosy. It runs in the family."

Informers? That figures.

"Do you ever hear from him?"

"Ach, I get the odd bit of nail now and then."

Nice one, Ma.

"Listen, you stinking rabble of Papist pigs, I'm not looking for trouble."

THE STAG NIGHT

As I staggered into the Club bar in Belfast I was not a pretty sight. Some, more churlish than others, would claim that I rarely am, but even my most ardent admirer would have been forced to concede that had some Hollywood producer been on the lookout for some derelict to play the part of a wino who has just been tied to the back of a Chevrolet and taken for a scrape around the block, I would have been 11/4 on to get the role.

"Jesus Christ! What the hell happened to you?" exclaimed Brian Artur. He sat there, surrounded by a group of our mutual friends and a sea of drink. It was the eve of his wedding; he had escaped up to Belfast and was intent on getting mindless. Although it was only eight o'clock he had made a good start. Few could doubt that, come closing time, assistance would be needed to get him back to my flat and sobered up for the next day's nuptials.

Neil Lyndon (may his name live in infamy), the foolish Brit journalist who was propping me up and who was the architect of my bleeding and battered countenance, tried to explain, as I slumped onto a seat and helped myself to a large whiskey which someone had thoughtfully left in front of me.

"It was like this," he claimed. "We were down at this bar near the docks where Sean knew the barman and we were getting free drink and I happened to start talking to this girl and tried to tape an interview with her and next thing this large thug comes up to Sean and says that he isn't an Orangeman and hits him a couple of times and then this crowd of Orangemen light on us and we are only saved by the barman yelling that he's called the cops and we got out and grabbed a taxi and here we are."

I gazed balefully (I'm good at that) at him through my one remaining open eye. "You lying wanker," I muttered. "You lying useless stupid wanker." I thought, given the circumstances, that I was being rather restrained, but then, the English never seem to pick up the subtle nuances of Ulster speech patterns. I think it's a basic flaw in their character, like being unable to manufacture whiskey or beat the West Indians at cricket.

"Listen, this is what really happened. We was down at the Liverpool House, getting a few free bevvies from adhesive Ray (named for his sticky fingers) who's leaving the bar tomorrow and was therefore in a generous mood with his employer's liquor, and this useless stream of Brit piss is getting yet another exclusive interview vis-à-vis the ongoing political situation in our fair wee Ulcer from yours truly when suddenly the bar is invaded by the Everton Orange Pipe band, on their way to the boat having been over for the Twalf. And they are tanked up and they are noisy and I says to Lyndon here, 'just put the tape recorder off, drink up and we'll head off elsewhere' and I go up to the bar to negotiate some free fags from young Raymond and when I come back what do I find but this cretin talking to this scrubber who would make Orange Lil look like one of the Peace People and he's chatting her up and saying that he'd like an interview with a real live Orangewoman and he produces the tape recorder. So, next minute this paranoid gorilla looms up and asks, not unreasonably, I thought, just who the hell we were, and before I can say anything this Brit buffoon admits to being an English journalist and claims that I'm an Orangeman who's a friend of bloody Ian Paisley. Me, an Orangeman! And before I can try to wriggle out and explain that I'm just a lapsed Prod and not one of the brethren, the gorilla has flashed a couple of mystic Orange/Masonic passwords, to which we haven't given the right response and I'm lying on the floor with a split lip, a bloody nose and a black eye."

Silence descended on the corner as my loyal friends viewed my wounds. Then Brian Artur staggered to his feet. "Comrades," he intoned solemnly, "this is clearly a case for social justice with the odd bit of bigotry thrown in. Let's get the bastards." Touched as I was by his obvious concern and his undying loyalty (exacerbated by the alcohol and his imminent doom), I felt constrained to mutter an insincere protest. "Forget it lads, sure they'll be on the boat by now. It doesn't matter."

"The boat doesn't sail until half nine." This contribution from Uncle Mal, a sober and serious Catholic bigot and car owner, carried some weight. "We can do it easy, the motor's outside."

Some of the team had some sense and 'volunteered' to stay in the bar and look after me. Sure wasn't it their Christian duty, as cousin Harry put it. Others were more loyal and less pragmatic.

Led by Brian Artur, my hero and champion, five of them swarmed out of the bar and into Mal's motor. Brian Artur was dragging a protesting Lyndon. "We need someone to finger them," he growled. His red drinker's nose led the troops like a beacon light Rudolf to the lions' den.

I gratefully accepted another whiskey and a Kleenex for my nose. Harry, the sensible coward, was philosophical. "Don't worry," he said. "They're too steaming to ever find them." We resumed our drinking and gradually the whiskey began to work its anaesthetic magic on my brain and wounds. As the man says, 'I was feeling no pain'. Other stag party guests arrived and the drink and banter flew. It was half ten when Uncle Mal threw open the swing doors and made his dramatic entrance. He was plainly ill at ease. Even in our pallatic condition we could fathom that all was not well. "What the fuck's up, Mal?" asked Harry, always one to come to the point.

"Give us a drink." He slumped onto a seat and downed the proffered whiskey in one. This was not his usual form. Uncle Mal is a half pint shandy or a glass of white wine, if he's really in the mood and the parrot woman has let him off the leash, man. He therefore had an attentive audience as he told the tale. Subsequent research has established that he was not, of course, totally accurate in his account. His own part was, for example, somewhat less heroic, but, by and large the story checked out.

They had hit the Liverpool House just before nine. Lyndon had been able to confirm that none of the attackers were still on the premises. Ray had told how they had stumbled off to the boat some twenty minutes previously. The gallant band, already starting to realize that they were somewhat foolishly absenting themselves from a night's drinking, had been prepared to accept that and return to console me and fortify themselves. But not Brian Artur. His blood was up. "Right lads, onto the boat!"

Uncle Mal, a former boy scout and perennial shit-stirrer and therefore always prepared, opened up the boot of the car and proceeded to hand out spanners and wrenches. It was clearly too late to pull back now. This was Brian Artur's stag night and what he said went. After all, the poor bastard would never get his way again after tomorrow. "I'll stay in the motor and keep the engine running," says Uncle Mal. No fool, Uncle Mal!

"Come on, you Brit wanker!" roared Brian Artur, clutching a

gasping Lyndon by the windpipe, "This is all your fault." Joe and the Digger followed. This was it. Over the top. It was Ypres all over again.

The imposing presence of Brian Artur was enough to intimidate the ticket collector. As a *coup de grâce* Brian Artur breathed over him. As the pensioner reeled back, Brian Artur airily waved the others through. "It's all right, mate, we're just seeing a few friends off."

The second class bar was crowded. The Orange people were tired and drunk, but, for yet another year, they had demonstrated their loyalty, crossed the Irish sea and marched to the field. They had shown the Fenians they were not to be trifled with. Lyndon, as he confessed to me later, did his best. He tried not to identify the gorilla, who, it later transpired, was an off-duty cop. He was standing at the bar, pint in hand, surrounded by his cronies. But the eagle eye of Skibbereen's finest was not to be denied. "That's the bastard, isn't it." Trembling, Lyndon averred that that was so and then, released from Brian Artur's grip, stumbled back and down the gangplank. Why had his editor ever sent him to this open insane asylum? Why wasn't he back in the saloon bar in Fleet Street! Who were these madmen!

Nothing would give me more pleasure than to relate how these Celtic heroes, outnumbered by forty to one, o'ercame the alien hordes. How Brian Artur, that doughty Cúchulainn, aided and abetted by the trusty Fionn and Cormac MacAirt (even if he was Australian) battled valiantly to a victory that put to shame even the mighty cattle raid of Cooley, the *Táin Bó*. However my mother, saintly woman that she is, reared me from infancy to be truthful. I must stress that it gives me no pleasure to record here the ignominious defeat of my gallant would-be avengers. If I tell how Brian Artur missed with his one and only punch and then proceeded to get his melt kicked in by the forces of reaction; if I relate how the Ned Kelly of Belfast threw one bottle which missed and then fled; and finally if I reveal that Joe Q., fleeing the scene without a blow struck and trying to vent his spleen, kicked a large Lambeg drum and broke his big right toe, I do so with no spirit of malice, but merely to set the record straight.

Brian Artur and I next met that evening in the City Hospital. Alcohol had successfully anaesthetized me to the extent that I had made only token protest when cousin Harry insisted on bringing me down to casualty to get stitches inserted in my lip. It was there, around midnight that comrades Brian Artur and Joe hobbled in.

Brian Artur's face was one puffy, vivid contusion. One eye was closed. Through the other one he recognized me and a smile spread slowly over the lunar landscape which he used for a face, revealing gaps where earlier this evening teeth had shone. "Sean, me oul son, we molucated them." "Revenge is sweet, eh, Brian Artur." "You better believe it, me oul mucker, you better fuckin' believe it."

I don't think I'll ever forget the wedding. The bride, a charming girl whose resemblance to a scorpion with dyspepsia was, I'm sure, completely accidental or one of those little jokes that our Lord likes to try out on us now and again just to show that He hasn't lost his sense of humor, was, quite understandably, not in the best of form. Apparently she had been prepared, just, to swallow Cousin Harry's tale of the unfortunate car accident which had resulted in her Brian Artur being covered in bandages, stitches and scars, but the sight of Joe with his foot in plaster and myself with six stitches in my lip, which I nonchalantly failed to pass off as herpes, undoubtedly resulted in a certain 'frostiness'. Years later Brian Artur, in a reminiscent mood, told me how she had spent the honeymoon, gazing across the Atlantic and viciously plucking out the stitches from his scalp.

"That's what you get for marrying a nurse," I opined. He thought for a minute and took a sip of his soda water and lime – for it was to this pass that a once legendary drinker had come – "That's what you get for marrying, fullstop!" And then, brightening up, he looked at me with that old grin and laughed. "Anyway, me ould son, we showed them, eh!" "Too right kid, too right."

And God's curse on the Everton pipe band!

Spiderman v. The Big Doc

"Do you want to make some money?" asked Brian Artur. I demurred. As a drinking companion Brian Artur was one of nature's gentlemen. As a tipster he ranked worse than the Scout, and those of you who follow the racing press will know that that's not great.

"I remember the last horse you gave me. It's still running if it isn't in the glue factory." He shook his head with impatience. "It's not a horse, you eejit, it's a sure thing. Spider's going up to the panel today."

I showed some interest. Brian Artur had told me tales of his friend Peter Quinn, the Spiderman of West Belfast, but I had never actually met him. A legend in his own lunchtime it was said. "Lead on, if we hurry we'll get a seat and maybe even a game of pool." "Sound," grinned Brian Artur and hailed a black taxi.

The Social club burst into spontaneous silence when Frank the doorman rushed in with the announcement that he was back. Everyone there that afternoon knew who 'he' was. The mighty Quinn. The Spiderman, and they all knew where he'd been. Hardened pool players put down their cues, the card sharks dropped their hands, big Kevin stopped pulling a pint mid-flow, causing Uncle Ted near apoplexy. All eyes swiveled towards the door. The bookies fumbled nervously for their notebooks. There was a lot of money resting on this one. This week had been a 'double dunt' on the dole, and the unemployed, who made up at least fifty percent of the clientele of the West Belfast Kneecapper's and Punters Club, had had extra cash with which to gamble. At home, did they but know it, many wives' housekeeping money depended on the outcome of this one.

He walked through the door and up to the bar. Amateur psychologists, in whom the club abounded, stared eagerly at his face for any sign, but he was as impassive as ever as Kevin pulled him his pint. He nodded over to where Brian Artur and I were sitting and joined us beside the 'A' team pool table and marking board.

The tension was electric but still no one spoke. The Spider sipped his pint and looked round. "Quiet in here today, isn't it. Has someone died?"

This was too much for the fans' patience and hubbub broke the silence. "Come on, Spider, how'd it go?" a dozen voices cried out. The Spiderman smiled slowly and took another sip of his pint. Raising his hand he got instant silence such as is only heard in the Club when 'The Solders Song' is played at the end of the night to quieten the drunken pint patriots at the end of a long Saturday.

"Wee buns," he said. "No problems."

Pandemonium ensued. The bookie who had been rash enough to give 11/4 against the Spider making it for the fifth time was caught trying to slink out of the door and roughly dragged into the hall by jubilant punters. Several hard men, including Tommy Boyd, who had been foolish enough to back the Big Doc were seen crying into their stout. One even approached the Spider where he sat, his table now laden with drink bought for him by his adoring fans and offered his hand and a groveling apology.

"Jesus, Spider, I'm sorry, I bet against you. I should have known better." "You will the next time, Bobby, ego te absolvo," said the Spider, graciously. I thanked him too, my faith in Brian Artur's tips restored. I was eleven quid better off.

Five in a row! Now that was something to tell your grandchildren. Luigi even kept the bar open an hour late that night and that hadn't happened since the B team won the Jack McCarten pool trophy, and that, dear readers is, I regret to have to tell you, a long time ago. "It was some day that," I said to the wife as I stumbled into the house that night, having dropped off Brian Artur, and evaded the breathalyzer patrol and those nasty little traffic islands which have a habit of attacking me and the car when I've had a drink or three. "Five in a row! Fair play to the Spider."

Spiderman. The nickname owed nothing to Stan Lee and Marvel Comics, you must understand. Quinn really had once, many years ago, been a Spiderman, a steeplejack, and he'd been good at his job and earning top dollar, while most were on the dole. That is until one day, five years ago, a gust of wind had swayed the scaffolding and hurled him fifty feet to the pavement below. He had been lucky. A broken arm, a broken leg and mild concussion, but he had survived where many had not. He'd been in hospital for four weeks and off work for another two months. He'd put in a 'compo' claim which would, three years later, eventually net him 20,000 pounds, but, in the meantime he was expected to go back to work, and this he would not do.

Don't get me wrong. He wasn't work-shy or scared. He expressed it all quite simply to me one afternoon in the club as we sat drinking beer between pool games. "A cat may have nine lives," he said, "but I figure I've used my one spare one up. Why should I get up on that scaffolding again and risk my neck for 100 pounds a week for a boss who never goes up, drives a Mercedes, and gets more than 500 pounds a week plus fringe benefits. It doesn't make a whole lot of sense."

And here's the didactic bit. He was not one of your armchair revolutionaries or your socialists or, as my old headmaster, God rot him, would have put it, 'a bit of a bolshie'. If you'd mentioned Marx to him he would have asked you, quite sincerely, whether you meant Groucho or Harpo. No, he was just an ordinary punter, who'd taken the decision that he wasn't going to risk his life again for someone who exploited him and, what's more, he wasn't prepared to work in some menial job for less than he'd been getting after he's spent twenty years of his life training for and doing a dangerous and relatively ill-paid job. Margaret Thatcher or Keith Joseph would no doubt brand him a skiver or parasite, as indeed might many of you, but it's remarkably easy to use such words when you own a lot of land, get 50,000 pounds a year and are in the unique position of being able to vote yourself a pay rise whenever you feel like it.

At any rate, the Spider decided that, for him, unless he turned to crime, which he didn't really fancy, for he had too many friends who were men of conviction – the chief one of which was that they wouldn't be caught – there was only really one option, and that was a life 'on the sick'.

Once you adopt such a course of action you enter an entire new subculture. In Belfast, and indeed, under the Blessed Margaret Thatcher, in the rest of the UK, it is one of the few growth industries. For those few prosperous members of our neat little society I should briefly explain how the system works, for many of you will have been reared, as indeed was I, on delightful folk myths about the idle unemployed driving up to collect their dole in Jaguars and sports cars and thumbing their noses at hard working citizens such as you and I.

In fact the dole is a system whereby you humiliate and enslave people. The pittance that they are paid is inadequate to support even a tolerable standard of living and so, of course, unable to get a full time job, many resort to doing 'homers' or 'nixers'. In other words, part time work such as car repairs, roofing, painting, plumbing, labouring, etc. to augment their pitiful dole. This is, naturally, illegal and also very useful for the state since they can then employ a veritable legion of snoopers, spies and touts whose sole job it is to track down and prosecute these evil malefactors.

The fact that the money that they eventually recover doesn't even pay a tenth of the salaries of these public spirited informers is neither here nor there. Some men and women apparently see it as their life's vocation to hide outside an unmarried mother's flat all night to determine whether in her unmitigated brazenness and concupiscence she permits a man to stay overnight. Such voyeurism obviously gives some people their jollies. They also have the bonus of self-righteousness when these vile miscreants are hauled through the courts to be judged and sentenced, not by their peers, but by some senile rich man pontificating about their deplorable lifestyle.

With luck the culprits may end up in one of the 'hotels' which Her Gracious Majesty provides for all who transgress the golden rule – i.e., he who has the gold, rules. Or, then again, you can go on the sick.

On the sick you get more money. Not much more, but a little. In order to do this you need a friendly doctor, not too hard to get in strifetorn Belfast. Contrary to popular opinion, some doctors do have a social conscience. Daily they see people suffering from the disease of unemployment, which is often terminal. Apart from doling out tranquilizers, they can, and some do, hand out sick lines. The mandarins in the bureaucracy know this however, and do not trust local doctors. Accordingly, they have created the 'panel', head of which is THE BIG DOC. There is not of course merely one BIG DOC, there are dozens of them scattered throughout the province, but their task, which they undertake with single-minded zeal, is to seek out the malingerers and throw them off the sick.

End of lecture. The reader, if he or she has lasted this far, will have realized that the author's late headmaster was quite right in describing him as 'a bit of a bolshie'. He is hopelessly partisan and probably has a massive chip on his shoulder. He is probably a waster too, and may well have done some time on the sick himself. Read, therefore, if you can, the rest of the story with extreme skepticism.

The Spider took expert advice before embarking upon his career on the sick. This was not hard to get. All he had to do was to go into the club any afternoon and there he could consult a wide range of experts, free, gratis and for nothing. There were the 'bad back men', the 'mysterious pains men', the 'bangers away men'. This last team were among the most erudite and esoteric. 'Bangers', for those of you unfortunate enough not to have lived in West Belfast, is slang for nerves. Throughout the years these men had acquired almost shamanistic powers in diagnosing and inventing mental conditions which could and would be described by overworked doctors as 'nervous debility'.

The Spider consulted everyone. He did not intend to come to any rash or hasty decision. He rejected out of hand however the 'bad back' strategy which so many advocated and used. This was, he felt, strictly for amateurs. Too many punters had been conned by experienced Big Docs who 'accidentally' dropped pencils and watched with delight as the 'patient' bent over to retrieve them for them, or who pretended to strike the patient in the back, only to see the 'sufferer' squeal before contact had even been made. Similarly he was suspicious of those who advocated 'mystery' diseases. It was all too easy for a zealous Big Doc to claim that there was a new 'miracle' cure, prescribe some placebo and send the protesting victim back to the dole queue. Clearly 'nervous debility' from which over half the population suffer in reality, did but they know it, had its merits, but the Spider wasn't totally satisfied.

He disappeared from the club for a whole three days, a fact in itself which provoked comment from the pool playing fraternity. No one believed Sweeny's assertion that he had been observed going into the reference section of the Andersonstown public library, but in doing so they maligned an honest witness, for, when he reappeared after his self-imposed exile the Spider was in possession of a new word. A word which was to astound even the most experienced malingerers. A word which, later on, after he had beaten the Big Doc three times in a row, many of them were to bandy about over their cups as if it were in common parlance. A word which on Quiz nights even Terry Young, the club's resident cretin, could define. The word 'Acrophobia'.

Now I shouldn't have to define this for you. As I've said, even Terry Young, the Quiz incompetent knows what it means, and TY, after all is the selfsame contestant who, on being asked who played the Lone Ranger in the TV series replied, 'how the hell would I know, he never took his mask off'. But, in case any of you out there in readerland have had a lapse of memory, 'acrophobia' means, quite simply, a fear of heights, which you must admit is a pretty fair handicap for a spiderman and damned hard to prove one way or another.

The first interview with the Big Doc was, as the Spider was later to describe it, 'a doddle'. The young inexperienced medic was no match for the Andytown man. As a result, three months later he went up in the rankings and had to see Gaffikin. Now you'll have to understand something about the Big Doc *modus operandi*. At most you get two days' notice. The letter arrives and contains not your Giro cheque but a demand that you attend the Big Doc's offices in Adelaide Street. The letter is edged in black.

Accordingly, trembling in trepidation, you voyage down to the town center at the appointed hour, clutching your little specimen of urine in a screw cap bottle and praying that it doesn't explode or leak, for there's nothing worse than having to urinate on demand. There you are shown into the waiting room where at least forty other potential victims are seated.

The Spider always described this as a psychological cock-up. If your appointment was for 10 a.m. there was no chance that you'd be seen before 11.30 and the bureaucratic shrinks who had devised this ploy had obviously felt that a ninety-minute wait amongst the genuine cases and the con men, in the bilious green painted room, brightened only by the most tasteless reproductions of an earless Van Gogh and a butch Florence Nightingale would unnerve most malingerers. This tactic may have succeeded with some, but not with the Spider. As he used to explain, in his weekly seminars between pool and pints, "It's ideal. It's so dreary and depressing that by the time you're called, you can have psyched yourself up to actually believing all the crap that you're going to come out with. By the time you go in you really are suffering from nervous debility."

Gaffikin was well known. Theoretically you are not supposed to know the name of the faceless medic who examines you and holds your destiny in the palm of his hands; but, of course, the grapevine knows them all. Gaffikin is marked a three on the scale. A hard man, but a sucker for the family problems angle. His own wife had left him and run off with a younger doctor after fifteen frustrated years of tedium, and so now, although a bitter man, he had a soft spot for deserted husbands. Any suggestion that your present problem might result in your wife flying the coop with another man and taking the children with her is sure to elicit a sympathetic response.

On the other hand, any admission that your condition has driven you to drink or religion was sure to evoke the utmost hostility. Knowing this, the cognoscenti were not surprised that the Spider surmounted this second hurdle with ease, but his third visit was to be the start of his epic encounter with THE Big Doc. The infamous McKenzie.

McKenzie. The monster of myth. Just as mothers throughout

the world threaten their obstreperous or boisterous children with the bogey man or the big bad wolf, so exasperated Andytown housewives threaten their husbands with McKenzie. In the clubs and shebeens his name was frequently used as a vile oath by hard men who lived in dread of him.

Alaistair McKenzie, although no one, not even his mother, if he had one, would have dared use his Christian name, was a dour fanatical teetotaler. The self-appointed Torquemada of the Welfare State. A man whose sole pleasure in life was to strike from the rolls of those receiving sickness benefit the crippled, the blind, the lame and the mutilated along with the malingerers, for they were all the same in McKenzie's book: parasites. Grown men, with years of experience of faking every symptom known to the medical profession had slunk out of his office in tears, a lifetime's work in ruins. Amongst the betting fraternity you could get 5/1 against anyone getting past McKenzie on their first try, let alone second, when the odds would be offered at 10/1 with few takers.

On his first encounter the odds were slightly in favour of the Spider in that he had done his homework. In the library he had studied every medical tome on acrophobia. He had memorized all the symptoms, all the quirks. He had, of course, totally eschewed the jargon. Nothing alerts a Big Doc quicker than if you come out with technical terms which you, a mere layman, are not supposed to know about.

But acrophobia was a new one for McKenzie and so the Spider had a slight edge. He duly collected his sick line, went back to the club to acknowledge the plaudits of the faithful, collect his winnings from the bookies, and plot his strategy for the next round. Meanwhile the word flashed round the grapevine: The Spider had beaten the Big Doc for the third time – and it had been McKenzie.

Four months later, when the word came that he had been ritually summoned again, the excitement and the betting was intense. It was a cert that it would be McKenzie again, and this time he would be well genned up on acrophobia. Only the Spider's most diehard supporters were prepared to bet on him this time, but those who did, like Gerry Osborne and Gerry Lowe, cleaned up, for the Spider had pulled another stroke – aerophobia. The fear of air or drafts (or 'George Rafts', as the elderly Onanist would have it). Somewhere in the course of McKenzie's sarcastic probing he casually confessed to this other fear, which, apart from heights caused him irrational panic. McKenzie was confounded. In front of him was either one of the smartest malingerers that he had ever encountered or a man who could make medical history and and, incidentally, McKenzie's name in the annals of medical science: The McKenzie Syndrome', the 'McKenzie Condition'. To ignore this was a risk he couldn't take, and so, while the Big Doc took down his textbooks and prepared to write a treatise for the British Medical Journal, the Spider got another extension of his sick line.

Back at the club the excitement was mounting amongst those who took these arcane matters seriously. A few people had beaten A Big Doc four times and gone on to strike gold – a lifetime invalidity pension – but no one had beaten McKenzie twice in a row before and the third encounter was starting to generate the kind of interest a World Heavyweight fight engenders in the hearts and minds of Belfast sporting fans.

Those who had studied the case intently with a view to making a few pounds in side bets had opined that the Spider would probably opt for Agoraphobia, the fear of open spaces next time, but, as he was later to explain to the faithful, Spider felt that this would have been a weak strategy. It would have been all too easy for McKenzie to recommend him for indoor work on the ground floor with no drafts. Instead the Spider pulled the *coup de grâce* and came up with neophobia, the fear of novelty. Acrophobia and aerophobia effectively precluded him from doing his old job; neophobia meant that he could do no other.

The Spider was not called before a Big Doc again. By letter he was informed that he had been awarded an invalidity pension for life. It was not a fortune, but it was the principle that mattered. Besides, he could always do homers and hustle pool. As for McKenzie, he died a few months later, his monograph unpublished, some say from a broken heart, but more likely from the injuries sustained when he was knocked down by a black taxi in Castle Street. The club celebrated, and even held a wake for him, where many of his former victims turned up for a gloat. We even put a death notice in the *Irish News* for him, which some felt secretly was in bad taste, and others felt was a waste of money since the bastard would never get to read it, unless the circulation department of the Vatican Telegraph was delivering to hell these days. But it was a simple message. I have it here in front of me:

"McKenzie, Alaistair. Dr. He has gone to that great panel in the sky. May St. Peter show the same charity to him that he did to us."

It was signed 'from Spider, Brian Artur & the lads'.

May The Farce Be With You

Unlike the other tales of Brian Artur this is the only one for which I have no conclusive proof. I have the word of the great man himself, which, I hasten to add, is normally enough for me or any other reasonable person. I have the vague recollections of Cousin Harry. The Bushman, alas, is no more. Proinseas Cleasa has vanished from human ken and the good Father Philbin, now resident in the home for the mentally bewildered run by the blessed Sisters of Perpetual Indulgence, was unable to confirm or deny the story, although his glazed look when I visited his sick bed, armed with the obligatory bottle of Lucozade leads me to believe that certainly something happened on that long week back in 197_. Finally, the cow has gone the way of all kine.

In religious discussions with my spiritual advisor, the Reverend Father Herbert of the Maccabees, he has chosen to express skepticism at this story. He does not believe in aliens or UFOs. He is quite entitled to his disbelief. By the same token, however, I am entitled to believe in them and to discount the anthropological facets of such Christian rituals as transubstantiation or the proposition that Jewish maidens can become pregnant because a dove gets stuck up their ear. That is, surely, what free will is all about. Anyway.

XT 69 put down the scout ship with all the aplomb that had made him a master space mariner at the remarkably early age of 562. ZT 46, his navigator, was sweating; well, at least as much as Largactyls can perspire, but his apprehension was needless. It was a smooth landing as the ship descended and squelched gently into the dank Fermanagh bog.

"Where are we?" asked XT 69. He had flunked intergalactic geography at Space Academy, but put him behind a console and program a few co-ordinates in and he was your man. Or rather, Largactyl. "A remote insignificant planet called Sol 3," replied ZT 46, consulting his pocket manual of the 'Galaxies Made Easy', a seminal work for the space voyager published by the Interdenominal Church of the Readers' Digest. "To be more precise, as far as I can determine, we are only three thousand zitts off course, due no doubt to that last meteor shower. We missed Betelgeuse."

"To be exact," chimed in the computer, "we are three Terran miles from a small village infested by Earthlings, or 'humans' as they call themselves, known to the indigenous population as 'Blacklion'. It straddles an artificial border between what is referred to as 'Ulcer' and 'The Potato Republic' by its denizens, on a small island off the European continent. It is designated in my manual as the 'arse hole of nowhere', whatever that may mean." Neither computers or Largactyls have arseholes.

XT 69 muttered a few Largactylian oaths to himself in which the threat of bloody carnage was inventively balanced against the accusation of incestuous carnality and gnashed his one fang (no mean feat in itself). He hated smartarse computers. "Never mind that," he grated, "Is there any nitrogen?"

"Affirmative," clicked the computer. "Although primitive, the planet has sufficient nitrogen to make up the deficit lost during the storm. I estimate that two point six zwerbs will suffice to replenish and effect basic repairs. That's six Terran days and nights," it added, showing off abominably. "The climate, due to an excess of oxygen, is not propitious, but the erection of a modest force field module should give us sufficient protection. I have already so instructed the auto repair crew."

"Question." XT 69 strove to regain control. He didn't need a bloody conglomeration of plastic and microchips to tell him what to do. "Is there intelligent life in the vicinity?"

The computer extended its antennae, assembled its data, and amid a plethora of hisses, stroboscopic effects and farts, produced its considered response.

"Sensors indicate that a primitive life force, of extremely limited intelligence, does exist. I have no history tapes to monitor, but on the basis of the limited data available, I would estimate that the local populace have the intellectual capacity of a slightly brain damaged Ptilian aardvark. There is no evidence that they present any danger, except to themselves, and statistically, it is virtually impossible that they can have developed weaponry capable of penetrating the force field."

"Recommend commencement of nitrogen replenishment immediately," snapped XT 69. "I already have," crackled the computer snottily. ZT 46 coughed. "Since we are forced to remain here for at least two zwerbs, permission to capture one of the local specimens?" he postulated, but XT 69 had already slithered off in a fit of pique to his slumber cocoon.

Brian Artur Grimshaw, a decidedly primitive life form even by Terra's fairly non-exacting criteria, weaving his way home across the border by a non-approved ditch, was the first Earthling to be vouchsafed a glimpse of the ET's craft. It being a Sunday and the Northern bars in Belcoo being closed, due to archaic legislation, puritanical insanity and the eternal vigilance of Constable McCrea, a Paisleyite who, not content with being born like the rest of us, had had to be reborn three times on account of his piles and dyspetic wife. Brian Artur had been slaking his omnipresent thirst with a few dozen pints of porter in the Bush bar in Blacklion, a hundred yards across the border in the Potato Republic.

The noise of the spacecraft and the glaring lights as it descended into the mire had not upset or surprised him overly. He had seen worse sights than that, and, come to think of it, stranger ones on other evenings after a few at the Bush. There had been that night when the Bushman had produced a keg of McAnoy's poitín – 'not a drop bottled until it's two days old' – now THAT had been a night to remember! In addition, being a 'good' Catholic, he had, like his peers, tended to believe that flying saucers were in fact diaphragms, discarded by nuns on their way heavenward.

Nonetheless, being of an inquisitive nature, he had felt bound to investigate when a 500-ton spacecraft had hovered above him with arclights ablazing. His first reaction when the spotlight hit him had been to get down on his knees and do his impression of Al Jolson singing 'Mammy', for, after all, one never knows when Opportunity will Knock and Hughie Greene and the TV crew will discover native talent. But, even in his befuddled state, he realized that this was neither the time nor the place.

Suddenly it hit him. "Jesus, Mary and Joseph," he muttered, "it's thon Captain Kirk. That Scottish bastard's going to beam me up."

The feeling of paralysis was only temporary, and within a few seconds he was stumbling his way across the bog, reeling, swaying and falling. "I knew that last bottle was a bad 'un," he gibbered, as like his Saviour, he fell for the third time.

SMACK! He staggered back, picked himself up and tried again.

WALLOP! There it was again! Even at the best of times, and this clearly wasn't one of them, Brian Artur may not have been the quickest, but when an invisible wall put him arse over tip for the third time he realized that something was up. He lay in the mud, not bothering to get up. What was the point? Some bastard was only going to knock him down again! He was clearly as unwelcome as a dead rat in the packing shed of a tampon factory. And then it came to him. Like Saul on the road to Damascus. A farce field!

He might not, in those days, have been a prolific reader. In fact, apart from the racing page of the *Fermanagh Herald* and page three of the *Sun*, the printed word had not bothered him too much, but while doing time for Ireland (six months in Crumlin Road jail for making moonshine) he had read no fewer than three Science Fiction books. "By Jesus, that's what it is! A fookin' farce field!" he muttered. Gingerly, he raised himself from the slime and began to examine this new phenomenon.

It took him some three hours, stumbling around as the dawn thrust its roseate fingers through the sepulchral morning mists. The aliens had turned the lights off – to economize? – which didn't help, but Brian Artur had roamed these bogs man and boy for thirty years and knew their wiles like those of his wife, Hilda. As the sun shone wearily and warily through the miasma Brian Artur had it sussed out to his satisfaction.

The alien craft, which had submerged itself in the middle of the *Fear a chonaic Murchadh* bog was the epicentre of a force field which stretched about a mile and a half around it, straddling the border. Parts of the village of Blacklion, on the southern side of the border, were included. So was Brian Artur's house on the northern side, but the actual village of Belcoo which housed the RUC barracks and the customs wasn't.

But four short hours after his initial encounter of the second kind Brian Artur's cerebral synapses had cranked out the answer. As the rain began its daily mizzle he found himself, not for the first time, outside the back door of the Bush Bar. A whole new era of the longstanding 'War of the Gaugers' was about to begin.

Meanwhile, back on the spacecraft, ZT 46 had been busy. He possessed an inquiring mind and, although no expert on alien subspecies, had always fancied seeing his name in the Interstellar Geographic. Already he had made his first capture: a Friesian cow. The cow had, at first, been somewhat bemused. One minute there it was, up to its udders in bog, vaguely trying to find some edible grass, and suddenly, – WHOOSH – inside an alien spacecraft, having been conveyed there by some kind of beam device. It was enough to make a cow shit itself. Solemnly, the Friesian did just that. Fascinated, ZT 46 looked on and recorded the defecation with an impressive array of instruments. Delicately he manoeuvred a small forcefield around the bovine and proceeded to insert the probe sensors. "Let the analysis commence," he muttered.

The Bushman was not happy. Here it was, 6 a.m., and him with only three hours of sleep beneath him, having been up to 3 a.m., clearing the bar of those Northern drunks and now here was that omadaun Grimshaw hammering on his back door for more porter. "Mother of God, who'd be a publican?" he mumbled, carefully forgetting that he was the richest man in the county, since in addition he was the estate agent, spirit grocer, auctioneer and loan shark. It was tough being a gombeen man, he thought to himself. "Divil a bit of thanks, only dog's abuse."

"Get the fuck out of there, Grimshaw, ye heathen bowsie," he bellowed. "I'm closed."

"Not for long, ye won't be, Murtagh," wheedled Brian Artur. "Not after ye've heard the proposition I've got for you."

In the village of Blacklion and its environs only one man could truly be said to drink more alcohol than Brian Artur and that was his cousin Harry, and yet their modes of consumption were totally different. Brian Artur was a sturdy, solid, reliable, regular drinker. One of his nicknames was, in fact, 'the Growth', because it was widely believed that the bottle of Guinness which was permanently in one hand had sprouted from his flesh like some warty appendage. Drink to him was no a problem. He drank, got drunk, fell down – no problem.

Cousin Harry was the exact opposite. The local schoolteacher, 'the Master', as he was called by one and all, was subject to furiously fluctuating bouts of exuberant drunkenness and tearful and stern temperance. For two or three weeks he would be a model of sobriety and rectitude. The clean shirt, the daily Communion and the pledge. Then, for no apparent reason, 'the black thirst' would come upon him, like one of the plagues of Egypt, and he would be off 'on a tear'. On a bash.

A small man with a pigeon chest, he would descend, as if a whirlwind, roaring drunk, upon any one of the dozen pubs in the vicinity, challenging one and all to drinking bouts (which he always won), to arm wrestling (which he always lost), and to table jumping, at which he was remarkably nimble. He had been '86'ed', or barred, from every bar within a twenty-mile radius at one time or another, but had always been allowed back since he paid cash and never asked for credit.

Broke again, he would stagger home and go to bed for two days before reappearing, spruce and immaculate as a conception, as if nothing had happened, armed with a 'sickline' from his good friend the local GP, and ready to 'batter some sense' into the local youth. The Bishop had been trying to sack him for years but the parish priest and the parents had a soft spot for him. When he was sober he was a good teacher, the best they'd ever had, and anyway, who else would put up with the 'future of Blacklion' for such a miserable pittance.

Besides, knowing that your children would be off school for a few days every month had its advantages. It meant that they would be available as cheap labour on the farm or in the shop.

Anyway, on the momentous night in question, 'the Master' was on a bash. Barred, temporarily at least, from the curtilege of the Bush Bar, he had been trying, for hours now, to drink the Smokey Tavern dry. At 4 a.m., the last customer in the bar, he had slumped off his stool and banged his head on the counter. This was not an uncommon occurrence and McKeever, the bar owner, was well used to it. With a grunt, he hauled the unconscious pedagogue over to the corner of the bar, threw an old horse blanket over him and retired upstairs to his scratcher.

Ten minutes later he was fast asleep and dreaming of winning the Irish Sweep and so missed the sight of the rural Rousseau throwing off the blanket and crawling behind the bar. There it was. Still on the top shelf where he'd been covertly admiring it all evening. McKeever's pride and joy: a bottle of 25-year-old Jack Daniels Kentucky Sour Mash Bourbon, a present from his cousin Barney in the Bronx. Trembling with anticipation and the DTs, Cousin Harry perched himself on a stool and reached for the nectar, but just as his fingers touched the sacred flagon he felt the earth move. Desperately he scrabbled to regain his equilibrium, to no avail. With a despairing oath and one hand still clutching the stolen liquor, the Bard of Blacklion toppled from his stool, described a graceful parabola through the side window of the Smokey Tavern and landed in the laneway.

Stumbling to his feet, he brushed the shards of glass from his best suit, spied the light from McKeever's window, heard his bellowing and the barking of his dogs and realized it was time to relocate, as our American friends, God bless them, would say. Gasping, he staggered up the road. He must have covered a quarter of a mile before he felt the liquid running down his leg.

"Sacred Heart of Jesus," he prayed, "let it be urine, not whiskey." It was. God is good. Now and again.

Shrugging off this minor inconvenience, he shook his leg and inspected his prize. It was unspoiled. The cobwebs were barely disturbed. But not for long. Prying the top off, he took a massive slug and wiped his lips. Stumbling along the laneway he took another, just as he came into the sights of ZT 46's tracking beam.

Seconds later, still clutching the Jack Daniels, he was sitting inside the alien vehicle. The first thing he saw as he rubbed his eyes was a placid, contented cow, apparently munching on a large heap of grass. The second thing was a bright green creature which waved its tentacles and emitted a string of high pitched gibberish. Admiringly the Master stared at the Bourbon in his hand.

"See them Yanks! When they make a Whiskey, they make a Whiskey!"

It is apparently an axiom in Largactylian text books that 'we are what we eat' – hence their predilection for wriggly green slugs. So it was hardly surprising that the first tests that ZT 46 conducted on his unwitting subjects concerned analyzing the contents of their respective stomachs. The cow had proven simple enough, and ever mindful of the Galaxy's rules of conduct when capturing primitive alien species, ZT 46 had programmed the computer to replicate its main staple. The analysis of the latest captive's entrails initially, however, proved more difficult. A priest at Delphi might have given up and just concluded that the entrail omens boded no one any good, but ZT 46 and his computer were made of sterner galactic stuff.

At first the analyzer had rejected the preliminary report on the grounds that no creature with such a metabolism could sustain life on a diet of 80% alcohol and a nauseous black fermented gunge which a scan through the creature's tortured brain synapses designated as 'Porter'.

Nevertheless, the creature did appear to show some sentient life features. On the surface it did not evince many signs of rating higher than the quadruped on any known intelligence quotient scale, and it certainly didn't qualify for inclusion in 'The Galaxy's Guide to Lesser Intelligent Lifeforms', but then, it didn't pay to take any chances, especially when what you were doing, even if for purely scientific reasons, was a direct violation of the Galaxy's ethical standards.

Accordingly, the synthesizer was programmed, and when a few moments later Harry recovered consciousness, he was confronted with a sight which would be emblazoned until death upon his retinae. Beside his three-quarter full bottle of Jack Daniels 25-year-old stood ten other three-quarter full bottles of what appeared to be a remarkably similar beverage. Rubbing his eyes he reached for nearest of the mirages and raised it to his lips. Holy Mary, Mother of God! If this was a mirage, he was going to join the Foreign Legion – as opposed to the Legion of Mary.

Suddenly, ZAP! Beside him appeared ten pint bottles of what appeared to be Porter. Better still, the first one tasted of Porter. Good Porter. "Thank you, God," he mumbled, his faith, always a dubious entity at the best of times, restored once more. "Thank you for bringing thine humble servant from that vale of tears where he moiled and toiled for so long to your celestial home. I always knew you would reward your true servants, and not pay any attention to what that old blatherskite of a Bishop said." He shut up. Maybe he'd gone too far. That mouth of his was always getting him into trouble. He shouldn't be badmouthing one of HIS servants, even if he was an old ...

Enough! But a quick glance around him proved reassuring. Neither the Bourbon nor the Porter had disappeared and there was no sign of the weird green thing that looked like a whirlybird clothesline. Graciously he toasted the cud-chewing cow with a large draft of Porter and, following up the salutation with a mouthful of Bourbon, he settled down to a monumental bash.

Proinseas, the good natured village idiot, had left school officially some four years earlier, and unofficially, three years before that. He had 'helped out' in various bars, working for a pittance, dug turf, dug sheughs and then filled them in again, and had even, at a particularly drunken local wedding party, attempted to grope the resident 'good thing' behind McKeever's barn. None of these ventures had brought him much success. While not exactly in the omadaun league, he was never likely to ever read a book, pass an exam, utter an original thought or attract the fairer sex. Or so he thought. Until that night.

Uncharacteristically, it had all started with a book. Well, at least a pamphlet. It had arrived all the way from London and had been sent by Proinseas's cousin Tommy, the former local head-the-ball, who had departed Blacklion a few years previously to seek fame and fortune in the metropolis and avoid the wrath of the local constabulary. He had ended up in a 'squat' in the East End, surrounded by the cream of the area's winos. Tommy however had never been much of a one for the gargle, but had quickly latched on to the weed and the resin, as well as a wide range of hallucinogenics.

The small book had been entitled 'A Guide to British Psilocybin Mushrooms' and bore an imprint of the Dalston public library from whence Tommy had liberated it. Its cover showed what were described as a group of psilocybin semilanceata standing in a field. To Proinseas they looked like wee mushrooms.

The text was fairly erudite and contained a lot of unpronounceable words in Latin. Tommy's accompanying note was rather obscure too, but after puzzling over both for the best part of a morning, Proinseas had decided that the message was that if one ate about twenty of them wee mushroom buggers, your head could do quare tricks.

The centerfold of the book contained a glossy colour pinup, not, as Proinseas would have preferred, featuring one of the big bosomed British bints wearing nothing more than a look of boredom and with their knickers around their ankles, but a double page spread of six Liberty Cap mushrooms. 'Them's the boyos', thought Proinseas. 'Them wee nipples on the top may not be as exciting as the real thing, but then you can't win them all.' Besides, things were awful boring around Blacklion.

The book had said that the best time to pick the magic mushrooms was at dawn, and that was why, at the same time that the cow and cousin Harry were experiencing close encounters of the third kind with ZT 46, young Proinseas was out and about in the morning dew, sampling the rather foul tasting Liberty Caps which festered in abundance around the neighbouring farms. He had only ingested about fifteen of them and had not as yet experienced any really interesting effects when he had wandered innocently into the path of ZT 46's beam. A millisecond later, there he was, sitting on the floor of the spacecraft beside an obviously stocious Harry and a contented cow.

XT awoke from his sleep tolerably rested. He checked the refueling dials and noted with pleasure that the nitrogen was being taken on board according to schedule. 'Soon be off this Federation forsaken meteorite', he thought to himself. He lapsed into a reverie concerning his first night of leave and big KW 51, it of the amazing tentacles in the Spacers' funhouse on Arcturus.

No! Time enough for such pleasurable and forbidden thoughts later. He ought to relieve ZT 46. Not a bad grubling really, though a bit immature. Well, the next couple of centuries would knock that out of him. Leisurely he floated over to the main bay and tentacled open the hatch. The scene that greeted him was not only amazing but horrifying as well to his tightly organized mind.

ZT had not been idle. In addition to the cow, Harry and Proinseas, he had managed to 'recruit' or scoop up Father Michael Philbin, the parish priest, who had been coming home from an all night call on a sick parishioner. ZT 46 was twittering to himself as he observed the glassy-eyed cleric, surrounded as he was by an ever-increasing pile of communion wafers and chalices of red biddy. Father Philbin, though he was to survive this night, was never to serve midnight Mass again.

Meanwhile, back at the Bush Bar Brian Artur had given up trying to explain his scheme to the bewildered publican and had resorted to tapping his main weakness – greed. "Never mind what I want the money for, Murtagh, here's an offer you can't refuse. You advance me ten thousand for just one month at 15% and if I don't repay you, you can have the Da's farm." The farm was run down and Brian Artur had never bothered to work it. The farmhouse roof leaked and Brian Artur usually slept in the barn or on the floor of some local hostelry but there were fifty acres of land with the property and with the price of land soaring, thanks to the apparently inexhaustible beneficence of the bandits in Brussels, Murtagh knew that he stood to make a lot of cabbage if/when Brian Artur defaulted. Even if, by some miracle, he didn't, well it was an easy fifteen hundred quid.

"I'd be needing the deeds deposited with my solicitor, Brian," he mused. What matter what the crazed loon wanted the money for, he thought to himself. It was probably to put on a horse at the Limerick races, what did he care.

"I'll be at the lawman's at 10 a.m. sharp with the deeds. You be there with the money. The banks open at 9.30 a.m. Yer man can draw up the contract."

They slapped hands on it, after ritually spitting upon their palms and contributing to the high rate of TB which prevailed in those parts. Murtagh went back upstairs to the wife, who was decidedly pissed off, until he crawled in beside her and whispered that if this one came off he just might be able to send her off on one of those cheap package deal tours to Lourdes. She even gave him a hug. Definitely not her wont.

"What in the sacred name of Xoth!" shrieked XT 69, tentacles awry as he took the holy name in vain, "have you been doing, you miserable excrescence? Where did all these creatures come from? What are they? Don't you realize you've violated every tenet of Inter-Galactic ethics that has ever been formulated! It'll be the Smilirgian marshes for you slimesac, if we ever get off this pestilential dungheap."

ZT withdrew his fourteen tentacles in horror. In all his 443 years no one had ever called him a slimesac. His dream was shattered. It became crashingly clear to him that he'd never be the Richard Attenborough of the megawaves. The wonderspawn of the Milky Way. In fact, he'd be lucky if he didn't end up as a retread on a three-wheeled swampmobile shitshifter. He might as well crawl up his own fundament and commit ritual self absorption. Swallowing his pride and saliva he babbled, "Research, O illustrious one, research."

"Research, you execrable particle of Grundlachian garbage!" roared XT 69, "Research! Have you any idea how heinous your action has been? What profound consciousness alteration have you occasioned to these primitives? What damage have you done to their metabolisms, to say nothing of their psyches, though, to be honest (he gestured at the bipeds), it doesn't look as if there was much to damage in the first place with these three."

Abasing himself ZT went into a prescribed grovel. "O superior one, I have scrupulously obeyed all the ground rules regarding the treatment of specimens," moaned ZT as he slithered across the cabin. "They have been well tended."

Had the captives been able to comprehend the twitterings of their hosts they would, perforce, have had to agree. To say the least, they were sated. The Master, through two pissholes in the snow, contemplated three empty bottles of Jack Daniels and eight empty bottles of Porter; young Proinseas, having consumed over 100 Liberty Caps, was spaced to the gills and far out in the Milky Way, and Father Philbin, up to his eyeballs in sacred wafers and altar wine was in an advanced state of ecstasy coupled with mental bewilderment. The cow was placidly chewing its cud and depositing mounds of malodorous manure upon the floor, which the robot cleaning unit hastened to sweep up and recycle at regular intervals.

Trembling with rage, XT swiveled round and fled for the sanctuary of his cocoon. Ascertaining that it would be at least 1.3 zwerbs before he had any chance of getting out of this mess, he administered a powerful tranquilizer to himself and zonked out. It's the same all over the Galaxy. When the going gets tough, the toughs cop out. Believe me, I've been there.

Meanwhile, back in the village, Brian Artur had not been idle. No one had ever seen him work so hard. He had the boy Martin working overtime cranking out the poitín while he, armed with a fistful of money was buying up every conceivable commodity, from luminous plastic statuettes of the Polish Pope (surplus from Knock), to cattle, pigs and cigarettes. These he conveyed across the border via the bog and stashed in every room and barn that he could procure. No excise or VAT tax to pay, he was made for life, he reckoned.

Within three days he was employing half the youth of Blacklion, who were all on holiday anyway since the Master's disappearance, to hump the merchandise across the temporarily nullified border and store it away from the prying eyes of the gaugers.

The customs men on the Northern side had, of course, by now detected the force field. Some indeed had even ridden their bicycles into it, but they had deemed it to be merely some new piece of weaponry which the British army were forever trying out along the border. The dedicated constable McCrea had attempted to get to the bottom of things, but the force field had disrupted the already primitive telephone service to Enniskillen and, while cycling the fifteen miles to HQ, he had unfortunately encountered a twenty-ton Guinness lorry which had hastened his departure from this vale of tears. His demise had been used as an excuse by the good folk of Belcoo for a three day wake and as a result no one had been in any state to worry about the mysterious barrier which seemed to hover over a small section of the border.

On the Southern side of the border the gardaí were too busy drinking the new free clothes allowance which had just arrived courtesy of their local TD to bother their heads about the rumors of strange goings-on which percolated through to the bars.

A few of them, in between pool games at Murtagh's had tried diffidently to contact the priest to ask his opinion, but he had disappeared and it was assumed that he was obviously off visiting the married sister in Sligo or doing another four day lie-in in the Fathers' home for inebriated and slightly tired clerics. Sure, wouldn't there be time enough in the morning to investigate, and, in the meantime, wasn't this a great bash altogether!

The computer awoke XT 69 and notified him that refueling was complete. Groggily he propelled himself to the video screen. His mouth felt like an Arcturian sewage farm. He flicked on the switch and inspected the bay. ZT was slumped in a catatonic trance, evidently dreaming of the Largactylian equivalent of hara-kiri. The aliens all appeared to be comatose but alive. It was now or never. Hopefully he could erase most of the memory tapes and tamper with the rest on the way back. ZT could be browbeaten into silence. The Federation must never find out ...

But what of the Terrans? Could he erase their memory banks? Did they even have memories? Rapidly he scanned with his EEG. Not much there. The quadruped appeared to have marginally more grey matter than the bipeds. Screw it! He would have to chance it. Swiftly he threw the ejector switch, raised the force field and deposited his erstwhile guests up to their uxters in the bog. The booster rockets whined, and, with an almost dignified fart, the ship sucked itself out of the mire and described a hazy curve into space. Within seconds it was out of sight, occasioning only one reported case of soiled underwear for the British army corporal at Ebrington barracks who had been monitoring the radar and dreaming of IRA 'doodlebugs' – 'just another mortar for old Ireland'. Within milliseconds the crew of the alien craft were treading boldly through new galaxies, leaving behind them two hungover villages and some bewildered individuals whose lives had been forever changed.

The fate of Father Philbin has been previously recorded, as has that of the Master. Young Proinseas emigrated and became a holy man to a group of brain-damaged Californian hippies before fading into obscurity. The cow was eaten. Brian Artur got rich, spent it all and moved to Belfast where he met the author. So it goes.

STEVIE

"That's a load of crap." We swiveled round in our seats. Who had had the temerity to insult Brian Artur? By the accent it must be a local. We peered through the nicotine haze towards the pool table. Grimshaw was the first to speak. "Is it yourself now Stephen, sure the Sergeant was just looking for you not half an hour ago."

The young man blushed, put down his cue, picked up his coat, made for the door, and exited into the night, followed by a gale of laughter. I turned to the great man and asked, "What was that all about?"

Grimshaw smiled. "I see you're not up to date with the local scéal. Well, it's like this ..."

Stevie was a fisherman. He lived in a small village in darkest Donegal and made a reasonable livelihood on the boats which operated out of Burtonport. Twenty-one, single, popular with the local girls and generally with enough shillings in his pocket to accommodate his already prodigious drinking habits, he was one of the few locals in the 'Teac Ban' who got on with and liked the Belfast men who came down to the Teac at weekends to escape the stress of their home town. The pub, an ex-RIC barracks, had been bought by a Belfast man and the tension between the owner, his Northern friends and the locals, although it rarely manifested itself until vast quantities of alcohol had been consumed, was always there like an ominous undercurrent.

Stevie was one of the odd men out. He liked the hard men from the North. 'The boys' from Andersonstown and the Falls and Ardoyne. The 'boys' who, with the stress of Belfast behind them for two or three days sat until all hours drinking and swapping stories about 'the troubles'. Stevie played darts with them and pool and kept up with their late night drinking sessions and this, alas, was to be his undoing.

It must have been all the tales of derring-do, of heists and hijackings, of kneecappings and even 'wet jobs', as the CIA, bless their little hearts, call murders, but whatever it was, Stevie conceived the idea that he too would become a 'desperado'. In sleepy Donegal the opportunities for a would-be Jesse James or Pretty Boy Floyd are somewhat limited, but, his mind made up, Stevie was undaunted. "You have nothing to fear but fear itself," he muttered to himself as he wove his way unsteadily back from the Teac one Friday night and found himself outside the town's only bank. "Nothing to fear, too fuckin' right," he mumbled as he fiddled with the catch on the back window. "Five grand, easy. That'll show those Belfast cowboys that we're not all asleep up here."

With an easy insouciance born of alcohol he forced the catch and climbed in, oblivious to the fact that he had triggered off the alarm which was wired directly to the local Garda station across the street. It was the first time that the alarm had ever sounded in the barracks and the sleepy night duty gardaí were at first amazed and then apprehensive.

Surely it must be the IRA, them feckin' Provos and they'd have guns. Donegal gardaí are used to dealing with the odd drunk, the errant driver and the occasional case of sheep shagging, but armed robbery is regarded as a bit over and beyond the call of duty. A man can get hurt by those trigger-happy boyos, and a free military funeral's not much of a substitute for the pension and the free clothes in anyone's book. Nonetheless, let it be said, Tirconnel's finest did not shirk in their town's hour of need. Pausing only to buckle on their Webleys, phone Letterkenny for assistance and to grab the station's one and only Uzi machine gun, they piled out and surrounded the bank. All three of them.

Inside, Stevie was peacefully engaged in rifling the tills when his equanimity was rudely shattered by the raucous voice of Sergeant McDaid, amplified and distorted by a bullhorn, urging him and all his murderous crew to throw their guns out and come quietly because the place was surrounded by a squad of crack marksmen.

It is true that the good Sergeant, in so describing himself and Constables McClatchey and O'Dowd in such terms may have been indulging in the odd bit of hyperbole, but, in the circumstances, such flights of rhetoric are surely permissible. At any rate, his announcement electrified Stevie.

Scooping up the handiest bundle of paper, he charged across the parquet tiled floor and launched himself, head first, through the front window of the bank, thinking only of John Wayne, Grainne Uaile and his own self-preservation, and not necessarily in that order.

With the luck of the daft and the drunk he fractured the plate glass, somersaulted, landed on his feet in the main street, right in front of the startled Sergeant, and took off out of town like a bat out of hell. At this juncture it must be confessed however, that, in the annals of crime, this particular exploit does not rate highly on the *modus operandi* quotient scale. The town, and I use the word loosely, has only one street. Indeed in the past some have rather unkindly referred to it as a 'one horse town'. And it died. Accordingly, adrenaline pumping as the would-be Cole Younger tore out of town, his choice of escape routes was strictly limited. As he pounded along, expecting a bullet in his back any minute, he was all too acutely aware that, with the sea on his left and the peat bog on his right and the next turn off three miles on up the road, his chances of evading capture must have rated as high as Margaret Thatcher being elected in West Belfast or Ian Paisley being accorded a civic reception in the Vatican. In short, not good odds. The squad car wheezed up alongside of him and Sergeant McDaid rolled down the window.

"Get in, Stevie, you stupid bollix," he said, more in sorrow than in anger. "It's the station for you, son."

Stevie contemplated the defiant leap onto the stony beach. It wasn't quite the drop Butch Cassidy and the Sundance Kid had had to undergo in the film, but it didn't look too promising. Briefly he considered a 'you'll never take me alive, copper', then he shrugged his shoulders and climbed into the back seat. He was knackered. O'Dowd, taking five to do a three point turn, drove them slowly back to the station. As he got his breath back, Stevie tried to regain some of his initial defiance.

"I gave youse a good run anyway, didn't I Sergeant?" McDaid, a compassionate man in his own rough way, glanced at the fistful of used cheques which Stevie still clutched in his hand, and nodded wearily.

"Aye, Stevie, yon Al Capone could have learnt a lot from you."

Stevie's notoriety in the village was shortlived. The Sergeant went bail for him and spoke on his behalf at the District Court. "T'was only the drink talking. He's not a bad lad, yer Honour." He got off with a 50 pound fine and 100 pounds for the window. The bank staff put up a plaque commemorating their only bank raid in history. To show there was no ill feeling, Stevie opened an account with them when he got his next paypacket. Alas, however, this blot on his career meant that he would never be admitted into the august ranks of the Cruit Island Liberation Front, that daring band of desperados led by the notorious 'Big Seamus'.

Still, soon the talk in the bars turned to other matters. I hear Stevie even got himself married. Sic Transit, Gloria Mundies.

BLUES FOR ALLAH

"Why are camels called ships of the desert?" It was Brian Artur at his most genial and pedagogical. A pint in hand, a half 'un nearby and a captive audience. His disciples in the Prisoners Defense Club looked at the great man expectantly. It was well known that Brian Artur, in his youth, had once spent or misspent an entire year in Saudi Arabia.

"Did I ever tell you about the lost city," Brian Artur asked rhetorically, for we had been discussing 'Raiders of the Lost Ark' which had been the night's video. "Sod the lost city, what about the camels?" commented O'Hare. The sage was not to be deterred. "It was like this ..."

"You camelfuckin' little bastard! If we're all gonna die, I'm damned well gonna make sure that you're the first." Brian Artur started up, banging his head on the crankcase of the lorry under which he'd been lying and getting a mouthful of sand for his trouble. The remarks were not directed against Brian Artur, but the wretched boy, Mohammed, and it was not the sentiments, with which Brian Artur heartily concurred, but the fact that they came from the lips of the normally placid John Wright, one of nature's gentlemen, that had surprised him.

Rolling out from under the truck Brian Artur squinted in the blinding sunlight and took in the scene. Wright was standing over the babbling Mohammed, a spotty, acne-ridden sixteen-year-old, a tire lever clenched in his hand, while the expedition's alleged leader, the Egyptian Mr. Mustafa was vainly trying to wrest it from him. The veins stood out on John's face, then suddenly he relaxed and dropped the lever, as the tension drained out of him.

"It's all right, John," Brian Artur said. "If we ever get outta this fuckin' desert we'll tie the wanker down and leave him for the vultures." "You're right, Paddy," Wright said, "the fuckpig doesn't deserve a quick death." The aforementioned birds, circling overhead, wheeled about seeming to agree.

"Effendis," whined Mr. Mustafa, the sweating, balding chief, and the asshole who'd got them into this insane expedition, "let us not fall out amongst ourselves. Mr. Brian, can you fix it or not?" "Look, mucker, I know as much about engines as a cow knows about having a holiday. Let Ali have a go." Brian Artur stood up, wiping the sand from his lips and spreading a pint of oil over his blistered face. Brian Artur was not a pretty sight. Neither were any of them, but then, what did it matter? If they didn't get the truck rolling in the next six hours they would all be dead anyway.

This was back in 1965. Brian Artur had had, in his youth, fantasies of dying heroically on the barricades, or, if all else failed, at the hands of a jealous lover who discovered him at age 77 in bed with his mistress, but this was too much of an anti-climax. Not with a bang but a whimper in the middle of the Saudi Arabian desert looking for the lost city of Mad-in-Saleh, surrounded by a crowd of incompetent A-rabs and two crazed English school teachers. Was it to this that a proud son of Kathleen ni Houlihan was reduced?

Resignedly he walked round to the side of the truck that afforded at least a little shade and squatted down beside Chris Faram, the other English teacher, who was placidly reading Winnie the Pooh in Latin. Is it any wonder that England lost its Empire? "Spot of trouble, Brian?" he said brightly. "Naw, Chris," the great one grunted, "everything's tickety-boo, old chap. John just tried to kill the boy Mohammed, we're a hundred miles from the next well, we've enough water to last until sundown, and we're all going to die." Sarcasm never was Brian Artur's forte.

Chris nodded, owlishly, and adjusted his sunglasses, before returning to the works of A.A. Milne. Brian Artur sat down and tried to figure out what the hell he was doing here. It had all seemed such a good idea when Mr. Mustafa had approached the rest of them. Teaching in Jeddah was one of the most boring jobs any of them had ever had, and the idea of taking off into the desert with film cameras to shoot the lost city of Mad-in-Saleh, which only four white men had ever seen, although not as exotic as flying across the Red Sea to catch a rare anti-social disease from the ladies of Ethiopia, which had been the plan until the Saudis refused to give them exit visas, was better than sitting in the apartment in Jeddah scratching their navels for two weeks.

Mr. Mustafa had even seemed to have his shit together. He had hired the truck, produced the cameras and arrived promptly with his friend Ali, a morose Palestinian teacher, on the designated day. Present also, however, was the unspeakable boy Mohammed.

He, it transpired, came with the truck. A package deal. His uncle wouldn't rent the wreck unless the nephew went along. In retrospect, it seems pretty certain that he hoped that the lorry would break down and that they would all perish under the inhospitable sun, their bones bleaching and their flesh torn by the omnipresent vultures who had followed them ever since they set out. Vultures can spot a lemon and a gang of incompetents from three miles high, just as a junkie hooker on Times Square can pick out a mark. To the hooker, it's a fix. To the vulture, lunch. To the lorry owner it would have been the will of Allah and a hefty sum from Lloyds of London.

Mohammed 'the mechanic' could not drive. Nor did he have the first idea about engines. This, of course, wasn't discovered until they were stuck in the middle of the desert, two days out. They had skirted the holy city of Medina, where no infidel had ever set foot, and no one in their right mind would want to, and headed north, following a map that the buffoon Mustafa had obviously purchased from the kind of gentleman who would sell you the Brooklyn Bridge. Brian Artur's reverie was interrupted by a string of Arabic oaths. Ali had had no more luck than the rest of them with the crankcase. Brian Artur began to reflect upon his wasted life. Jesus! He hadn't even made it with big Margie at the pea factory, and the entire night shift had managed to do that!

"What seems to be the trouble with this old camion?" It was Chris. Mustafa and Ali tried to tell him. John and Brian Artur just sat there and swapped ideas about how the boy should finally get to meet Allah. "I say, has anyone got a pencil?" By now Chris was under the chassis. "He's finally cracked," said John. "He never was too sane to start with. It's all the flogging they get in those public schools." John was a grammar school product. Brian Artur was there on the strength of a forged diploma from the Fermanagh Technical College. "Ali, there's a good chap, try to give the old motor a spin, will you?" Resignedly Ali got into the cab. Unlike Mustafa and the boy Mohammed who was still insanely babbling bits of the Koran, Ali was not a devout Moslem. When you got him to talk, over a gallon of sediki, the rotgut illicit liquor that one had to swill in that prohibition-ridden theocracy, the only thing he wanted to talk about was massacring Israelis and getting back his father's patch of dried-up desert in Palestine, from which his family had been evicted when he was but a child. As the sediki ran down his throat like a torchlight procession, he would, in broken English, curse Allah and all his prophets and ask his English and Irish friends to toast Karl Marx and Joe Stalin. They had always obliged. What the hell! A drink is a drink is a drink, even if it tastes like paint stripper.

Ali turned the key. The engine sprang into life, showering Chris with oil and sand, and the rest of them jumped to their feet. Chris crawled out and stood up. John ran round and kissed him but then John always was a bit like that, and ten months in the Saudi land had made him forget any heterosexual pretensions he might have once had. Five minutes later they were on the truck again and trundling along, Brian Artur's suggestion that the boy be towed behind with a rope around his ankles having been narrowly outvoted. At sunset, they hit the oasis.

Now the traditional picture of an oasis, as seen by P.C. Wren and Beau Geste, conjures up a pretty sight of cool water, surrounded by palm trees, a simple but dignified tent with a noble sheikh contentedly sucking on a hookah and watching a couple of nubile and scantily clad ladies from the harem as they undulate in an erotic belly dance. This may be all very well on the back lot at Warner Brothers, but Brian Artur assures me that it is not strictly accurate.

Their oasis was the second class waiting room of a ruined railway station, stuck in the arsehole of nowhere. The noble sheikh was a wizened old turd who sat on a decrepit rug and managed to simultaneously suck his big toe (one of the Saudis' more endearing habits), and clamp a tinny transistor radio to his ear, from which came the delightful A-rab cacophony which was euphemistically called music.

So there they were, squatting on the tattered rug, being forced to drink the vile diesel oil that masqueraded as coffee, lest, as Mr. Mustafa put it, "we offend his Excellency", and waiting for the great man to acknowledge their presence and give them some water from his well. The first hour and five cups of 'coffee' had been merely tedious. The rug had made a change from the jolting of the lorry. The second hour was rather boring. Now, it was becoming, in Grimshaw's words, "a fuckin' nightmare". John and Brian Artur got up, bowed, indicated that they had a call of nature to attend to and made their way outside into the darkness. They gazed again upon the rusting railway engine and traced the bullet holes in the cab with their fingers. John scratched 'T.E.L. luvs Mohammed' on it with his penknife, while Brian Artur had a slash. Inside, Mr. Mustafa sat crouched like a panting acolyte at 'his Excellency's' feet. It was too dark to see the vultures, but they knew there were out there somewhere.

"I'd give my left testicle for a pint of Watney's Red Barrel at this very minute," muttered John. "Make it a pint of Guinness and you can have mine too." No genie appeared.

"Fuck this for a game of darts," Brian Artur grunted. Comment was superfluous. They stubbed out their cigarettes and went back inside. Chris had disappeared, doubtless off to catch up on the exploits of Winnie The Pooh. Ali had fallen asleep, dreaming of bloody massacres and revenge for Deir Yassin. Mr. Mustafa was still acting the fawning puppy, but even his stoicism was wearing thin.

Just then Chris came running in. "I say, chaps, the 9.30 from Medina's just pulling in at the platform. Maybe they've a copy of the Times that'll tell us what's happening in the Test Match."

They cracked up. In retrospect, it wasn't funny. It was insane, but they'd had a long hard day. Wright rolled on the carpet, giggling hysterically. Brian Artur tried not to laugh and ended up banging his head on the sand. Ali woke up and spasmodically gripped a non-existent sub-machine gun. Even the sheikh paid attention. Languidly he removed his filthy toe from his equally filthy mouth, switched off his transistor and asked Mustafa in halting Arabic just who the fuck they were.

They got their water, freed the boy Mohammed, whom Wright had insisted on tying to the axle of the lorry, and drove off along the remnants of the railway tracks. As dawn came up, Mr. Mustafa woke them with a cry. "Behold! Behold the lost city!"

"I didn't expect to see a Petra, 'the rose red city', or even any really wonderful ruins, standing majestically in the desert, but that!" recalled Brian Artur. Four crummy rock caves in a blind canyon. Jesus wept! So did John and Brian Artur! Mustafa frolicked happily with his cine camera. They hadn't the heart to tell him that he was using the wrong film and that nothing would come out. The boy prayed to Mecca, which was, in fact, in the opposite direction by Chris's simple calculations. Ali slept.

Chris started to write up the trip in his exercise book for the old school magazine. John carved graffiti on the wall of one of the caves and Brian Artur mused that the so-called 'lost city' had not in fact been lost but merely thrown away, like a used condom.

"What's the moral of it all?" asked Cisco, one of Brian Artur's thicker disciples. The great man looked at him with scorn. "The moral is, son, when some asshole tries to tempt you into looking for a lost city, take a dose of the Ethiopian pox instead."

"Why DO they call camels 'ships of the desert?' asked McAnoy. "Because they're full of Arab seamen." Everyone knows that.

I Danced With The Man Who Danced With Chuck Berry

I woke up with a splitting head. God's curse on Fats Nolan and his recycled rotgut! I should have known better, but then, wasn't it cheap? Not in the long run. Never again, I vowed, yet again.

"Get up, you lazy drunken scut." It was the dulcet tone of the lovely Beryl. The wife. There she was, a vision of loveliness, dressed up like a nun at a whore's wedding, standing over me, threatening me with a cup of tea. "Whaffor?" I croaked, my thick tongue trying to tight its way through a swamp of phlegm. "Don't come that with me, you bastard. Don't try the old amnesia bit. You know fine well you're coming to Kevin's wedding." I do so admire the wife's command of the vernacular.

The wedding. Christ! I'd forgotten all about it, even though it had been one of my excuses for going out and getting mindless with 'the lads' the night before. Not Kevin's stag party, you understand, which doubtless was held in some poxy lounge bar in a hotel full of chinless twats and would-be lawyers, but a quiet evening in the 'Armalite' shebeen on the Falls Road, where I had some vague recollection of making a complete tit of myself and having to be carted home in the early hours. Kevin's wedding. Fuck it! I hardly knew the bugger, but the wife had been best friends with his sister, a prominent member of the Catholic Mafia, and so had got an invite to this society piss up.

"I'm not going, kid. I'm not up to it. You get a taxi. Sure no one will miss me." The pursed lips, the stony stare, the headsplitting silence soon told me it wasn't on. No way. Muttering the odd Biblical imprecation I crawled out of the scratcher and groped for my Levis. "Just what do you think you're doing?" It was a voice that could stop cancer. "You're not going to disgrace me by wearing those filthy old things."

Cowardice is the better part of discretion and I was in no shape to argue. Trying to keep the top of my head in touch with the rest of my skull, I edged over to the wardrobe and selected a none too clean pair of cords. Prudently I rejected my Guinness stained 'Smash H Block' T-shirt and opted for my red and black Moroccan shirt. Beryl wasn't impressed, but she was in a hurry. Hell hath no fury like a woman late for a wedding or a funeral. They hate to miss any fun.

The drive itself was fairly uneventful. The nuptials were to be held in some hick chapel in County Down, some fifteen miles from Belfast. The only trouble was, we didn't know exactly where the pineapple was, and I didn't relish asking directions to the Catholic chapel in Comber, known to fearful Teagues as a black hole, full of tight-arsed Protestant Orangemen, all running round looking for haemorrhoid ointment or a Kafflik to tar and feather. Beryl, however, was resolute. "Stop the car," she bellowed, or at least so it sounded to my suffering ears, and in the main square of the small market village she jumped out and engaged a rustic worthy in earnest conversation. As usual, with unerring accuracy she succeeded in picking the only Teague in town – I think they can tell each other at a glance by the gap between their eyes which comes from too frequent perusal of rosary beads – and, seconds later, armed with a series of complicated directions, we were speeding out of town and along the narrow back roads of County Down, past the little boxes owned by would-be stockbroker/commuters and over the cowshit strewn lanes. Miraculously, when we found the bowling alley we were only ten minutes late.

Standing outside, in the tiny graveyard, I recognized two familiar faces. Pat Agnew, roué son of a Belfast publican and my old chum Brian Artur. Beryl, hitching up her outfit, scuttled for the church door and was therefore unable to do more than shoot a venomous glance over her shoulder when I shouted after her, "I'll just stay out here and have a rap with the lads, luv." The oak door slammed after her. Peace at last.

"Bout ye, lads." "Bout ye, Sean." I leant against the graveyard wall as each of us contemplated a boring forty-five minutes.

The last time I'd seen Pat had been a couple of months ago at the Chuck Berry concert at the ABC cinema – now, alas! a bombed-out ruin. It had been a great gig and Pat had almost stolen the show by getting up on the stage and jiving with the Maestro himself. When the bouncers had tried to intervene Chuck had told them to "fuck off! This here's a fren of mine. I wan everyone to hava good time. Let's boogie." He and Pat had then duckwalked across the stage to tumultuous applause, until Pat, full as a pisspot, had fallen off onto the front row. A great night!

"How's she cutting, Sean?" "Fair to grim." "You're not going in?"

"Some fuckin' chance. Every time I go into one of those places the holy water starts to sizzle!"

In silence we took in the rural scene. It left a lot to be desired. It was a fair bet that there wasn't a pool table for ten miles. Desultory conversation and then the inevitable question. "Have youse any gargle?" Pat produced a hip flask, rather grudgingly, I thought. That lasted us all of ten minutes and I reached into my pocket for a cigarette. Then I found it. Only a small lump, wrapped in the ubiquitous silver paper. A bit of the old Uncle Robert aka Bob Hope aka dope. Dimly I remembered Uncle Mal slipping it to me a couple of nights previously.

Pat's eyes lit up. Not a pretty sight, by the way, resembling as they do a traffic light permanently stuck on No Go. "Is that some Bob?" "Yeah." He beamed. "We should roll a number, eh?" I could see that Brian Artur, for all his blasé sophistication and rented suit was a bit confused. "Got any straights, Brian, me ould mucker?" He obliged, and Pat skinned up the hash.

The skins (cigarette papers, not prophylactics, you fools, this was holy mother Ireland) were tired and stuck together. The shit wasn't that fresh either, so we just bucked it all into a five skinner. What the hell!

Solemnly we lit up and toked. Not bad. Not great, but better than a kick in the slats. A few minutes later the wedding party streamed out, and as freshly coiffured young ladies squealed and threw rice, the cameras clicked. Then it was a mad rush, piling into motors and heading off for the reception, spelt B-o-o-z-e. I'd taken the precaution of turning the wheel and so was one of the first to hit the roadhouse.

"Here, bate this into you, you look as if you need it," said Brian Artur, handing me a Black Bushmills, the *sine qua non* of graceful living in my former part of the world.

"Very civil of you, my son, very civil indeed." The three of us had managed to get into our second double whiskey before the wives emerged, chattering and chittering from the toilets, or 'powder rooms' as the 'Old Crow', a hostelry which actually did, believe it or not, serve crow to those foolish enough to order it, called their bogs. They were just about to get their 'aperitifs' when the groom staggered in, ashen faced.

"Hey Kev, what's up? Did you find out she's up the spout?" a coarse oaf ventured. "Sod that, lads, everyone out, the fucking kitchen's on fire."

"You mean Crow's off, Kev?"

"The whole bloody thing's nearly off, but we'll transfer to the 'Highwayman'. I know the manager there and he'll fix us up with a buffet or something."

"Do you know the way, Pat?" "Yeah, OK! I'll lead." "At least it saved us buying the ladies a round." "You always were a mean bastard, Pat."

"Don't worry, they'll hit us for a few before the day is o'er." They did.

The Highwayman was a bit upmarket from the Old Crow, but nothing to give Egon Ronay an orgasm. The prices were a bit of a revelation, compared with my local, the 'Armalite', but then they did serve the drink in glasses and at least they had toilets unlike the shebeen. (Quigley has been threatening to put one in the next time a load of copper falls off the back of a lorry outside Casement Park, but we're not holding our breath or our urine either.) Emerging from the 'Caballeros', I got stuck into the drink, but, to be candid, the atmosphere was not the most congenial. The little weed was nagging at the back of my cerebellum but not doing too much damage, and the party was swarming with relatives of both bride and groom who were mostly priests or nuns. Worse still, many of them were in plain clothes.

That is, I believe, to say the least, sneaky behaviour and should definitely be outlawed by the Geneva Convention. I mean to say, there one is, telling some innocuous joke about the Queen giving Prince Charles a jigsaw puzzle of Lord Mountbatten for his birthday, or some such piece of badinage, when some miserable bastard coughs and says that that sort of talk isn't right and fitting in front of a little sister of the poor, whom you had taken from her garb to be some bleeding hippie from Berkeley who possibly wouldn't be beyond doing a turn now and again, to oblige, so to speak.

And then there's the fifty-year-old soak, who's been knocking back the G and T's as if Prohibition is coming in at midnight who turns out to be a Rev. Mother who was Beryl's teacher years ago and is now in charge of a convent school in England. Like, she's been the one telling the really dirty stories and trying to grope the younger men's bums. Worse still, she's called Sister Wilfred – as if it isn't confusing enough having these stale buns in mufti, they have to call themselves by male names. Still, fair play to the old trout, she did buy a few rounds.

Anyway, after some delay, we are herded into the reception and seated at our respective places. I'm seated next to Beryl, who has defrosted slightly after a few whiskeys and is gossiping with Sister Wilfred and a few more old class chums from the Alma Mater. Opposite me is Brian Artur, wedged between a Stale Bun and a Far East and now that I look at him, he's looking a bit trick. I mean there's something about the eyes. Half an hour previously he'd stopped me in the bog and asked me the origins of the Bob Hope. I'd told him its ethnic roots (viz. N. Africa), and apologized for its age and ineffectiveness. Certainly Pat and I were hardly getting too much of a buzz from it now.

The speeches started. They were the usual predictable and boring offerings. Everyone laughed when they were supposed to and applauded on cue, but for me at least, it was just another pain in the dong. Brian Artur, I noticed, however, seemed to be really getting into it. He started to guffaw loudly at even the feeblest jest and thump his cutlery on the table whenever he apparently felt that some form of emphasis was called for. The clerics flanking him began to cast startled glances, covertly, at him. So did I. Next minute, before I could kick him under the table, he started to heckle the best man's admittedly deplorable effort. Looks of disapproval began to flash in his direction, particularly from his wife, the good lady Hilda, but he carried on obliviously.

Suddenly the groom was on his feet, immaculate in his hired tux. It was his turn. "Come on, Kev, let's hear it, old mate, you can do better than those wankers so far." "Shut up, Brian," I hissed, lunging for him under the table with my boot.

Alas, my days of playing hooker for the Under-14 Rugby team are long gone and I only succeeded in making contact with a nun's bony ankle. She yelped, but fair play to the plucky little handmaiden of the Lord, she didn't give way to any of that filthy language. Julie Andrews would have been proud of her. But there was no stopping Brian Artur anyway.

The groom, embarrassed in front of his new in-laws, didn't know that. Harking back to his days as President of the University Debating Society, he came up with the old ploy of trying to embarrass the opposition into silence. "All right, folks, if I may digress. The yobbo making all the noise at the center table is my good friend Brian Artur Grimshaw. It seems he wants to say something, and so, in the spirit of ecumenism, I'll gladly vacate the floor to him for a few minutes. Come on Brian, let's be hearing you."

Good tactic Kev? Collapse of stout party? Brian Artur redfaced and embarrassed slumps down abashed? Nine times out of ten it might have worked. Brian Artur was not normally known as an after dinner speaker, even when drunk. Not even a during dinner speaker. But the groom had reckoned without the little weed. Rising to his feet, and swaying amid the horrified clerics he waved grandly towards the top table.

"I have only three words to say to this company," he roared.

"MOROCCO!"

Stunned silence. Pat and I started to giggle hysterically and then tried to stop, but it became contagious, and when one ceased the one would set the other off. Majestically, Brian Artur drew himself up and gracefully described a swan-dive of which Greg Louanis would have been proud, into the sherry trifle. Glasses went flying. Clerics were soaked. Hilda started wailing and a few of the other wives joined in, in a weird form of solidarity.

It was five minutes before three of us could manage to drag Brian Artur down the stairs and help him throw up in the magnolia bushes. He still had a blissful smile over his trifle-stained face. I don't think I've ever seen him so happy. Kev never did get to finish his speech.

Everyone retired to the room laid on for the serious drinking and dancing for those athletic and foolish enough to even consider corybantics. I ended up in the company of the formidable Sister Wilfred, who, after consuming a bottle of gin, insisted that we call her 'Wilf Baby' or some such idiocy. She was all for accompanying us to the party afterwards, until her pinched-faced Pioneer section of the drunken nuns protectors and minders came and dragged her off to her hotel. That night the little car drove itself home by remote control. "Well done, little car," I muttered, as I shoveled the inert corpse of Brian Artur and his still weeping wife out and made it to my front door.

"Some wedding eh, kid?" I muttered as Beryl and I stumbled into bed. "What about old Brian Artur, then?" She muttered something I couldn't catch. She tried again.

"I danced with the man who danced with Chuck Berry." "Who? Pat Agnew? Fuck him! The bastard still owes me a fiver he borrowed in the Club bar three years ago." Still, there you are now.

"Morocco!"

NORMAN I

Not many people know this, but Brian Artur was once a paramilitary. I know most think of him only as a wit, scholar and drunk, but this view of Ulster's greatest man is very far from the truth. Renaissance man has to do many things, most of which we cognoscenti cannot bruit about until the war is over, and going to your country's aid when she is beleaguered by the foreigner is only one of them.

As I've indicated, the full extent of Grimshaw's heroic actions in the Resistance will not be known until the war is over and old Ireland is free and the pensions are being given out, but I can reveal that in the year 197_ the great man was on the run and hiding in the maiden city of Derry.

Those scoffers who allege that he was only on the run from the wife and not the forces of repression only cheapen themselves. I will not deign to answer their sneers. Suffice to say that the men who know about these things are not fooled. When the time comes to write Emmett's epitaph one name will be up there among the heroes and heroines of the Emerald Isle, and that name will be Brian Artur Grimshaw, for was he not, at one time, Norman's O/C!

Norman was from Derry. Short, stocky, intense and thick as a plank. That was probably why he fancied himself for the job of I/O when it became vacant in the local unit. The previous I/O had left to become the guest of a gracious Queen in Long Kesh camp.

For some time, and this is going back to 197_, Norm had taken it upon himself to act as the unofficial guide to the Bogside for all visiting pressmen. I was a reporter at the time and became used to Norm waylaying me in various bars and insisting that I and any other unfortunate journalist in the vicinity accompany him for yet another 'scoop'.

Sometimes he would appear as himself; on other occasions he

would wear a mask and try, in vain, to disguise his voice, but it was always poor Norm whose 'scoops' never quite seemed to work out. I remember, for example, his taking a party of us to see the local paramilitaries' latest acquisition in military hardware. He managed to get the car in which we were travelling hijacked and burnt by some overenthusiastic teenagers.

I can also recall the time when he was driving me to another rendezvous for yet another 'exclusive' when he ran out of petrol. We pushed the vehicle half a mile up the road to the filling station only for Norm to discover that he had no money. Adopting a menacing stance he informed the petrol pump attendant that this was "the staff car of the IRA. The bill will be paid when the revolution is won." "Fuck off, Norman," replied the grizzled old age pensioner, and proceeded to drag him from the car and kick his melt in. I had to rescue him from the wrath of the geriatric and pay the bill before we could proceed to the rendezvous which was, as usual, in the wrong place. Oh well, another exclusive down the drain.

Anyway, we press habitués of the City Hotel were, to say the least, amazed when it came over the grapevine that Norm had been appointed the new I/O. We had no idea that 'the bhoys' were that hard up. It didn't last long, of course; a week, to be precise.

I was in 'the Rocker' having a quiet pint and idly hoping to pick up some scéal or gossip which my Editor might actually print instead of throwing into the waste paper basket, when Brian Artur came in, laughing so hard that the tears ran down his face. "Give us a pint, comrade."

Well, what else are news sleuths' expense accounts for? "What is it, O great one? You look as if you'd just seen a member of the Royal family fall off a horse." "Better than that, my son, I've just seen the new I/O in action ..." "Not Norman?" "The very same." He downed his pint and ordered another. Oh well, what are newspapers for if not to supply free liquor to the underprivileged?

"The big tube was sleuthing round the town," said Brian Artur, wiping the froth from his lips, "and he spots that new photographer, you know, the one who's just checked into the City." "Aye, Healey. He's OK!"

"I know that. You know that, but does Norman? Does he what! He susses him out immediately as a Brit undercover agent and tails him all over the town. Eventually the guy goes into that chinky restaurant at the bottom of Shipquay Street and sits down to have a meal." "The Kit-e-kat Lounge," I shuddered, recalling a recent bout of botulism and toxic poisoning that a visit to the self same establishment had occasioned. "The very same. Anyway, the boul Norman spots this wee kid and gives him ten pence to run and get Art and I and to be sure and tell us to come 'well tooled up' because he had cornered a dangerous spy. Well, we didn't really believe it, but Art gets a rod from the nearest safe house because we figured you can't afford to take any chances, and we nip down to the restaurant, only to discover the fire brigade outside it, hosing it down and Norman lying unconscious in the gutter, surrounded by enraged Chinamen who are trying to kick his tripe in. So we weigh in, drag the clown up the street and into the Bogside, sit him down and get the whole story.

Apparently Norm went inside to observe the 'undercover agent' more closely and sat down two tables away from him. Next thing a waiter arrives so Norm has to order sweet and sour pigeon or something to get rid of him. Well, the Chinaman goes off to kill the pigeon and Norm decides that he's too conspicuous and had better hide, so he whips out his *Derry Journal*, puts it up in front of his face and pretends to be reading it, but then he can't see yer man, so what does he do? He lights a fag and tries to burn a wee hole in it so he can look through and keep the 'spy' under observation. Next minute, the paper's ablaze, Norman burns his hands, drops the Journal onto the floor, the wall coverings go up in flames, the potted plants start to smoulder, the Chinese come running out of the kitchen throwing buckets of water. Unfortunately, one of them has chip fat in it and the whole place goes up.

The 'Brit' gets up and strolls out without paying his bill, the fire brigade comes storming in, eager to try out their new hoses and the Chinese drag Norman out and proceed to give him an exhibition of Oriental martial arts. If me and Art hadn't arrived they'd have molucated him."

We were still laughing when Art came in, with his unerring talent for discovering a source of free drink working overtime. "You've been telling him about Norman, haven't you," he said accusingly to Brian Artur. Then, to me, "Well, get us a pint and I'll tell you a better one about that bampot." I went up to the bar, musing about whatever had happened to the IRA of old: the dedicated non-drinking, non-smoking and practically celibate characters of yesteryear. Funny how you never ran into any of them these days.

"It was the *Derry Journal* that reminded me of it," said Art, sipping what turned out to be the first of many pints. "It was last year. We used to go over the border to get gelly. It was a regular weekly run, standard drill. There's no harm me telling you it now, we've got a different routine.

You used to drive the car over the border about forty miles to this wee village, park outside the pub and go in carrying a copy of the Journal under your arm. You'd order a pint and sit down and very soon someone would come up to you and ask for the car keys. You'd give him them, have another slow pint and sit and read the paper. About an hour later another guy would come in, hand you your keys, having stuffed the door panels with gelly at some neighbouring farm and you'd drive back over the border with the gear. For a couple of months it was almost routine. Anyway, this day we'd an 'op' on and a couple of the regular drivers were out of town so we were really short handed and Norman volunteers to go the gelly run. Well, there was no chance of us letting him along on the job, so the O/C reckons, why not? Surely even Norman couldn't cock up a simple gelly run!" We sighed and stared into our pints.

"So, off goes Norman in this brand new Avenger that we'd hijacked. Across the border and drives to the village. He even manages to get the right pub in the right village. Sits himself down at the bar, orders a pint and starts reading the Journal. About ten minutes later this punter comes in, orders his drink and asks Norman if he could have a look at his paper. Norman gives him a big wink and hands over the car keys. 'You can't miss it. It's the big red Avenger parked outside.'

The fellow looks at Norman as if he's mentally deranged. I mean, like he was short a few neurons or something, shrugs his shoulders, downs his pint and saunters outside with the keys and that's the last anyone saw of him. We figure he must have driven straight to Dublin and flogged it. Anyway, a quarter of an hour later, the local contact comes in looking for the keys and a massive row breaks out.

Norman can't believe that he's given them to the wrong punter and accuses Bucky of trying to con him and being a Brit agent. He ends up getting another hiding and has to hitch all the way back to Derry with his arm in a sling."

We all laughed and then I put my foot right in it. "What I can't understand is how you allow head-the-balls like Norman anywhere near the movement in the first place," I queried. The minute I said it I knew I'd made a mistake. The atmosphere became decidedly chilly. "Listen, mucker, who are you calling a head-the-ball! It's all right for us to slag the likes of idiots like Norman, but he's our head-the-ball, not yours. You haven't the right. You're a foreigner."

"I'm from Belfast," I protested.

"On yer bike, if not it's a rainy night in Shantallow! Do you want to be history or geography?"

I like to think that I left with due dignity, but it's hard to maintain one's *sang froid* when one trips drunkenly over a beer keg and tumbles half the way down Waterloo Street. So it goes.

Post Script: You don't really want to know what a rainy night in Shantallow entails! Believe me!

Who The Fuck Is Demis Roussos?

I am a great fan of poor old mad Billy Blake. Indeed, today, as I was reading my *Guardian* newspaper I chanced on an article about a visit to London of the immensely fat and untalented Demis Roussos and I was reminded of Blake's maxim – 'if the doors of perception were cleansed, everything would appear as it is – infinite'. 'True, Billy,' I mused, 'too fucking true'. But what is truth quoth jesting Pilate. What is real and what is not real? But this is not the place for metaphysical meanderings. According to Demis the greasy Greek he was once a preacher in ancient Egypt and a Jewish rabbi at the end of the last century. He is Greek Orthodox but loves reading the Koran. He also was, as he modestly admits, 'a love God in the 1970s in Britain'. The unforgettable 'Forever and Forever' is 'one of the top ten songs of all time', he proudly proclaims. He denies that he wore oversized maternity dresses, masquerading as 'kaftans' because there was an Albanian dwarf secreted underneath licking his balls so he could hit the high notes which drove many a man to drink, my good self included.

In 1985, either as a publicity stunt because his career was floundering or because Shiites are exceptionally stupid, Demis was allegedly kidnapped by Muslim fundamentalists. He 'sang' his way to freedom by subjecting his captors to a few bars of one of his more popular tonsil-torturing oeuvres, causing them to flee in search of the nearest exorcist thus facilitating his escape from durance vile. And it must have been vile for his idiot guards. Demis denies that he 'ever gave them the pleasure' of his vocal range and, for all I know, he may be telling the truth. After a lifetime as a serious investigative journalist I accept that 'truth is a black cat in a darkened room and justice is a blind bat', as the late lamented Bert Brecht so aptly put it. But I think the wanker warbled.

But enough of this persiflage and enough of cheap shots at one of Europe's greatest songbirds. What the article triggered off in my few remaining brain synapses was the recollection that although Demis may once have been an Egyptian priest and/or Jewish rabbi he had never claimed to be a McGuffin and I had once been Demis Roussos.

It all happened in Dublin way back in 1976. Now, I may have mentioned this before, but I do not like Dublin. I am a Blefuscu man, as Wolfie Toni would have said, and I don't know of any Belfast or Derry man who does like Dublin. To many of us black Northerners the 'Celtic Tiger' resembles nothing more than old Buck Alec's mangy toothless lion with which he used to scare the weans on the Custom House steps. It's not just because W.T. Cosgrave and Mulcahy and Ernie Blythe and Kevin O'Higgins and them freestaters sold us out in 1922. It's not just because they don't know how to make a decent glass of porter, even though the Guinness factory to this day pollutes the Liffey. It's not just because of the tawdry, plastic, pseudo American 'Kultur' and omnipresent Turd Burger franchises. It's not even, though God knows this would be reason enough, the chi-chi 'boutiques' and 'restaurants' and 'nite clubs' that have spread like the bubonic plague through the pestilential place. It's not just the trendy 'arts' community, with the likes of Colm Tóibín and Rose Mary Doorli et al., and their shameless denial of their history in the ruthless search for the almighty Euro/Yank gravy train.

It's not just because of the Cruiser O'Brien, a man described as 'a lighthouse in a bog' – illuminating but no fucking use to man or beast. It's not just because of their sleazy politicians, their Jack Lynchs and Chuckie Haugheys and their Garrett Fitzgeralds and their Smurfits and Reillys. It's not just because of their shameless hacks like Kevin Myers and Eamonn Dunphy and Eoghan Harris and Ruth Dudley Edwards and the Forsterite revisionists. It's not just because of the stale buns with begging bowls in the streets. It's not just because of the heroin junkies vomiting on your feet as they wave Stanley knives in your face. It's because the banana Republic with no bananas, in the aftermath of the senile Spanish/American mathematician who wanted the boys and girls to dance at the cross roads, was allowed to become infected with the feculent presence and all pervading influence of the anti-Christ himself, Gay Byrne.

So I suppose this tale is about Gaybo, and Demis Roussos and, of course, Kevin Healey. And it's hard to know where to start. So kann's gehen.

It was a dark and stormy night ... naw, that's been done before. It was the usual damp dark night in Blefuscu when the phone call came to Cobweb Castle, my mean abode off the Malone Road. There were a group of us sitting in front of the fire and using an LP cover (Migod! Could it have been by Demis Roussos – nay, too much synchronicity, get back Jung man) to skin up a joint. Grimshaw was there I'm sure. Brian Artur was always there. The taximan was there too. AKA 'The Cisco Kid' and I can date this whole sordid episode to 1975 because he'd just got out of the Kesh. Jimmy 'the weasel' McKeown, who went on to become a top Union leader had come down to join us for he lived on the top floor of our Victorian commune. McIlvogue was of course there, sitting quietly in the corner, biting the head of a whippet and taking notes. We were happy. That's a word I haven't had much use for in a long time, but, yes, we were happy, we were young (relatively), solvent and were going to have fun. Fun. There's a strange word. A funny word.

The reason for our bonhomie was that I had just published a modest book entitled *In Praise of Poitín* and we were planning our appearance on Nationwide Television tomorrow afternoon, 17th March, the day of the sanctified Patrick, where we were to be interviewed by none other than the blessed Valerie Singleton. Why, if one of us played his cards right he might even get onto Blue Peter and have some incontinent wombat piss all over us or learn how to make a totally useless artifact out of used condoms and string. The 'hook' we had sold to the TV was that I, as the first author to write a book exclusively on moonshine whiskey in Ireland, aka poitín, had been running all year the great All Ireland Poitín championship which would be decided on air direct from the BBC studios in Blefescu. My co-conspirators were to appear, suitably masked, and be introduced as the 'Irish Expert Poitín Adjudication Panel' who were to reveal live on air the winner of the title 'Best Poitín Maker of 1975'. I had procured eight bottles of the finest illegal *uisge beatha* and labelled them 1-8. My masked experts (masked because poitín is still illegal) would blind taste them (and after tasting them go blind) and pronounce the Island's winner to a bemused British public.

And then the phone rang. It was my publisher, a slimy reptile whose name shall never be mentioned in polite company unless accompanied by large ingestions of mouthwash. (Oh all right, since this is the era of name and shame, it was John D. Murphy.) He was phoning to tell me that RTÉ, Potato TV, had just called and wanted me on the Gaybo Late Late Show tomorrow evening to promote my book. Happy days. Fame at last. McIlvogue kept skinning up and I broke out a couple of extra bottles of liquid death, all the way from Connemara, to complete the evening.

The next day dawned fair 'Hark, hark the lark at heaven's gate sings, and Phoebus 'gain arises' (not one of the Bard's better staves, but then, he was young). Through the bosky Quantocks we wended our merry carefree way past the gasworks and murals of a homosexual Dutch dwarf upon a white horse, and into the foyer of the British Broadcasting Corporation.

The hospitality was splendid. The program was pre-recorded in mid-afternoon and went without a hitch. Valerie Singleton, over the line from London, was her ineffable charming self. She giggled girlishly and asked us to assure the viewers that 'we weren't really drinking that illegal 'cratur'' as she called it. Tee hee! What a romp Val. Isn't this a great St. Patrick's Day show. Sure aren't those natives quaint and lovable when they're not blowing the fuck out of us. *Uisge beatha* was consumed in immoderate quantities and the masked experts and my good self were wafted out on a cushion of that esteemed Egyptian Al Kohol's finest C^2H^6O and into a motor with a sober driver who's task was to convey us 100 miles down the road to dear old dirty Dublin, there to mix with the Gaybo glitterati on The Late Late Show, which, in those dark days all rural Ireland watched since they couldn't get the filthy BBC channels.

I seem to recollect a fleeting thought as we wheeled into Dubh linn, the black pool, that all had been going too well. Were we mocking fate? Lumberjacks, as we were, usually don't get away with having a good time unpunished. That's why God created Puritans. Still, as the good book says 'wine is a mocker' (Proverbs 20:1). Whether this is Aramaic for 'motherfucker' I don't know, my linguistic skills in Essene have been shot to hell since John Allegro gave me those mushrooms. Nonetheless, the journey down had been splendid. More poitín had been consumed, herbal remedies were flowering and flowing, the driver was sober and we even managed to stop just outside of Dublin and watch ourselves on TV in the local pub. Not only that, the locals had recognized us as 'celebrities' in their midst as they watched bemusedly us appearing in their physical presence and also on the flickering TV screen (the concept of 'pre-recording' had apparently not percolated as far south as Balbriggan). Their hospitality was a tribute to Munster. I had, vainly, thought that the locals had recognized me, the only unmasked participant in the programme from my vivacious good looks but this misplaced vanity was banished from my mind when McIlvogue pointed out that McKeown, ever security conscious, had still not removed his balaclava mask.

Trotzdem, as we entered O'Connell Street, Dublin's main drag, we had every right to feel good about ourselves. It was then that Grimshaw vouchsafed a comment. "Where the fuck are we going, and, by the way, to you realize the driver's stocious." Christ of the shaven tholes (Jeffrey 'I was a teenage Jesus' Hunter)! The driver was steaming. The Balbriggan culchies must have nobbled him. Not that he'd have need too much encouragement.

The chauffeur, who had been rented for the day, was a Prod from Sandy Row who would only answer to the name of TT. We had been assured that this stood for 'total temperance' but now I feared that the soubriquet's origins owed more to 'toping twat'. "Where d'ya wanna go, ye Fenian fucks." Ah! How quickly drink loosens the tongue. Still, we weren't paying him, RTÉ were, so, let's cast aside sectarian strife.

"Cabinteeley," I replied, "We have to pick up Auntie Rita."

"And where would that be, Sir," TT sneered. "It's south side," I responded. "You can't get lost. Just ask anyone for Cabinteeley and they'll put you straight. When you get there wake me up and I'll fish out the exact address. I must perchance close my eyes briefly to arrange my thoughts for tonight's interview." Soon my snores joined those of the other judges.

I was awoken from my reverie by McKeown. His little red Fenian eyes glittering ferally. "This fucking taximan's trying to pull a fast one on us." Groggily I tried to return to the land of the normal (whatever that may be). There came a rapping at my windowpane. It wasn't a raven, it was TT. Now I think of it, perhaps it was an omen. After all, didn't Edgar Allen die Poe? My dreams of fortune turned leeward and slid into the gutter, as did I when TT opened the door and I fell out onto the street. "Ye all right Sir? Don't worry, I've found him. He's in here." He pointed to a low shebeen by the side of the road. It was dark and I hadn't a fucking clue where we were. The battered sign on the ginmill door proclaimed, when deciphered, 'The Rat and Raven'. 'Edgar Allen again!' I shuddered. "C'mon, he's in here." Our conductor grabbed me by the arm and, followed by a ragtail band of erstwhile masked marauders, I entered the Raving Rat.

The decor was early Arthur Carleton, he of 'Tales of the Irish Peasantry' a modest little seller back in 1840 if I recollect, but mercifully the light was as dim as us. I was propelled up to the bar by TT and introduced to a florid faced gentleman, standing at the bar and drinking what appeared to be a treble Jamesons. "Here he is, sir," gibbered TT, "here's Kevin Healey."

What the fuck? Kevin Healey was a septuagenarian. Lean,

cadaverous. He looked like the guy who is always the first to see 'the Creature' and whose face is frozen in a terrified rictus. He could have been a mortician. Shit! He might even have been Edgar Allen Poe's nephew. "What do you want of me?" he asked, fear flickering behind his eye sockets. I tried to explain that I didn't want him at all, but as soon as I began to speak and he heard the Blefuscu accent and saw my ravaged band, teetering behind me he adopted the path of the true craven and ordered 'double whiskeys all round' for his new found friends from the black North. It would have been churlish to refuse and, I must confess that although our party contained thieves, rogues, rapscallions, *âmes damnées* and slubberdegullions, we were deficient in churls. Three generous rounds later, all paid for by the estimable Mr. Kevin Healey, who, although he had a voice like a goose farting in the fog, never let the giving hand cease, we reeled out into the motor, dragging a comatose TT with us. I looked at my watch. Bugger it! We were running late. No chance of getting to Cabinteeley. As O/C my primordial instincts slipped into gear. I called Auntie Rita and said we'd meet her and her team at the studio. She who normally must be obeyed was not the best pleased, and insisted that I must know the way to subversive HQ. I hadn't the heart to tell her that although I had indeed been there on a few previous occasions, I had either been blindfolded by her minders or blind drunk on my own volition when I had crossed the portals of her and Brendan's pied-à-terre. Nor did I feel that it was really necessary that my illsorted troops be presented to her esteemed self in their present state. Nowadays the Mafia (middle aged fat Italian arseholes) don't worry about 'going to the mattresses' – after all, they're now posturopedic and they have remote controls for the digital satellite TV and phone in pizza, but in those days 'going to the mattresses' meant just that. Therefore, I was not too dismayed at giving Cabinteeley a body swerve and heading directly to the bastion of Kultur, RTÉ.

I have little recollection of my drive to the studio, with TT and the troops unconscious in the back. I had asked the taximan to drive but he had just laughed and made a suggestion that was not only extremely vulgar but anatomically impossible, especially for a fat bastard like myself. Fortune favours the bold however, and, 15 minutes before airtime I was ensconced in the Green Room in the Entertainment facility off stage in RTÉ 1's flagship. The troops had been shovelled into seats in the audience, which seemed to consist mainly of a cross between Dublin 4's finest and tweedy culchie ladies with a sprinkling of bespectacled Far Easts and Stale Buns. (Why do most clerics appear to be myopic? Is it the rosary beads?) I was still hoping that Auntie Rita and the troops would arrive and had left tickets for them at the box office. But for now, all I could do was grin, bear it and meet my fellow guests.

In the Green Room we made a merry crew. (Secretly I was hoping for Frankie Vaughan to emerge from behind the shamrock door, but, alas, it was not to be.) As I was the last arrival, my fellow panellists all made a point of approaching me and introducing themselves. The first was, not surprisingly, one of God's anointed. He was not your traditional Far East however. He didn't offer me a Jehovah Sarnie as so many do but warmly shook hands and told me that although he was a priest he was also heavy into Zen Buddhism and had pole vaulted for Ireland at the latest European games. He was dressed in mufti and glowed with health. He refused my offer of liquid refreshment from the bottle of poitín I had smuggled in. Generously, he offered to help me if I felt overwhelmed by this kosmic karmic moment. As he patronisingly groped my shoulder, he whispered "Just call me Terence, I'm an old stager at this game." Yeah, Terry baby, later for you, you smug parasitical cocksucker.

Next up in the welcome line was a fresh faced forty-something-year-old lady. She had a blank, helpless sort of face – rather like a rose before it is sprayed with pesticide. "Hello, I'm a Protestant missionary's wife. This is the third time I've been on the programme. I've recently changed my medication ..." "Thank you for sharing that, Deirdre," I responded, discerning her name from the badge pinned upon her ample bosom.

Chemical relief of any kind was clearly essential. Ostentatiously I took a slug from the unlabelled bottle.

"Got any more of that, Paddy?" It was the third guest. The American. Six foot six long haired hippie. Not only that, and remember that this was over twenty years ago, he rather startled us by having a pierced nose and an earring. No big deal these days, but back then if the Provos had done it to him they'd have clearly been in breach of any ceasefire. Before we were summoned onto the stage the American, who turned out to be Walter Bowart, former editor of the East Village Other and author of *Operation Mind Control*, the ultimate conspiracy 'cryptocracy' book in those days, was happily pissed.

But first we had to be welcomed by God himself. Gaybo oozed into the room and smarmed his way through. He wore little white mittens presumably so that he wouldn't actually have to touch us *hoi polloi* with his naked fleshy and sweating hand. I expected a few anodyne remarks from our genial host and was therefore somewhat nonplussed when he brusquely said "loved the book, just what we need for Paddy's day – by the way, have you ever been a Republican or Anarchist? If so, you can't appear." Bit late now, I thought. If his assiduous assistants hadn't discovered my political and metaphysical form by now I wasn't about to enlighten them. "No problem, Gaybo, *nihil obstat*, but can you just answer me one question. I can see why you have a mad pole vaulting Zen Far East, the Yank's written an important and controversial book, but why on earth have you got the Prod missionary bint on – she says this isn't her first appearance?" The great one rearranged his vulpine features and essayed what in hindsight I suppose was meant to be a smile. "Ah, but hasn't she got gorgeous tits!" Well, nothing special I thought, glancing over at Deirdre's heaving bazooms. "But Gay, she just told me she turned down a part as Helen Keller because she didn't think she could remember the lines."

Ignoring me the great one swept out and soon the applause of the audience filtered back to the Green Room. The minute Gaybo left the staff whipped away the complimentary beverages, but Bowart and I, who were due to be on in the second half of the programme, were unfazed. I still had my bottle of West Cork's finest moonshine.

Half an hour later, and feeling no pain, I was ushered onto the set. Peering through the gloom I could see Grimshaw et al. sitting in the second row. Better still, Auntie Rita and some heavies had arrived and were obviously enjoying the show. I had watched on the monitor with increasing boredom as the Far East and the lovely Deirdre had sparkled and only woken up when Wally Bowart attempted to explain the nature of the secret mind control experiments which the intelligence services were then conducting in America. Gay, and the audience apparently had trouble with his accent which, I could not help but regret, had perhaps been further obfuscated by my ever generous pouring hand.

I sat down heavily in the seat provided and placed the remnants of the poitín bottle on the table in front of me and Gaybo introduced me to the audience as the author of 'a wonderful lighthearted book about Poitín which he had enjoyed immensely'. I guess I've never been a team player – probably a fatal flaw in the publishing game, but this bastard was really getting on my tits and they weren't as big or as 'gorgeous' as Deirdre's.

"But Gay, you haven't even read the book. Your researcher only got it two hours ago and you've been too busy swilling down the gin and ogling Deirdre's tits to even look at it. Here, at least have a slug of the good stuff," I proffered the bottle.

Gay was, to say the least, somewhat taken aback, but, experienced trooper that he was he laughed gayly – "I hope that's not any of that illegal stuff." What the fuck did he think it was! I took a slug and passed the bottle to a grateful Wally Bowart who took a large gulp and vouchsafed "Fuckin' A, this stuff's all right."

Gay turned grey and decided that this Northern upstart had better be put in his place. "Look, it is St Patrick's Day and we all like a bit of fun but you are not allowed to drink on this show and certainly not something which I suspect is an illegal substance. Besides, let's be responsible – poitín can make you go blind."

Ah fuck it. Now or never. Leaning over I took a startled Gaybo's palm and examined it intently. The superstar hastily withdrew his moist appendage but we irredentists would not be thwarted.

"There, Gay," I continued, "I'm sure when you were a wee boy they told you that certain solitary activities would make you go blind, but I don't see any hairs on the palm of your hand and you don't have a white stick and a wee blinkie doggie."

A sussuration crept around the studio on tiptoe. Surely he wasn't about to say the 'W' word? I didn't have to. From the second row my hungover fans began to chant, led, as always by the great Grimshaw:

"Gay Byrne's a wanker."

Rita and the team at the back took up the chant. Bewildered elderly ladies turned to their spouses and asked what a 'wanker' was, only to emit squeals of horror when informed sheepishly by their consorts. Bowart fell off his seat. Deirdre put her hands over her ears, the Far East squatted and attempted a calming Zen mantra and Gaybo announced a commercial break.

As the RTÉ goons escorted myself and Bowart (who'd decided he wanted to join the Lumberjacks) out and we joined our fans outside my last sight of Gaybo was him shaking his fist and screaming "you'll never appear on RTÉ ever again!" Big hairy deal, Gaybo, we were off to the reception at the Third Policeman.

My memories of the reception are blurred by time. I do recall Grimshaw throwing up into the punch bowl which our generous hosts had provided, and Cosgrove stealing a huge potted plant which he walked out with through the foyer determined to present it to McIlvogue's poor wife as a token of his undying love. I do recall waking in a house in Glasnevin, the home of a Kraut Komrade, Uncle

Ralf. The sainted Aine, his long suffering wife served me a triple by-pass breakfast which did the trick however – Amazing Grease – and informed me that the Blefuscu team had hi-jacked a car and taken off back to the Athens of the North. Some of them were actually supposed to work that day. Poor fools. The hired car was outside the door however, and was presumably being paid for, albeit unwittingly, by RTÉ, and there was no sign of the obnoxious TT.

On awaking Ralf insisted that we go down town and get our heads together over a few pints. I was always weak. By mid-afternoon we were in the dreaded McDaid's off Stephen's Green and suffering no pain. We had even formulated a vague plan. Ralf would go off and check up what damage we had done to the Third Policeman and I would take the hired wheel and drive back to Belfast. Baldric might have thought it 'a cunning plan' but somehow I knew it was unlikely to be such smooth sailing. For once I was right. Ralf had just left and I was sipping my last bevvie when Tom McGurk entered, spied my large self and slid into the booth. We had not met for over a year and obviously reminiscences and back stabbing were *de rigueur*. He bought a round. That was a shock. McGurk was notorious as County Tyrone's meanest man. But, it seemed, now that he was down in Dublin he had landed a newspaper job and was flush.

"What are ye doing tonight," he asked. "I saw ye making a tit out of that pratt Gaybo last night." "I better head up the road, Beryl will be waiting." A daunting thought, as McGurk shrewdly discerned. He'd met the wife. "Here," McGurk reached into his pocket, "I've a few tickets for a free drink reception tonight. I can't go, but you might as well use them. It's in Howth. Sure it's on your way."

He left, weaving his way out into a crowded and dreary Dublin dusk. I got on the phone.

It's no fun drinking alone, besides, I hadn't had a real chance to pay my respects to Auntie Rita and the nameless but feared. By 8 o'clock I found myself in Cabinteeley. Rita and Mickey were there. They were broke and readily agreed to accompany me to a free drinks reception. We Northerners do not look gift horses in the mouth. Soon we were threading our way around Dublin and heading for Howth.

As we pulled into the car park of the luxurious hotel, perched on Howth head with its garden of tropical palms and plants running down to Dublin Bay I pulled the invites out of my pocket and handed them to Rita. She took one look and subjected me to her withering gaze – not a pleasant experience – I mean this is a hard woman. "McGuffin, you do realize that this is a reception for Demis Roussos, don't you?" I lied. "Of course, but it's free gargle." In fact I had stuffed the freebie tickets into my pocket without even looking at them once McGurk had told me where the soirée was to be held.

"Who the fuck's Demis Roussos?" asked Mickey.

Mickey had recently escaped from one of Her Majesty's Hotels in our wee Ulcer and consequently his musical listening pleasure for the past five years had been restricted to 'The Men Behind The Wire' and the entire repertoire of Eamonn Largey and the Flying Column.

"You'll not like him, Mickey," said Rita, somewhat snidely I felt. "He's a big fat eejit like McGuffin here."

"C'mon," I retorted, my throat dying to be slaked, "we'll not even see him. It's only 9.30, his show at the Olympia or wherever won't be over for hours." I parked the wheels and we merry three sauntered up the broad steps and through the august portals of the Howth Majestic. "I don't like the look of this," muttered Auntie Rita. "the decor's the color of a cancerous lung! And all these flunkies in monkey suits. Just get us a quiet table and some vino collapso quick McGuffin or I'll turn nasty." Even Mickey shuddered at that.

"No bother," I bluffed quickly and hastened forward – all right, I was pushed – towards the maître domo, reaching for the invites. Christ! Rita had left them in the car. The head functionnaire took one look at me and bared his teeth. They were as white as Johnny Winter. "Why Mr. Roussos," he breathed ingratiatingly, "we've been expecting you, what an honour. Come this way, we've reserved the best table for you and your party." He looked at my 'party'. "These are just two journalists," I improvised, "the troupe will be along shortly." He beamed and ushered us into the banquet hall, bumping into two tables on the way. "My apologies, Mr. Roussos, I seem to have displaced my contact lenses." 'Thank fuck for that', I thought.

He seated us underneath the sparkling chandeliers, snapped his fingers imperiously and, miraculously, a bottle of Moët and Chandon's Premiere arrived. We got stuck in. This was going to have to be a quickie, I figured. While we basked in the opulent splendour and more and more bottles of champagne arrived members of the staff sidled up to the table and soon I was signing Demis autographs as if to the manor born. Other guests soon filled up the room and not even Mickey demanding a 'pint of plain' in a loud voice could spoil the evening. Auntie Rita was most impressed and I felt that for once I had redeemed myself. Even Mickey was enjoying himself.

"Hey, here's a good one! What smells of piss and does the hokey cokey? The Queen Mother!" He laughed uproariously. I glanced at my watch. Jesus! It was almost midnight. Mickey had already turned into a pumpkin but the fat Greek and his bodyguards were due any minute. I nodded imploringly to Rita. Sound woman that she is, she grabbed Mickey before he could tell his joke about the nun and the sheep and dragged him out to the foyer. "Don't forget to tip the staff Demis," she trilled over her shoulder. Bitch! "Must go to the restrooms," I slurred – five bottles of the old Moët will do that for you – and made my way out, through a politely applauding crowd of Dublin 4 wankers, several of whom even wanted to kiss my hand – and that was only the men.

From the foyer it was a short trot to the car where Rita, only somewhat the worse for wear, was standing. I opened the doors and proceeded to get in. Suddenly, "Where's Mickey?" I asked, fear gripping my scrotum. "You shouldn't have let him out of your sight." Rita got into the front passenger seat. "Don't worry, here he comes now, start the engine." I glanced out the window. Mickey was indeed running towards us across the tarmac, clutching a rake of wine bottles in his arms. "Get in, you malacca, we're out of here," I shouted. He opened the back door and thrust the bottles onto the seat. There was a glazed look in his eye. He looked up at me. "McG, I started out with nothing and I still have most of it left. We are the men who stole Trevelyan's corn."

"Gotta get more," he gasped, and stumbled back up the steps. "For God sake, get him, Rita." She ran after him and back into the Majestic while I nervously tried to keep the engine running. Four minutes later, although it seemed an eternity, they both emerged, each laden down with what appeared to be the entire stock of the wine cellar – which, it later transpired, had been conveniently situated underneath the main staircase and left open by some employee who was doubtless fondly going over their Demis Roussos autographed underwear – I tell ye, the things some of these groupies ask you to sign, I feel sorry for that poor Tom Jones. "Andalay, vamanos" I roared as I started to gun the car. "Wait," bawled Rita, "Mickey's not in yet." "Where the fuck is the head-the-ball?' I screamed and then looked in my rear view mirror.

Now I know that objects in the rear view mirror may appear closer than they are, but this was no time for metaphysical speculation about the space time continuum. Leaping out of the car I made a run across the grass where a bedraggled Mickey was engaged in a titanic struggle with a eight foot tall palm tree. "What the fuck are you playing at you brain damaged omadaun?" I bellowed.

"Give us a hand, Mac I have to get this for the Ma. She loves tropical plants." The time was not opportune to remind Mickey that his dear mother lived in a Portakabin near the municipal rubbish dump in Newtownards in the Black North when last heard of and was unlikely to have the necessary facilities for palm cultivation. Between us we dragged the protesting palm to the back of the car and popped the trunk, stuck the roots in, leaving six foot of palm fronds exposed and got the fuck out of Dodge. As I swerved down the driveway, we sideswiped a limo that was coming the other way. There were curtains across the rear windows but I swear to this day that I heard some clown singing 'Forever and Forever and For fucking Ever' as we careened off into the mystic.

We were so gargled and exhausted – Mickey had insisted that we plant the poor palm in Rita's back yard in Cabinteeley lest it die before he could ship it up North to the Ma – that the mattresses actually felt all right. I arose early the next morning and tiptoed out, pausing only to trip over a few champagne bottles, slumped into the car and headed North. Ten miles outside the Pale, on the main road I stopped at a petrol station. I fumbled for some gas money. Only a torn fiver left. Still, it should get me out of the grey mists and back under the blue skies of our beloved statelet.

A grizzled attendant shuffled up and peered in through the window. I flinched. I hadn't changed my clothes in two days and was suffering from what the grandda used to call 'the whips and jangles'.

"Come here Mary," the honest toiler of the soil closet shouted. His wife shuffled out and joined him at my window. "It is, I tell ye, it's him." Not more Demis fans surely?

"He's thon boyo who called Gay Byrne a wanker on the Late Late last night. Give us your autograph. The wife and me's being saying that for years."

All together now:
               "Gay Byrne Is Still A Wanker!"

Paxo

He fell at León. Just half an hour before the young Sandinistas took the town, driving Somoza's demoralized National Guards out with a series of daring and, at times, almost suicidal charges. I didn't see him die, but I saw his body. There was a lull in the fighting and we journalists had come crawling out of the hotels to view the aftermath of battle.

He lay where he'd been shot, on the front steps of the police station. His rifle lay beside him. It too was old. The Sandinistas were too radical or idealistic for the Americans or Russians to bother arming them with the modern technology of death. That they had to capture from the Somocistas. The U.S. had, as usual, backed the wrong side, and when Somoza fled had frantically tried to promote the aims of yet more puppets, this time from the middle class and the responsible elements of the Army. Too little, too late. The usual story.

In death the old man had a look of composure on his face. A young dark-haired student, wearing the distinctive anarchist red and black colors on the scarf tied loosely around his neck, cradled the old man's body in his arms. He had draped a Sandinista flag across the old man to cover the gaping bullet wound through which his tired life's blood had flowed. He was crying softly over the old timer, and, with all the ghoulish insensitivity of a true reporter, I sensed a story or at least a feature.

"What was his name?" I asked in my execrable Spanish. He looked up at me through tearstained eyes. "Paxo, Señor." "Paco?" "No, Paxo." And sitting there, with his dead friend's head cradled in his lap, he told me the story of Paxo.

He was born about 1930 in a small village just south of Chinandega. His father was a peasant, just as his father and his father before him had been.

He too, by the nature of things, was also a peasant and would doubtless have lived and died as such had not two men from the village, Jose and Manuel, left it to join the FSLN, a small band of rebels who named themselves after Sandino, the almost legendary folk hero of the peasants who had fought against the Yanqui gringos and the dictatorship until treacherously murdered by Somoza back in 1934. Sandino had believed in expropriating the land from the exploiters and giving it to the peasants, in co-operative farms, in freedom, you know, all the things that look so nice on paper and for which so many brave young fighters like the Sandinistas are fighting and dying for today in many other countries and which they will see stolen away from them by the first devious politician who comes along, if history is any judge – and it generally is.

Anyway, Paco, then about 30 and bored with the drudgery of the land, was recruited by his two fellow campesinos and joined up to fight tyranny, save the oppressed – you know, all those sorts of romantic, wonderful, futile and stupid reasons that people have for doing beautiful and idiotic things. 'Better to die on your feet than live on your knees'. 'If in dying, my example will have encouraged another to take the rifle from my dying hand and continue the struggle I will not have died in vain' etc. etc. You know that sort of nonsense. You should. Hacks like me have been churning it out for long enough.

Well, for whatever reason, Paco took to the hills with Jose and Manuel and joined the small band of would-be freedom fighters, and there, in the low Sierras north of León, he met O'Toole.

O'Toole of the flashing eyes and the flaming red hair, now flecked with grey grizzle. O'Toole from the county Sligo in holy, apostolic, murderous Ireland. O'Toole the romantic, the drunkard, the adventurer, the failed revolutionary. O'Toole who, as a boy, had run messages in and out of the GPO in Dublin in 1916.

Who had been sentenced to death and then reprieved because of his age. Who had escaped from his penal cell in England and made his way back home to join the newly formed IRA and fight the Black and Tans and the Auxies, the English murder gangs. O'Toole who had been one of Michael Collins' Apostles, his elite hit squad, and who had helped win the war only to see Collins, his idol, lose the peace and sell out the Republic. He had fought on the losing side (of course) in the internecine civil war and been sentenced to death by his former comrades who had forgotten their vow and their dreams and were busy 'fulfilling the work of the foe', and had only been reprieved by the ceasefire and Frank Aiken's call to dump arms.

He had been involved, some said, though no one could ever prove it, in the assassination of Kevin O'Higgins in 1927, the Free State Minister who had been gunned down on the steps of the church after Mass by people who had an old score to settle, men who had vowed to never forgive, never forget. Whether he had been involved or not, he left Ireland the next day, never to return.

The next years of his life were swathed in mystery, although scattered sightings were reported as far apart as Australia, America, Brazil and even China. What is certain, however, is that he appeared, phoenix-like from the ashes, in Spain in 1936. That his gaunt face was definitely sighted by members of the Irish Connolly Brigade at Jarama and Brunete and Teruel and finally, at the last stand in Madrid. Yeah, Madrid, when by this time with the anarchists of the FAI, he had fought from building to building in the University to keep the fascists at bay, sending the bombs up in the elevators with only ten-second fuses.

Always the first up out of the trenches, his flaming red hair already flecked with grey, and bellowing, in his still untamed brogue, "Up the Republic, up the feckin' Republic!" with his captured gun clenched in his hand.

The British were even to claim that he had been part of an IRA unit in the abortive bombing campaign in England in 1939 after his escape from Spain, but although it would have been his form, I doubt it for I have spoken to many survivors of that fiasco and none can recall him. Doubtless he fought in the Second World holocaust, but where and for whom is not recorded.

Nor is there any word of what he was doing in the fifties, when he should have been drawing a pension somewhere and taking it easy. No, all that is clear is that, like some aged Zapata, he appeared from nowhere with a band of ragged and poorly armed peasants and a few university students on a hilltop in dusty Nicaragua in the hot dry summer of 1961, and it was there that the thirty year old illiterate peasant met the sixty year old mad Irishman.

Apparently they hit it off from the beginning. O'Toole had only rudimentary Spanish, a hangover from his Madrid days, and Paco had no English, let alone Gaelic, but they got on together. And it was there in the hills with O'Toole dying of dysentery and God only knows what other diseases and the abortive rebellion sputtering its way nowhere, like so many before it, that the Irishman taught the Nicaraguan about Paxo and gave Paco his name.

"Ah Paxo! That's the quare stuff, me boyo!" he used to say, as they squatted on the dusty hillside trying to find some shade from the blistering sun. "That's the stuff to give the Brits and the Fascists a dose of the runs. Paxo, that's the people's weapon." And, although he was dying, and knew that he was, he slowly, laboriously and patiently taught the peasant all he needed to know about Paxo.

"T'was invented by a friend of mine," he used to say. "Big Jim O'Donovan, God rest his soul." (He was never to know that Jim O'Donovan, the IRA's first 'Director of Chemicals' or Explosives expert was not to die until 1979, in a hospital outside Dublin, forgotten by everyone but his wife, who just happened to be Tom Barry's sister.) Big Jim! The man who called Mickey Collins a traitor to his face and lived. The same Big Jim who drew up the S Plan to bomb England. As Grimshaw says, 'I wonder if they realize, Sir, artificial fertilizer'.

Paxo. Homemade explosive. Primitive unstable stuff. Nowadays the IRA has refined it, improved it. It's now called co-op mix, but back in those days it was the Paxo and so it was called by the dying O'Toole, on the bleak inhospitable hill, the arsehole of nowhere, where he died, wracked with pain and tended only by his new-found peasant friend. And Paco listened. Listened to his friend, the giant, half-mad foreigner, whose brow he had to wipe and whose shit he had to clean up when the Irishman became too weak. And he tried to understand his ravings and he studied the drawings, traced in the dusty earth with a pointed stick.

One night that summer his friend died. Weakened, sick and aging, his last words as he looked up into the peasant's face were, "Up the Republic, Paxo, me oul mate, and fuck them fascists."

Paco buried him there in a shallow grave scooped out with his machete. He put a simple wooden cross above the mound of earth, picked up the two old rifles and trudged off down the hill.

The others had left two days previously, unable to take the sick, dying rebel with them, and dispersed, some into exile, some into jail, some to die before the dictator's firing squads. Some, like Paco, managed to drift back to their own villages. Paco was lucky. The new police chief in the area had been drafted in and records had been lost.

No one inquired too closely where he had been for the last six months, assuming that like so many others he had been trying to eke out a livelihood in the city. Paco took up his old life on the tiny piece of land his family owned. His father died soon afterwards and his mother didn't survive him long. A sister died in childbirth and two brothers drifted away to Managua, to try to survive in the shanty town jungle of the favellas. By 1966 he was alone on the small family plot, laboring all day as his ancestors had before. And then, one day, the road came.

The road. A broad four-lane highway that cut a swathe 150 miles long from the United Fruit Company's plantations to the port. The consumers in Yanquiland wanted bananas. United Fruit wanted their dollars; hence it was important to get the bananas to market as quickly as possible. Yanqui consumers have money; Nicaraguan peasants do not. It is the inexorable law of the market, and Somoza, who was not an ignorant peasant but a cultured puppet whose penchant for the good things of consumerland was world famous, ordered that the road be built. After all, it didn't cost him anything. The World Bank and various A.I.D. agencies agreed to finance the loan.

It was a fine road. Straight as a die, right from the plantations to the port. Forests were razed, mountains were blasted, peasants steamrollered off their pathetic little strips of economically impractical land. When the road was finished it would be possible to get the bananas to the boats a whole five hours earlier than hitherto. It was a magnificent feat of engineering. National Geographic and the Construction Times both vouched for that. The American construction engineers, under dynamic young men fresh out of M.I.T., demonstrated real Yanqui knowhow.

It cut right across Paco's tiny plot of land. Alone now, for he had never married, he was 36 years of age and looked 50. Poor diet and ceaseless toil had aged him. His hair was white, his hands gnarled and calloused. Few in the village talked to him. It wasn't good to be seen with him. Sometimes in the cantina, which he would visit maybe once a month to drink mescal or tequila, he would come out with remarks that were 'dangerous'. He was 'un poco rojeta', a bit of a red. He was suspected of being 'mal de la cabeza'. Mothers warned their children to stay away from him. He was probably harmless but a bit crazy. And the road came.

The first thing Paco knew was when a man from the ministry came to his shack and handed him a piece of paper. Paco couldn't read it and the man didn't bother to explain. He had a lot of pieces of paper to hand out that month. So Paco had to take it to the local priest. The priest was surprised to see him. He had a reputation as a 'bit of a troublemaker', he didn't attend Mass regularly and when he did he didn't contribute a peso. He was perhaps even an atheist, although he never actually said so.

The priest, however, was a man of God and the spiritual ruler of the village, so he read the piece of paper to Paco, just as he had had to do for a dozen or so other peons in the past week whom the government official had visited. He explained that the Government was requisitioning two-thirds of his land for the new road. Then he explained what requisitioning meant.

Paco shook his head. "Father," he said, "it is not just. It is not fair." The priest, who was a man of God, had to disagree. "Paco, it is the will of God. It is progress. When this road is built it will bring civilization to our poor village. The Government is only acting on our behalf. Trust me. It is all for the best."

Paco went back to his shack with a bottle of mescal and thought for a long time. He went to the tin box which was hidden under a pile of rubbish at the back of the hut and counted his money. That didn't take long. Then he went back to the village and sat by himself at the rickety table in the flyblown cantina and killed another bottle of mescal. He thought of the Sandinistas and his days in the mountains. Most of all he thought of his dead gringo friend, O'Toole.

That night Paco was thrown out of the cantina. He was drunk and he didn't bother to try to protest. Anyway, protest was not for peasants like him. Somehow he managed to stagger back to his hut, stopping only to vomit beside the dusty track.

In the morning he got up with a sore head and went and tended his land, just as he had always done. That night, before he lay down to sleep he counted once more the few pesos that represented his life's savings. The next morning he went into the village and asked the sweaty, fat store owner Raoul for some weedkiller.

"Weedkiller?" Raoul said, scratching his head. "Weedkiller is expensive, Paco. It is not for peasants like you. What do you need with weedkiller, anyway? Your land can barely grow anything as it is and you are going to lose most of it." But Paco was stubborn. He persisted and eventually Raoul, when Paco produced his tin box, agreed to send to the town for an assortment of chemicals, most of which he had never heard of and which he had great difficulty in spelling.

Work on the road commenced. It started at the plantation and snaked across the land. Within months it had advanced eighty kilometres; soon it approached Paco's village, where Paco still worked on his piece of land. He had given up drinking mescal now and was never seen in the cantina. Every month, after selling his crops for a few pesos, he would visit the local store and purchase a few more chemicals to make his weedkiller. By now Raoul had got used to ordering the stuff and no longer used to regale the drunks in the cantina about the antics of 'the mad Paco'.

The road approached with leaps and bounds, as helmeted Yanquis supervised sweating peons. One day Paco looked up from his toil in the field to see a great metallic monster grate up the rough track. It was the first bulldozer he had ever seen, and like his neighbours, he stood back and watched as the machine gouged out a track across the tiny fields, savaging the earth. His earth and his ancestors' earth.

Within a month it was done and the road had passed by. Where Paco's best field had been was now a towering rampart, atop of which was the concrete highway. Inexorably the road and those who worked on it had moved on, en route to the sea. Raoul, whose cantina had been the only business to benefit from the brief influx of workers, mourned their passing. No one else did.

Paco's little bit of land was now split in two by the highway. Every night when his day's toil was over he would walk the few hundred metres to the concrete colossus and talk to it, curse it, insult it, piss on it.

He would take his pick, the pick which he had stolen from the workers who were the servants of the road. The monster hadn't missed it. It had many tools. Every night, for over an hour, he would attack the side of the monster, hacking, savaging it with ill-coordinated swings of the pick, and as he swung and cursed the monster he would often think of his gringo friend.

O'Toole had used a pick. He had told Paco of how he had been what he called a 'navvy' in far-off London, wherever that was, and he had talked of skyscrapers and giant office blocks which were bigger, far bigger, than Paco had seen on his one trip into Managua to visit his brother many years ago.

Each night, muscles torn, and drenched with sweat, he would labor at the wall, and when he could work no more he would cover up his work with sagebrush and branches and stumble back to his shack to throw himself down on his sacking and dream the night away with sweaty, violent dreams.

Each month he would buy another small sack of weedkiller, manufactured in Yanqui land. Each month on his way back to the shack he allowed himself a grim smile at the irony of it. One month he even permitted himself a laugh, which he hurriedly stifled as he glanced around. That day, in addition to his quota of weedkiller, he had in a plastic bag a small shiny object, which the miner who had sold it to him called a detonator. It had taken a month's earnings and several evenings buying drinks for the miner in a neighbouring town to get it and a small length of cortex, but he didn't regret it.

Nine months to the day that the work on the road had started, the highway was completed. It was a marvelous work of modern technology. Somoza himself surrounded by his goons, pale imitations of Papa Doc's 'Tonton Macoutes', was to officially cut the tape at the port. His deputy, a corpulent general called Ramirez, with the chief of police, was to officiate at the plantation.

Then, after the speeches, the drinks and the handshakes, they were to drive with the United Fruit's Nicaraguan agent and the brilliant young engineer the two hundred kilometers along the new road to receive Somoza's congratulations and attend a state banquet.

The great day was declared a National holiday, even for the peasants. Paco's village was decorated with bunting and tattered flags. The priest ordered a special thanksgiving Mass that morning and all the village attended. Even Paco. The priest, clad in his new ceremonial robes, noticed him standing awkwardly at the back of the tiny church. He permitted himself a smile and then preached the wonderful sermon that he had spent weeks composing, and called on the congregation to join with him in praying for El Presidente, who had brought this progress to their humble village.

After the service he bade the congregation join him beside the new road, which he would bless as Señor Ramirez and the police chief and his party flashed by in their limousine on their way to meet the President.

And the villagers did as they were bidden and joined him by the highway to wave flags and cheer as the Mercedes Benz bearing the dignitaries (and only ten minutes behind schedule) flashed by on the new road, which had been officially designated the United Fruit Highway.

Paco was not among the cheering throng. He had slipped out of the church before the final blessing and made his way back to his shack. He sat there a while, as a kilometre away, the man of God and his flock waved flags and prayed for the success of the road. Then, resolutely and almost as if he were in a trance, he walked across his field to the road, carrying a crude wooden box.

The limousines sped down the magnificent road, slowing only slightly to acknowledge the cheers of the villagers, and accelerated on towards the port.

Paco crouched in the shadow of the monster which had stolen his land. As he pressed the plunger he said, softly, to himself, "Up the Republic."

As the car passed, the great white snake which was the road

erupted. In slow motion it lifted itself, like some primeval beast rising from the slime and rippled, sloughing off its skin and falling apart. The Mercedes was hurled twenty feet in the air before plummeting down the embankment. The occupants barely had time for an act of contrition let alone a scream. Lying in the debris, concussed and bleeding, Paco saw through his closing eyes the car somersault and burst into flame. He was smiling when he blacked out.

Paco was arrested of course and taken to the Securidad in Managua and tortured to reveal his accomplices. It was only the second time Paco had been to the capital and he didn't get to see much of it. After a week they stopped applying the electrodes to his genitals. There wasn't much left to which to attach them anyway. They issued an 'all points bulletin' to find the gringo O'Toole, who, had he been alive, would doubtless have appreciated being Public Enemy No. 1 yet again.

Paco lay for months, burnt and scarred, in his filthy cell. Then he was dragged into court and sentenced to death for the assassination of the Minister and of Hiram Fish, Vice President of United Fruits. The day before he was due to be executed they came to his cell and told him that he had been reprieved due to El Presidente's generosity. They did not tell him that the Tupamaros in Uruguay had kidnapped the Nicaraguan Ambassador and a CIA man and were demanding Paco's release. More dead than alive he was transferred to St. Heloise of the Angels Penitentiary in León.

He was there for twelve years. He was an old man when he went in and the beatings, humiliations and the meagre diet all left their marks on him, but he remained unbowed. By now he was known as Paxo and many of the guards thought that he was crazy. Maybe he was.

One day his cell door opened and he looked up, expecting another beating, but it was not the guard but a young student who stood before him.

"Paxo?" "Si," the old man replied. "Kill me if you want, I'm tired." The student began to cry. "You are free, Paxo, free. We are liberating the town. Somoza is on the run and the Sandinistas are freeing the prisoners. Join us."

Paco did not know whether to believe him or not. Was it another trick? But as he stumbled out into the light which hurt his eyes and saw the young guerrillas with their red and black scarves and face masks and the bodies of the guards he too began to cry.

"Have you a gun for old Paxo?" he asked. "I used to know how to handle one." They offered him his choice of weapons and he marvelled at the M1s and the Armalites which they had captured from the Guarda Civil, but he chose an old gun which reminded him of O'Toole and the mountains and marched off with the rebels.

He died, two weeks later, on the steps of the police station. He killed three policemen before they blew him away. As I said, I never talked to him but I saw his body. I would have liked to have talked to him. He would have made what my Editor calls a thinkpiece feature. Instead I got drunk with the rest of the press corps on free Cuba Libres at the León Hilton. I missed my copy time, but then, as I said to my Editor over the International line, who in Britain wants to read about Nicaragua anyhow?

Hi-Jack In The Hong Kong Horror Hotel

It was all Toy Boy Roy's fault I suppose. Yee Nor has a lot to answer for as well. If she'd kept her eyes open or listened to all the stories she'd have been sure to have caught him groping some piece of Chinatown tottie in the back of my Mercedes and not allowed him to invest in real estate in San Francisco. She wouldn't have ended up in the club Fed slammer, Raymond wouldn't have ended up slinging hash in a low dive in Kowloon, Jomo wouldn't have been hit by a runaway rickshaw and ended up in Horror Hotel, but, then again it's an ill wind – I wouldn't have ended up with my faithful Mordred, the Toy Boy's Mercedes.

My involvement in this sordid saga began early one morning in 199_ when I was peremptorily summoned to Jomo's law office located in downtown San Francisco. When I arrived I found the great attorney ensconced with perhaps the ugliest Chinese woman I have ever seen. I mean, if my dog had been that ugly I'd have shaved its arse and taught it to walk backwards. I was introduced to Yee Nor and Jomo attempted to pass me off as a stellar international lawyer and financial wizard. Yeah! Right! Beside Yee Nor sat her husband Roy the toy boy. He was at least fifteen years younger than Yee Nor, but no oil painting himself and clearly had been hiding behind the door when the brains were being doled out. But there is always a silver lining, if one thinks positively. It had been a benevolent act by the divine despot in bringing these two fine people together in holy matrimony. It meant that only two people suffered, not four.

Yee Nor may not have been pinup of the month but underneath that frizzy balding skull there was a mind like a steel rat trap. Ten years ago Yee Nor, a refugee from Hong Kong, had arrived in San

Francisco and set up a couple of sweatshops which had prospered. Being an immigrant she had not fully appreciated little matters such as paying tax, social security and the likes and ended up getting charged with a theft of some $250,000. This is a felony. By any State's standards. Fate however had sent her to Jomo and through devious legal chicanery he had managed, to the outrage of the District Attorney, in having the offence reduced down to a misdemeanor which resulted in a small fine. The judge involved was within one week of retirement and hated the DA more than he liked Jomo. Nonetheless, it was a mighty victory.

Since then Yee Nor, with some help from her elderly father, a Hong Kong crook – but a gentleman crook – had prospered. By the time she came to see us she owned no fewer than fifteen sweatshops in Baghdad by the Bay and had paper assets of some $67 million. There was only one snag – oh all right there was more than one – but the main problem was that this wealth existed on paper only, based on the enormous bank loans which the crooked Chinatown banks insisted on 'giving' her to acquire new properties. Five of the companies were still profitable, mainly because the crooked bankers had instructed her as to how she could lease a wonderful new machine – the Shimmy Shaka.

Ah the Shimmy Shaka! A joy to behold. A vast gleaming metallic loom, which had to be hoisted into the run down tenements where Yee Nor installed her workers and her machines, through the second or even third floor windows (yes, you pedants, both workers and machines were regularly hoisted in and out). With a Shimmy Shaka, manufactured of course in Hong Kong, one had only to feed in a couple of dollars worth of wool, push a few buttons and out the other end came a lovely sweater, in whatever shape, size, design or colour one wanted. This could be, and was, sold to such 'reputable' outlets as The Gap, Levi Strauss, Banana Republic and Maceys who flogged them to the yuppies for $60 a pop.

Shimmy Shakas cost about $200,000 each and Yee Nor had twenty of them so the money rolled in. Well, that's not quite true. As far as the leasing companies were concerned Yee Nor had 20 machines, in actuality she had eight. The other 12 were phantom machines which were used to borrow yet more millions from the leasing companies themselves as well as the bankers. The toy boy's job was to switch ID numbers on the machine anytime a lessor came by to check on his investment. These shrewd businessmen were quite prepared to accept as collateral a little statement from an alleged chartered accountant testifying to Yee Nor's annual statement of financial solvency even though they knew that Yee Nor had merely typed it up herself on a piece of paper which had a Woolworth's stamp on the top of it proclaiming it to be the work of a non existent accountant. The bankers and loan officers knew this – hadn't they shown her how to do it, but they were greedy. They were making $50,000 bonuses every time Yee Nor borrowed another odd million and she had to keep borrowing more and more to rob Peter and pay Paul – the old Ponzi scheme. Yee Nor was the toast of the town and was photographed with everyone who was anyone from the Mayor (now Senator) Diane Feinstein to the top politicians who regarded her as a most generous contributor to their electoral war chests. The chief of police was a fair-weather friend as well, until the shit hit the fan. And all could have continued to go swimmingly (except for the poor workers in the sweat shops) but for the idiot Toy Boy. Yee Nor loved her little Roy and lavished him with cars, jewellery and every Yuppie gadget to delight his little heart. Alas, Toy Boy, smarting under the sneers of his fellow Chinese gangsters that he was only a gigolo, decided that he in fact was born to be a real estate speculator, nay, mogul. In truth, Roy knew as much about real estate as a cow knows about having a holiday which was why, by buying high and having to sell low when the bottom dropped out of the market, he managed to squander some $20 million in the space of a bad two years. When they found out Yee Nor and her bankers were not the best pleased, though to be fair, Yee Nor was hurt far more by Roy's increasingly blatant dallyings with a parade of Chinese and Vietnamese tarts. Word got out, the vultures circled and loans started to get called in. The FBI were alerted, an investigation begun and in short Yee Nor arrived in Jomo's office only a few days ahead of the long arm of the law.

    Worse still, from our legal point of view, she had left it a bit late coming to us, having wasted $20,000 on some law shark down the street who was supposed to be a financial expert and merely took her bread and then threatened to tell the Feds that she was a crook. It's nice to know that the old profession still lives up to its reputation. (This, of course, is just sour grapes – 'it should have been me, driving that Cadillac' as Ray Charles used to sing, although what a blinkie wants with a Cadillac I'd rather not speculate.) It soon became apparent why Jomo had called me in. He was intent in snaring a retainer from Yee Nor but he clearly could not represent both her and the toy boy – the dreaded 'conflict of interest' – i.e. Yee Nor might want to turn on the Toy Boy or vice versa, and therefore, for a much lesser fee, he would suggest mygoodself as Roy's mouthpiece. The deal was done. No sooner had the guilty pair scurried off to their mansion in Hillsborough than the writs started filing through the door. Every creditor who had got wind of the all too imminent collapse of the Yee Nor empire was frantically trying to get first in line to salvage whatever they could. Tough shit. The only people who were going to make anything out of this mess were the lawyers and the big receiver firms.

Jomo as usual panicked and instructed me to prepare answers to the complaints – each at least fifty pages long – which were pouring in. While not pretending to be any kind of financial expert or business lawyer – after all I generally only dealt with ODCs, or Ordinary Decent Criminals to you, I realized that the entire Yee Nor empire was shortly to be taken into receivership. Their lawyers would, for hefty fees paid out of the estate, sort it all out. Accordingly I devised a filing system which I would recommend to any other budding attorney involved in boring civil litigation. Every day I would stroll into the office where Darlene, the ever efficient secretary, would give me the latest batch of Summonses and Complaints and a list of some fifty hysterical lawyers who were screaming that I must call them immediately. I would sit down, light a joint and solemnly take each and every Summons and Complaint and place it in a large cardboard box. After the little weed had plied its wicked way with my brain cells I might, out of the goodness of my heart make the odd phone call to New York or Chicago or Philadelphia and engage one or other of these apoplectic mouthpieces in telephonic communication. Needless to say, I always called collect and they always accepted the call. On a fine afternoon I might even stroll down to one of the sweat shops and watch SF's finest preventing teeth gnashing attorneys from hoisting Shimmy Shakas out of third floor windows

It was at times risible to hear these legal titans threaten and then cajole, begging me to get them into the first line on the starting grid for litigants in order that their corporate clients might at least salvage something from their greedy endeavours. I would soon tire of this, put down the receiver and repair to the bar there to contemplate how Jomo and I were to benefit financially from this debacle. We had already looted the main factory just before the receiver arrived and made off with some 700 sweaters, which made nice presents for the homeless of San Francisco (for I donated most of them to the Cannabis Buyers Club so that in addition to giving AIDS, Asthma, Glaucoma and Cancer victims a little bit of medicinal herb for a brief period they also got a nice new woolly) but Jomo was keeping all the retainer that Yee Nor had grudgingly handed over in used twenties from her voluminous handbag and I was, as usual, fiscally in pain. I did manage to squirrel away the phoney books used by Yee Nor's companies but these were in handwritten code in Chinese by an enigmatic lady called Grace and probably wouldn't have helped the investigators from the Receiving vultures much. I also rescued a very indiscreet photograph album which showed Yee Nor and Roy in happier times cavorting with the rich and verminous of our fair City but this little piece of potential blackmail would have to wait. (The cheque still in the mail Hongisto?)

The receiver had seized five of Roy's Mercedes before I could get round to it but I finally did acquire the mighty Mordred, as I christened him, a 1970 Merc – my one and only, which turned out to have been used as a passion wagon by Roy, judging by the used condoms and strange bondage implements I found in the trunk. But man cannot live by Merc alone. The Feds and the State were closing in and it was time for plan B. Jomo hastily sent me to the law library to research current extradition laws and, next time I encountered Yee Nor and Roy in the office I was able to give them a list of countries in which they would be safe from the rapacious hand of Uncle Sam. There is only one drawback to these countries – they are all shitholes, where the not so happy family would not really enjoy their exile. Roy believed that he could go to Texas and that there was no extradition treaty there. Alas, I had to point out to him that Texas actually was a part of the great US of A, a piece of information that shook him. Taiwan was decided on, but first we had to stop our esteemed clients from getting arrested.

Plan C was a piece of cake. We persuaded Yee Nor to stage a mental breakdown and we whipped her into the psych ward in SF General Hospital. This wasn't too hard to do. She was really cracking up and the death threats emanating from her legions of creditors were more potent than the Prozac on which she was daily dosing. As the Feds descended Yee Nor and the Toy Boy were on a flight to Taiwan and thence to Vietnam and Laos. And there it might have rested. The initial media frenzy died down after I had stood on the steps of City Hall and assured the assembled hacks that my client the Toy Boy was 'beyond beeper range'. Roy hadn't been charged yet and the Feebs chance of serving him were remote – and Yee Nor was a fugitive and unextraditable. But Yee Nor got 'homesick' for her adopted home, the good old US of A. Hadn't she paid to be a citizen and was the proud owner of a US passport. The long distance phone calls started. Even Royboy got in the act and I would return from a strenuous afternoon in my local shebeen to find incoherent messages on my machine, begging to be told when they could return home. These people were unclear on the concept – but then, aren't most people on this mound of misery.

And then we got a call from the Feebs. As luck would have it the call had been placed by one Padraig Murphy, a fine upstanding Irish-American and Federista. Would we come into Fed HQ and discuss our clients' whereabouts or would we prefer to have the office raided and our financial dealings subjected to some scrutiny? Personally, being assetless and judgement proof I didn't give a rat's arse, but Jomo had a legitimate business and a family. And so, one sunny day we found ourselves on the 20th floor of the Philip Burton Building on Goldengate, in the Fed's inner sanctum. Murphy was, by and large, not the worst sort, but I couldn't help but notice that his eyes never joined in when his lips smiled.

I attempted to break the ice by telling him an Irish joke – well he was wearing a green tie. You know, the one about the guy who goes into an Irish bar in Kilburn in London with a rucksack, has a pint of Guinness and asks the bartender if he can leave the sack behind the bar "for an hour or so". Suspicious, the bartender asks him "What's in the rucksack?" "Seventeen pounds of Semtex." "O that's no problem, I thought it was a fucking bodhran," says the bartender. Jomo tittered nervously. I smiled. So did Murphy. "Very funny, I must tell that to the Buck," he ventured. The Buck had been for years the Bay Areas supposed super sleuth who infiltrated every Irish group to suss out 'the terrorists'. Corrupt, incompetent and vindictive. I'd already met him on several occasions. Not an auspicious start to the interview.

"I'm afraid we can't help," muttered Jomo, "we don't know where our clients are though I believe it's Taiwan and you know there's no extradition from there."

Murphy grinned, vulpinely, and pushed over copies of Jomo and my recent telephone bills. "I don't believe that Hong Kong is exempt from extraditing American citizens," he sneered. A fair point. "I'll get to the point. You lure the assholes back here and we'll cut a deal. We'll ignore Roy and guarantee Yee Nor no more than ten years if she'll rat out the Chinese bankers and corrupt lease companies." I was about to tell him to fuck off – ever so politely of course – but Jomo beat me to the punch. He may be timid at times in front of authority but he was solid when it came to ratting out a client. "No deal. But here's an alternative. You come out to Hong Kong and we'll allow our clients to be interviewed. If they want to squeal maybe we can cut a deal, but I won't advise them to return to the mainland." I liked this one better. "Come on Pat, this way you get a freebie to Hong Kong. You've got to see it before the red hordes of bureaucrats take over in '99. I'll even take you to Ned Kelly's Australian bar." This clinched it.

And so, two weeks later Jomo and I were in the fleshpots of Kowloon, sitting in an English bar and drinking gnats piss with the Brit ex-pats. Our flights had been arranged by a comrade in Malaysian Air who had endeavored to get us cut rates while billing our Chinese criminal clients full fare and we'd even managed to have two days of tourism in Japan en route – a mistake in retrospect but then that's another story. So, for once, I actually had a few Hong Kong dollars in my pocket and the prospect of a sin filled week in Honkers. Jomo even had a $20,000 fee from Yee Nor in the hotel safe – not that I'd see much of that, still, Macao and the gambling tables beckoned. First, all we had to do was baby sit Yee Nor through an FBI interview in the Hong Kong Hilton the next day. Murphy and his sidekick had arrived and were awaiting Yee Nor on the morrow. Jomo was real cheerful. He'd just had a new haircut and believed himself to be a dashing example of American male superiority. I hadn't the heart to tell him he looked like the victim of a drive by perm. Nevertheless, it was clearly a night to celebrate.

It is 10 p.m. and we are in Juicy Lucy's or some such pick up bar in the heart of Kowloon. We are only a hundred yard stroll to the hotel and I'm getting ready to split and get a few hours kip before Yee Nor descends upon us at 8 a.m. and we have to escort her on the ferry over to Hong Kong. Roy, needless to say has been exiled, on pain of death, to the New Territories for a few days. The last thing I want is for the Feebs to have a chance to even speak to the omadaun. I have, of course, reckoned without Jomo the Playboy of the Western World. He is trying to pick up bored Colombian callgirls who, he claims, apparently find him (and his bulging wallet) irresistible. I turn to say goodnight to Jomo only to discover that he is involved in an altercation with a florid faced Brit about who(m) the bored South American demi-monde is going to shag first – Jomo or the Brit. Personally, I have always agreed with Cyril Connolly who described his fellow English countrymen as 'sheep with a nasty side' and this particular illegitimate offspring of Margaret Thatcher appeared to be no exception. His command of the vernacular may have been far from encyclopaedic but even he could take offence when Jomo, the archetypal Ugly American, called him a 'muthafucka', a soubriquet much in use in the courts of justice in California. "I think what my colleague meant," I vouchsafed, "is that this is merely a jocular reference to your collective Oedipal complexes." Blessed are the peacemakers. For they shall be shat upon by all and sundry, particularly sundry.

Picking myself up from the floor and gingerly wiping the claret from my nose, I waved aside the ministrations of the two extremely disproportioned genetic throwbacks whom Juicy Lucy (who was probably a syphilitic male Asian eunuch in real life) employed as bouncers and unsteadily made my way towards the exit. "See ya, Jomo," I muttered over my shoulder. "I'll be along later, I've a date with Miranda." (Or whatever the Colombian Belle Du Jour was calling herself. Personally, she reminded me of Greta Garbo, whom the late great John Gilbert succinctly referred to as 'a broad who would make you eat a mile of her shit just to smell her asshole'. The Colonists do have such a quaint way with words, don't they.)

Ten minutes later I had managed to stumble my weary way back to the hotel, ignoring the blandishments of those 'adventure capitalists' who offered me, and any other 'furriner', their offspring, siblings and even grandmothers along with a wide range of potentially interesting pharmaceuticals. Sometimes we Ulcermen are made of sterner stuff. A naggin of Bush and I hit the scratcher after setting the alarm clock (a proud souvenir stolen from the glorious Peoples' Republic of China which featured the late Chairman waving a little red book and which went off with a Maoist cacophony of unintelligible slogans – perfect to arouse an inebriated Paddy from his ill-gotten slumber).

I awoke at 7 a.m., bleary-eyed, and with a jaundiced orb surveyed the hotel room. It looked like Jonestown on the morning after. The room phone was ringing. I answered. It was Yee Nor. "Where Jomo?" I looked around the room. His bed appeared to have been untroubled by either his or the Colombian tart's presence. "You better come up, Yee Nor." I hit the shower. Ten minutes later I was having to calm down my esteemed co-counsel's client. "Where Jomo? Where Jomo?" A good question Yee Nor and certainly enough to stump this brain battered Paddy. The phone rang. It was the Colombian tart. "Where Jomo? Where Jomo?" O happy day. I was able to ascertain that 'young Lochinvar' had split from Juicy Lucy's an hour after I had and had arranged an assignation with the young ambassadoress for the land best known for the dandruff of the Gods. Only he hadn't shown. She was worried. Yee Nor was worried. Shit, even I was worried. The phone rang again. "Patrick Murphy here, are you bringing your client over to the Hilton now?"

"Pat, me ould segocia, you're not going to believe this, but Jomo's gone missing." "You bastard! I sure as shit don't believe this! It's an obvious dirty ploy by you bastards!" Murphy was not a happy budgie. "I swear, Pat, on Paisley's grave." "Tell me what happened." He started making calls. To the Hong Kong police – he didn't have a problem in this, the HKPD were more corrupt than even the Feebs. I called the hospitals. I sent Yee Nor to the coffee shop, finished the Bushmills and hit the phones.

It was not until 11 a.m. that Jomo was located. He had been hit by a runaway rickshaw (actually a taxi) on his way back to the hotel. Taken, unconscious, to 'Horror Hotel', the public hospital on top of the hill (hey, Jomo, the views are great from up here!) he had drifted in and out of unconsciousness on a blood-stained gurney in the corridor beside two Chinamen, both of whom had snuffed it during the night. His jaw had been broken, his arm and leg fractured and he could not speak.

"How's she cutting, mucker?" I asked as I entered the ward, sidestepped the blood on the floor and located his bed. He couldn't talk. That was the upside. The downside was that he was genuinely seriously injured and the eager Chinese doctor whom I tracked down was most interested in operating immediately upon his jaw in what could only charitably be described as 'primitive conditions'. I passed over a scrap of paper to him. His eyes flickered with recognition and he painfully scrawled:

Get me drugs
Get me out of here
Phone the wife

I scrunched the note up and brought in Murphy who had been waiting outside. To be fair to him, he was genuinely shocked at Jomo's condition. Much to his surprise I hadn't been pulling a scam. He was however over there on a mission. "Jomo, can McGuffin represent Yee Nor at our interview?" Jomo closed his eyes and emitted an eldritch moan. "So, that's a yes!" "Come on Paddy, let's get this over with."

That afternoon I sat on the 21st floor of the Honkers Hilton and looked out over the view. Fairly spectacular, I had to admit. Murphy and his team were interrogating Yee Nor about the entangled web which she and the Chinatown bankers had woven. My task was *de minimis*. Every time Yee Nor didn't want to answer a question she would look at me and ask if she should answer. "No way, you foolish fool from foolsville," I'd generally reply. Nonetheless the Feebs were happy. Yee Nor gave up three crooks – who were already out of the country – indeed, I even saw one on the streets of Kowloon – and Murphy was happy. He even asked me to introduce him to the bars of Kowloon before he and his young assistant returned. They wanted knock-off Rolexes, a commodity which was not too difficult to locate. I left them drunk and hungover in Scruffy Murphy's – an Irish dive bar which I rather liked and decided that, for once, I should behave with a certain modicum of responsibility. The Feds were splitting but I still had to save Jomo.

Dr. Woo (I swear, that really was his name) was insisting that he operate on Jomo's jaw the next day and the hospital were demanding $5,000 from me as 'his only contact'. Yeh! Right! As old Vladimir Ilyich used to say (when addressing the Central Committee of Bolshevism) 'what the fuck do we do?' My mind was as empty as a hermit's address book. I'd managed to get Jomo sedated with a heavy dosage of morphine obtained, quite legally, from a local pharmacy but what of the mad Woo who was just itching to try out his periodontal skills on a comatose Yank? And then there was the dreaded Hadj!

We had airline tickets out of Hong Kong but they were for six days ahead. So much for our little vacation. I called the airline. My request for an alteration of our return tickets was met with incredulous giggling. Did I not know that every flight out of HK was fully booked by Hadjis, Muslim pilgrims intent on travelling to Mecca and throwing their shoes against the sacred Kaaba – look, this is sacred to them camel jockeys. Get real, it's no more ludicrous than celebrating a homosexual Dutch dwarf's victory over a cowardly Jacobite at some polluted puddle in Ireland in 1690 as the Orange Ordure does or the Yank's habit of respecting Easter Bunnies, Tooth Fairies and electing Alzheimers patients and crooks into the Presidency. After all, Americans are a nation who laugh at witchdoctors and spend over $2bn a year on fake weight reducing systems so I don't knock mad Muslims. But the Hadj did present a problem.

God bless Onkel Heinrik and his contacts. Several international phone calls later and I had Jomo and I booked on the last flight out of Honkers, tomorrow. I had had a visit to the local police station and their attitude had, to be honest, not been that sympathetic. Now for Actionman. A last pint in Ned Kelly's and I hailed a taxi – perhaps even the same one that had tried to cut down the legal career of one of San Francisco's finest attorneys.

"Wait here, mi amigo," I said to the cabbie and entered Horror Hotel. The sun was setting over the peaks. Phoebus was wending his weary way – the shades of night were coming down – you get the picture, do I have to send youse a postcard! The staff were off on whatever extra-curricular activities they favoured – glue-sniffing and advanced Kama Sutra probably – and I found no problem in hijacking a wheel chair on the ground floor. Luckily, one of the lifts was working. Up on the seventh floor it was a simple task to shovel a semi-comatose Jomo out of bed and into the wheelchair. Ignoring startled gasps and execrations from the staff and the few live patients we scarpered along the corridors, screeching to a halt outside the lift doors and pressed the button. Behind me pandemonium was breaking out, but the gallant Paddy was not to be deterred. For was I not on a mission from God.

Bursting out of the front doors at a rate that would have gratified Michael Schumacher and hauling Jomo into the taxi I extracted fifty HK dollars out of his wallet and thrust it into the hands of our slightly bewildered Asian chum. "Carlton Hotel," I bellowed. As we swung out of the hospital grounds and headed down the hill my last glimpse of Horror Hotel was of an irate Dr. Woo, gesticulating furiously at the front door. 'Bring me the head of Jomo' he seemed to be barking, but it was too late. The hotel staff helped me get Jomo up to our room. They were most co-operative and made up the bill. They were not as co-operative when I insisted on them opening Jomo's hotel safe deposit box and securing the $20,000. "Mr. Jomo can't sign for this – he's not compos mentis," insisted the manager. Fuck the critics! They're as useless as eunuchs at a gang bang! "I've got a power of attorney," I screamed, and launched into a spew of fake Latin. It worked. The next morning the staff of Malaysian airlines and I hauled a brain dead Jomo (his brain may have been dead but he was happy – so he should have been after the amount of morphine I'd been feeding him all night – well, I had to sleep, didn't I!) onto the plane.

Feeding my disabled comrade pot noodles through a straw stuck up his nose – well, his jaw was broken you'll recall – I finally got him back to the belly of the beast where his tearful family were all ready to look after him. It was just as well. When he was hauled off to a top SF dentist his equipment showed that if Dr. Woo had done his planned operation Jomo would have been permanently vocally disabled. Instead, he made a complete recovery and has ever since inflicted his rhetoric upon us poor mortals. But apart from tearful thanks what did your faithful scribe receive for his stellar work of corporeal mercy. Bugger all! Yee Nor did eventually come back and did a couple of years. Royboy is still selling sweet and sour God knows what in

Kowloon. Murphy is retired and Jomo is still practising – maybe one day he'll get the hang of it?

Still, as Frank Kermode used to say:

"We live in chaos and are equipped for co-existence with it only by our fictive powers." Whatever the hell that has to do with the cost of a hill of beans.

But He Never Coveted His Neighbour's Ox

He's been called a desperado. Even a terrorist. Certainly a hooligan. It's been alleged that he broke every one of the ten commandments. Some of them several times over. But I'm here to put the record straight. I've tried to write this down for years and never succeeded. Maybe I won't get it finished this time either, because of tears – of laughter, of sorrow, of joy and of pain – or maybe because of the drink. Who knows. Here goes.

His name was Mickey. He came from Newtownards (or N'ards as the signposts and the locals used to say) in the Black North of Ireland. I met him in the South when he was on the run for various alleged acts of freedom fighting, ranging from sniping at the British Army of Occupation to 'vehicular endangerment'. I remember one drunken night after Mickey had tried to kidnap a palm tree for his mother (a keen horticulturist) from the front garden of the overpriced hotel out near Howth and Rita and I had got him and the palm tree – or what was left of it – into the 'borrowed' car and I'd asked him what he'd done back up North before politics and the cops had forced him into exile. "And by the way, what the hell is 'vehicular endangerment'?" He'd laughed. "Jesus, didn't I have a steady job, McGuff. Wasn't I a tail gunner on a milk float."

Aye, that was Mickey. Always one for a joke (or a helping hand or a rare antisocial disease) but then, maybe it was true. Stranger things have happened in our wee Ulcer. Still, this isn't really a story about what we Ulcermen euphemistically call 'the troubles'. This is about Mickey. Mickey and the sheep.

Now don't go jumping to conclusions. There is nothing carnal about this story. Mickey was not like that. No wellington boots and midnight assignations at the ovine pen for him. He was strictly a ladies' man. True, where he grew up in N'ards a debutante was any girl who wasn't on penicillin, ("that's Protestants for ye," said Mickey); but, as usual, I digress.

Mickey's close encounter with our four legged woolly friend occurred one dark night in December 197_ when Big Eamonn was driving – all right, weaving his way back from Portlaoise jail across the bleak and unlit Curragh of Kildare with Mickey as his passenger.

They'd been visiting Big Eamonn's brother Francie at the jail where he was doing ten years for shoplifting (he'd lifted Woolworth six inches off the ground with 200 pounds of gelignite). Now let's be straight about Big Eamonn. Bright he was not. A fine fellow, no doubt. He believed in having fun until at least one part of his body turned blue, but to be fair, he was mercifully free from the ravages of intelligence. If ignorance were bliss, he'd be the happiest mortal on this mound of misery. And again. To be candid, they'd both 'had the odd gargle or three'.

Visiting the penal establishments of the Emerald Isle will do that for ye. You enter in trepidation to visit your kith and kindred and are so damn glad when, obviously through some incredible bureaucratic oversight, they actually let you out after the visiting hour is over, and your nearest or dearest hasn't forcibly changed clothes with you and trussed you up in his stead, that you immediately repair to the nearest hostelry to celebrate. Then, after a few, you have to have another few to commiserate with the beloved left behind in durance vile. And so it goes.

And so it went, that on that fateful night on the windswept Curragh of Kildare, of immortal memory in patriotic Irish song, while bloodstock slumbered, trainers dreamt of Epsom and Kentucky Derbys and the ghost of Shergar roamed free – for this is horse country, my friend – that our dynamic duo were surprised when the front fender of the Ford Cortina which they had expropriated from an unsuspecting Dublin suburbanite that morning, was violently struck by an insomniac sheep which had rashly chosen to wander across the dual carriageway to seek greener grass.

The bump woke Mickey from his slumber in the front passenger seat. "What the fuck was that, big lad?" he inquired. Big Eamonn was a little confused. Not an abnormal occurrence.

Nonetheless, his interrogation training seminar tape clicked into the few remaining brain cells which were functioning at 1 a.m. in the morning. When in doubt, deny everything.

"It was the SAS, Mickey. A fucking SAS man camouflaged in

them snow clothes. He jumped right out in front of me. He had an Uzi." The stolen Cortina had ground to a halt. Mickey glanced in the rear view mirror.

"You hit a fucking sheep, Big Eamonn."

Big Eamonn looked in the mirror. This might be a tough one to talk his way out of. Mickey outranked him. Let's face it, EVERYONE outranked Big Eamonn.

"Well, yeah, it looks like a sheep NOW," he admitted, "but these SAS men are real sneaky. And remember, they shagged a lot of sheep in Aden."

Mickey thought for a moment. This was true. Britain's elite counter-terrorist group were notorious for their unusual sexual practices, to say nothing about the odd bit of bestiality. Nonetheless.

"You hit a sheep, Big Eamonn."

"It was self-defence." Not for nothing had Big Eamonn been voted 'most likely to succeed' when he had graduated from Head-the-Ball Hall school for the mentally bewildered. "What are you going to do about it?" Mickey was inexorable.

Big Eamonn looked for the magic lightbulb. The one that illuminated itself to let you know there's an incoming message awaiting on the old cerebral answering machine.

"Get the fuck offside?" he ventured. Mickey shook his head. "Big Eamonn," he said, "do you know how much lamb is fetching on the Dublin meat market this very minute?" The lightbulb lit up. Big Eamonn opened the door, got out, and walked back up the road. Mickey took the bunch of 'open one, open all' keys out of the ignition and walked round to open the trunk. Five minutes later the two caballeros were spinning along the road to dirty old Dublin.

They were about twenty miles down the road when the Cortina started to vibrate like a ouija board. "Were you expecting a message from the spirit world, Big Eamonn?" inquired Mickey. Big Eamonn looked concerned. "I'm a good Kafflik, Mickey." Mickey nodded. "It's coming from the trunk, Big Eamonn. Your SAS man doesn't seem to be dead after all."

Big Eamonn beamed. The supernatural had always bothered him. He pulled the car over, got out and opened the trunk. Two minutes later he was back in the car. "He is now, Mickey," he said. "Aye, Big Eamonn, so it seems."

They hit the quiet Dublin suburb of Rathgar at 2.30 a.m. Mickey had decided that the 'billet' for the night would be 'the sister's'. Unlike her brother, Dymphna, although 'sound on the national question' was not a political refugee. Rather, as a highly trained nurse who was unable to obtain work in a Northern Health Service dominated by born again Paisleyite haemorrhoid sufferers and other 'good Protestants', she had opted for economic refugee status and worked as a health care practitioner for the Sisters of the Blessed Armpit in Baile Atha Cliath (or Dublin, to youse who lack the Gaelic).

The sheep-shocked Cortina pulled into the driveway of No. 37 and shuddered to a halt. Mickey gestured to Big Eamonn to quietly open the trunk while he used his bunch of keys to unlock the front door of the ground floor apartment.

"Put our ovine friend in the bathroom, Big Eamonn," was all he whispered. "Why?" "Because we don't want the shaggin' sheep to bleed all over the shaggin' sheep shag rug, do we, Big Eamonn?"

Big Eamonn nodded to himself as he humped the ex-sheep in through the hall door. That made sense. Didn't it? Big Eamonn liked it when things made sense. It meant his brain didn't hurt as much.

Tired, 'stressed out' (and/or full as sheughs) and desirous of not waking 'the sister' our two heroes crashed out on the sofa bed and the floor respectively.

Ms. Edith Purselips, headmistress, spinster of the parish and doyenne of the Pioneers of Total Abstinence, awoke as was her wont, at 5 a.m. She stretched herself, yawned and slipped out of her bed and walked to the shower. She groped back the shower curtain. Her piercing scream shattered the early morning calmness of bourgeois Rathgar.

It was the Bates Motel all over again! Blood dripped all over the tiled bath stall, freshly and lovingly spackled by her beloved brother Declan only the previous week. A shaggy gore-stained corpse hung, dripping red, from the shower stall. As the draft from the open door twitched the plastic curtain the corpse twisted, shimmering in the morning dawn and revealed its gaping molars in a ghastly rictus.

Many a member of the alleged weaker sex would have had recourse to a swoon. Not so the fair Edith. She came from British stock. Throwing her hair curler box at the grinning apparition – which reminded her, she later confessed, of the late and unlamented Lord Brookeborough (himself no stranger to perverse ovine practices if local gossip could be believed), she whirled around like a Dervish and gave vent to a wail that would have caused even a Banshee to reach for the Roche tablets, stumbled down the hall into the living room, tripped over the recumbent form of a sleeping Big Eamonn and fell through the open front door into the arms of the startled milky who had been stooping to deliver two pints.

Ms. Purselips' screams awakened Dymphna in her flat next door in No. 35. Dimly she remembered that her ne'er-do-well brother hadn't showed up the night before, but then, that was typical. Mickey was careless about his appearance – sometimes he didn't show up for days. What was the old bat next door yelling about? She groped her way to the window and peered out.

The old biddy had finally flipped out completely. There she was, naked as the day she was whelped, sexually assaulting the milkman! Disgraceful! It was all that sexual repression.

Unaccustomed as he was to being tumbled by naked spinsters (even in Rathgar, for despite rumors to the contrary, I have it on good authority that a milkman's morning round does not consist of being constantly seduced by lascivious negligée-clad house-wives) Finbar O'Leary reacted with all the aplomb that goes with being an employee of the Dublin Milk Marketing Board.

"All right, missus," he said, thrusting the hysterical Edith aside, "you don't have to go on about it. I promise I'll bring the strawberry yogurt tomorrow."

"How much did you finally get for the sheep, Mickey?" I asked. He tried to laugh but the effort was too great. The cancer had eaten its insidious, pernicious, malicious way through him amazingly quickly. I hadn't recognized him in his hospital bed, so changed, utterly changed was he from the laughing, smiling, funloving Mickey I had seen only a few months previously. Even more horrifying (and yet in some almost perverse way, inspiring for those who knew and loved him) was the fact that although he was in constant pain and knew that he was dying, he could still laugh and joke about the vicissitudes of fortune and insanity of life and death. We rapped about old times – the palm tree and Demis Roussos, the poitín launch, the sheep. He asked about Big Eamonn, whose whereabouts were unknown. He talked about his forthcoming 'big adventure in the sky'. He promised to get 'those scab angels' out on strike within a week. A sound Union man was our Mickey. Rita came in and I made to leave them alone together. He too had loved her.

As I made to go out he reached over and gripped me with his emaciated hand. He smiled. A look that I carry to this day. "McGuff," he said, his eyes twinkling in his shrunken face, "they say I've done a lot of bad things in my time. No," he waved aside my protests, "I've been a bad budgie, but," and he paused and that old laugh forced its way out of the body that had once been our Mickey, "I'll tell you something. I never coveted my neighbour's ox."

Nor did ye, Mickey. Slán agus beannacht. Go to sleep my weary Provo, let the times go drifting by, can't you hear the bazookas humming, that's the Provo's lullaby.

The Badger

"George Ade. Now there's a name to conjure with. Hardly a household one, I grant you, but, according to the International Thesaurus of Quotations (and who are we poor mortals to contradict such an august publication?) George was the man who first coined the famous epithet, 'Some are born great, some achieve greatness, and some have greatness thrust upon them'."

"What the fuck are you talking about now, Artur?" said Uncle Mal, a man with a vocabulary noted for its succinctness and prosaic limitations. Brian Artur and I, being of an intellectual bent, only tolerated the oaf because he happened to own the bar in which we were drinking on that fateful wet winter's night in Donegal when I first heard of the Badger.

Brian Artur gazed disdainfully at his interrupter and indicated with a tilt of his wrist that another whiskey would not go amiss. Our genial host, aghast at his faux pas, hastened to make amends. I generously permitted him to include me in the round. Grimshaw regaled the company with a smile. "As I was saying," he pontificated, "the good George Ade forgot one category when he first penned this aphorism: those who thrust greatness upon themselves."

We acolytes gazed on in admiration, much as the stupider apostles must have done when JC started telling one of his stories. Brian Artur nodded in approval. Was he not one of the province's many prophets? Did he not deserve attention, even if it was from the usual hangers-on? Sipping his Bushmills, he fixed the company with a bloodshot eye and began his tale: The Tale of the Badger.

"I don't suppose any of you have ever met the Badger," he essayed. Behind the bar Uncle Mal snorted. Hadn't he thrown the bum out of the 'Teac Ban' more than enough times. The rest of us, out of towners from the mean streets of Belfast, however, were all ears. The night was young, the weather outside foul, we were drunk and Uncle Mal was paying.

"Tell us about him, Brian Artur," begged Cosgrove, helping himself to another pint of Guinness while Mal's back was turned.

"He was a great man," said Grimshaw solemnly, "a great man."

And so he was. A man's man who carved out for himself, and upon his own body, a small slice of history in that remote corner of Donegal, Ireland, known as 'The Rosses'.

To look at, as I found out, he was not a prepossessing character. Twenty-five going on forty-five. A fading fringe of ginger hair, a stubbly ginger beard, a moon face and a battered straw hat, with real straw sticking out of it, these were the characteristics that bring his image back to me as I write, seven thousand miles away from the rugged Donegal coastline and the warmth of the 'Teac Ban', the bar in which Brian Artur and I spent so many happy and drunken hours.

The Badger was an alcoholic who had been barred from nearly every bar in the Rosses and, particularly, in the neighbourhood of Dungloe, and that's quite a few bars when you have a car or a lift, as he generally did. He used to be a fisherman, like most of the locals, for there was little other work in the area, and if they weren't going off on the boats and getting drowned (due, in part, to the congenital local superstition that it was 'unlucky' to go out on the boats if one could swim), they had to labour on the building sites over in Scotland or England but the Badger had forsaken the sea for the pleasures, albeit dubious, of alcohol.

Accordingly, he could always be seen around the bars. The Teac Ban, the Harbour, the Caves, Neilly's, the Thatch, the El Paso – the list is almost endless. Grimshaw first met him in the Caves, a sordid bar which only opened when all others had closed and the proprietor, 'the Caveman' had awakened from his daily slumber. The Badger was being gently propelled through the front door, with only the odd kick to the head. His last big red twenty pound note had been expended, and, for the past two hours he had been molesting the pool players and scrounging for more drink. That was his form.

He wasn't driving that night, his latest car having been written off in one of Donegal's notorious ditches and his licence having been confiscated by what the locals termed an 'over-zealous' judge.

As he wandered off into the night, howling imprecations at the bar staff and threatening to report them to the Garda for permitting late night drinking (it was 4.30 a.m.), Brian Artur asked the Cavemen who he was. That's how he got the first part of the story.

Two years previously, while staggering out of Bonner's, a local hostelry, the Badger had experienced a form of satori. This had been occasioned not by his conversion to Zen Buddhism by a wandering Samurai archer or mendicant hippie, but rather by being struck by the front wing of a Ford Granada, driven by a visiting American tourist, who had succumbed to too much of the local 'hospitality', and was unaccustomed to licensing hours which could most charitably be described as 'flexible'.

Precipitously hurled into an omnipresent Donegal ditch, the Badger had experienced his existential moment of catharsis. It may not have lived up to Kierkegaard's 'Dark Night of the Soul' or Saul/Paul's trip on the road to Damascus, but, at that moment the Badger discovered his purpose in life. He learned, furthermore, that drunken tourists, in addition to having feelings of guilt and remorse, had insurance companies.

Awakening in Dungloe hospital the following morning, swathed in bandages and suffering more from his massive hangover than his physical injuries, the Badger had found an equally hungover and much more guilt-ridden American by his bedside, begging forgiveness and offering $1000 if the Badger would forget all about it. Chickenfeed, but, from such acorns, great oak trees grow, if I may mix a metaphor.

After ensuring that the Yank paid for his hospital bill and handed over the 'compensation' in used big red Free State twenty pound notes, the Badger discharged himself from the hospital and launched himself upon his spectacular albeit brief professional career.

Now some cynics have said that such a profession had already existed for years in the US of A, where experienced tumblers and bunco artists had perfected the art, and I'm sure that this is true.

Any nation that can claim to have 'discovered' a country before the local indigenous population, had a first President who grew marijuana but got away with it by calling it hemp and had another esteemed President who 'freed' the slaves while still owning some twenty souls himself, are hardly lacking in what might be termed 'native cunning'. At this juncture, however, I should like to put a word in on behalf of the Badger.

I cannot claim to have known the creature very well, but from that brief acquaintanceship and from the words of those who knew and tolerated, as opposed to loved, him one can state categorically that his literary research had never extended beyond the page three pin-up of a Rupert Murdoch smut-rag or the racing page of the *Daily Mirror*. Accordingly, he must be given credit for the scheme/scam that he was to perpetuate upon the denizens of Donegal over the next two years and which was to make him the bane of those insurance companies unwary enough to insure any motorist who ventured out at dark along the county's fairy-like and uncharted hills and vales.

On old maps when the cartographer knew little or nothing about a region he generally wrote 'Terra Incognita', or, more imaginatively, 'Here be Dragons'. In the years 1970-1972 a maker of an Automobile Association map would have been quite entitled to inform those seeking information that in the area of the Rosses 'Here be Badgers'.

Within three weeks of his release from Dungloe hospital, the Badger and his fair-weather cronies had managed to drink the American's grand. Once bitten, twice wise. The staff of the hospital were dismayed/perplexed/resigned, depending upon their degree of cynicism, to go on duty one Monday morning and find the Badger being stretchered into casualty with a worried English tourist fussing around him.

"It was so dark, and he just seemed to jump out in front of me out of the ditch. There was nothing I could do but put on the brakes. God! I hope he's all right. Here's my insurance company." From his stretcher the Badger extended a conciliatory hand.

"No hard feelings, fella. You were drunk as a skunk, but I'll not say a word."

Seven weeks later, just as the Badger was being discharged by a relieved hospital staff, for he was not the easiest of patients, a little man from the insurance company in Letterkenny arrived and presented him with a cheque for four thousand pounds. It was, the Badger decided, definitely better than working on the boats.

It didn't last too long, of course. The only real beneficiary was the garage owner in Mullaghduff from whom the Badger bought a brand new Avenger, which he managed to write off two weeks later coming home from Burtonport in the early hours of the morning, and those hangers-on who congregated at the various bars around the Badger like dogs sniffing turds.

And so it was back on the road again for the intrepid Badger. In the space of the next ten months he successfully hurled himself, with feral cunning, skill and the luck of the drunk, across the path of no fewer than four unsuspecting drunken drivers. He sustained two broken arms, a broken leg, six cracked ribs, and at least two cases of severe concussion (although with the Badger these were often difficult to diagnose), but the money rolled in. Fourteen grand, the locals reckoned.

Another car was bought and duly written off. The publicans got the rest. Brian Artur wasn't up there much and had to rely on long range gossip. The next time he'd been up staying at the Teac the Badger had not been about. Barred for life, Brian was told. No one seemed to know what had happened to him, or they weren't prepared to talk about it to strangers. Someone did say that he'd cracked up and tried to hang his mother from the only tree in the Rosses, which was on the tiny plot of land that she farmed, but this could not be confirmed.

But Brian Artur wouldn't let it rest at that. His wife was off with the blessed Sisters of Perpetual Indulgence or some such sodality and Brian Artur had the weekend in which to pubcrawl. Somewhere down near Mullaghmore, late at night, and after many pints and half 'uns, he had cornered his quarry. The Badger had been run to earth.

As Grimshaw tells it, he was now only a shadow of his former self. A pint of porter sufficed to get the tragic end to his story.

"He was swathed in bandages which wouldn't have shamed Christopher Lee or any other mummy from a tomb, but sick as he was, he was still prepared to unburden his soul to me," said Grimshaw. "I inspire confidence in people, have you ever noticed that?" We nodded. It was Grimshaw's shout. The great man fished in his tweed jacket, announced that he's left his wallet upstairs, and graciously permitted me to buy the round.

"As in so many instances in history," he continued when the drinks came, "greed had been the poor man's downfall." He had had a good run but had become careless and over-ambitious.

In the past he had always ensured that the cars which assaulted him had been driven by drunken foreign tourists. But it had been a slack year for the tourist trade and the publicans and the boarding house owners hadn't been the only ones to feel it. Northerners from Belfast had been short of cash due to 'the troubles' and there wasn't a Jap or a Kraut, let alone a Brit or a Yank to be seen in the Rosses from one month to the next. The Badger had decided upon desperate measures.

And so, on a dark and windy night, fortified only by his intrepid courage and a bottle of Bushmills whiskey, the Badger had taken up his midnight vigil in his favourite ditch outside Gallagher's deserted caravan site to await, as he put it, "the first class motor that came along."

As usual, his timing was immaculate. The Mercedes had, it is true, cracked three ribs and broken both his legs, as well as fracturing his skull, but this was, after all, only an occupational hazard. The whiskey had deadened the pain. What really hurt, however, was to awake, as usual, in hospital, to discover that the driver of the car had been his own cousin, a priest returned from the missions in darkest Africa.

It is bad enough to suffer for a cause or in pursuance of one's work, but it is a much bitterer blow to realize that there is just no way that one is going to get one penny piece of compensation and is, furthermore, going to have to pay one's own medical bills.

Hoover aka JEHoovah

"The Uncle met Jedgar Hoover, ye know!" Brian Artur was at his most pontifical. It was his round and he'd do anything to deflect the idiot bartender's eye away from the pint dispenser from which he was surreptitiously filching another pint of foam and the bottle of Black Bushmills which he had managed to move six feet nearer him in preparation for his sudden departure later that night if all went according to plan – which it rarely did.

We were in the Teac Ban – where else? Deep in the heart of the Rosses in darkest Donegal where many's a ruction ourselves had a hand in – (knock it off, ye fool! That's Dungannon. Stop trying to steal one of the Orangemen's few decent rhymes).

"Ye're joking!" Malachy the owner was bored. Brian Artur's stories were guaranteed to inspire a thirst in anyone and these Blefuscu bowsies (as Dean Swift might have said) had been robbing him blind all night.

"Is that the uncle who shot District Inspector Swanzey on the chapel steps in Lisburn back in 1922 with MacCurtain's gun?" asked Joe, our local Republican historian. "The very same," beamed Brian Artur.

"But didn't you tell us that the uncle who shot Swanzey had ended up a henpecked old age pensioner?" queried Joe, always a stickler for historical accuracy.

'A cheap shot', I thought, but indeed I did recall the great one telling that tall tale only a few months ago. O ye of little faith!

"That was uncle Proinseas," bellowed an irked BA. "Did I not tell yese that it was three of the uncles who gunned down that damn dog! They were all interned on the Argenta, ye know." This at least was true, for I had consulted the prison ship records, though whether it proved the indomitable loyalty and soundness on the National Question of the entire Grimshaw family back in those dark days or merely proved that it took three Lurgan men to shoot down one unarmed war criminal is a question open to varied interpretations. For myself, having met at least two of the fabled uncles I sensibly and prudently adhere to the politically correct version.

"The uncle who met Jedgar was Uncle Gerry. When he was released from the prison hulk he emigrated to Amerikay. To cut a long story short ..." The bartender groaned. This was not likely to happen. The blessed Bard may have contended that brevity is the soul of wit but he'd never met Brian Artur.

Undaunted, the great one continued "... to cut a long story short, Uncle Gerry ended up in Chicago in the thirties and, through the local ward heeler, got a cushy job in the the local mortuary. He enjoyed the work. It was a doddle. No one bothered him on the nightshift."

"I thought necrophilia was dead boring." This from Coyle, a Yank who'd joined the company, and had been having a quiet nap at the end of the bar after a few pints too many of the blessed Hippocrene.

"Go back to sleep, ye tube!" Sure what can ye expect from an unfortunate who lives in a country that has the Statue of Liberty as its symbol and compulsory urine testing as its sacrament. The ex-colonial went back to sleep and BA fixed us with his basilisk gaze.

"Then came the black day of infamy in 1933 when, fingered by the lady in red outside the Roxie cinema, the great John Herbert Dillinger, Public enemy No. 1, was cut down in his prime by the murderous G-men led by that transvestite Hoover ..."

"It was 1934, not 1933. July 27th. And it was the Biograph theatre not the Roxie. The woman in red was Anna Sage."

We sat stunned. This boorish interruption had come from Stevie, the resident failed bank robber. A man not noted locally for his knowledge of history. Ah! But still waters run deep. Only the Shadow knows what evil lurks in the hearts of Donegal desperados.

"As I was saying," – Brian Artur was not an easy man to shut up – "it is a little known fact but the late unlamented J. Edgar and his catamite buddy Clyde 'babyface' Tolson had a perverted fascination with the alleged sexual prowess of Big John Dillinger."

"Aye, they didn't call him Big John for nothing," muttered Stevie, obviously a fan.

"That was why they put him No. 1 on the most wanted list. Sure Al Capone and his boys rubbed out far more than Gentleman John, but Jedgar and Clyde wanted to see Dillinger's dong. They need tangible evidence to prove the old adage 'big car, small dick'. Sure didn't the boul Jedgar always drive around in a wee coupé. Don't ye know how much it hurt Jedgar that Dillinger was driving around in hot rod Lincolns and souped up Fords, robbing banks and escaping from jail with a gun carved from a bar of soap, making fools out of the G-men and the great unwashed public lapping it all up and claiming that Johnnie had a mighty member. Why it was more than a God fearing old Queen like Jedgar could stomach."

"Get on with it," mouthed Malachy, "if ye want another drink." Uncle Mal drove a very big car. He had a vested interest in this story.

"Anyway, the night of the shooting outside the cinema," Brian Artur continued imperiously, "the uncle was working as usual when they wheeled the corpse in and ordered the uncle to rack and stack it and then to shut up shop and admit nobody until the next day when they'd do the autopsy. Now, to picture this the way I heard it you have to imagine one of them movie scripts. The way I see it is Uncle Gerry had settled in for the evening with a drop of the cratur and is reading the racing form when, in the middle of the night, there's a blattering on the door. He opens it and who's there but the boul Jedgar himself. Of course Gerry recognized him. Wasn't his ugly mug on the front page of the paper along with that asslicker Walter Winchell near every day. But Gerry hadn't come up the river in a bubble. *Carpe diem!* He knew how to seize the time. So next thing the drooling Jedgar, who's wearing a rug which would fool no one, slips the Uncle $200, no mean sum in 1933 ..."

"1934!" This from our would-be Donegal mastermind.

"... and tells him to get offside for the next hour and keep his mouth shut if he knows what's good for him. So Gerry does as he's told. No point in getting on the prevert's bad books or in turning down a buckshee two hundred. But, of course, after letting Jedgar in and ostentatiously leaving, he sneaks back into the adjacent storeroom and spies in through a wee window. And what does he see?"

The more prurient of us held our breath. Grudgingly Malachy poured the seanachie another nippy sweetie.

"The camera pans in," intoned Brian Artur, now fully convinced that he was as good as that Martin Sore-arse any day when it came to directing gangster movies, "the senile delinquent reaches into a black doctor's bag, whips out a cutthroat razor and begins to sharpen it on this whetstone. Next he produces a bottle of mint julep essence and moves over to the drawers where the stiffs are stashed. He checks the names and pulls out the drawer labelled 'Dillinger'. The camera focuses in on the corpse which is covered by a white sheet. A moment of tension and then Jedgar pulls up the bottom of the sheet to reveal a miniscule wizened dick attached to a withered scrotum. He gasps and draws back. He takes another look. Then he slyly chuckles and pulls out a camera and proceeds to photograph this sad sight.

Elated, he apparently abandons his plan to fellate the flaccid member after pouring mint extract over it. "You cheap hood," he snarls. "I knew yours was no bigger than mine." Contemptuously he tries to jack off, but he is startled when the uncle next door accidentally knocks a box of suppositories off the shelf in the storeroom. Hastily he retrousers his flabby joystick and, obviously content with his photos and his vindication, he replaces the sheet and exits the room, closing the door behind him.

There is a pause. Then a figure stealthily slides into the morgue and locks the door behind him. It is the Uncle. He approaches the Dillinger drawer and pulls it open. He approaches the head of the corpse and pulls back the sheet. The cinema audience gasp. We see the head of an elderly white haired Anglo-Saxon. He is at least seventy years old. He is clearly not dapper Johnnie Dillinger. Softly the Uncle replaces the shroud.

He takes the John Dillinger tag off the corpse's toe and exchanges it with the tag on the corpse in the next drawer. It reads 'Cecil Trimble' aka Buck Cecil, a former Orange gunman who had had to flee Belfast after shooting more than his quotient of Fenians and had ended his days working for Alphonse Capone in the liquor wars which had claimed his miserable life only the previous day.

The Uncle chuckles, reaches into his pocket and extracts ten twenty dollar bills and a hip flask. He takes a slug. 'Here's to you, John, sure weren't you from fine Irish stock.' As the camera fades we see him pulling open the drawer which had contained the real Dillinger body. The last shot is of a corpse. It is a black man. Cut! It's a wrap."

The Master took another sip of the *uisge beatha* and basked in our awed reverence. Even Stevie could not forbear to cheer.

"Sure I knew they never got John D," he exulted.

"I knew them FBI men were faggots," exclaimed Malachy. "I knew one called Patrick Murphy. He'd suck the chrome off an exhaust pipe!" A few heads nodded in agreement. We'd all heard that canard. We also knew that Malachy, who had failed to get a Morrison visa to emigrate to the US of A was perhaps a little jaundiced when it came to American law enforcement.

"Well, that calls for another round," piped up Tony the Cadger. Brian Artur had already preempted him having slipped the bottle of Bushmills to his faithful amanuensis and scribe (my goodself) to secrete in the copious pockets of my full length black leather paramil coat while our genial host was distracted.

Malachy rushed to oblige. When did he and the locals get to hear such arcane historical smut and trivia as this. We were toasting the seanachie when up spoke an aged crone who had been lurking beside the turf fire nursing a hot port and eavesdropping.

"Was that Gerry Grimshaw from Lurgan?" she inquired brightly. "None other. My esteemed uncle," beamed Brian Artur.

"Sure didn't I date that old blaggard back in the twenties," she cackled suddenly. "He was always a cold fish. He was run out of town for interfering with the dead. He was one of them necrofillers."

The master paused mid-swallow. Turning a baleful eye on the eldritch hag he intoned solemnly, "He must indeed have been, madam, if he ever deigned to play the humpbacked camel with the likes of you."

Incensed by this blatantly sexist remark, the harridan stood up and revealed a side of herself hitherto unknown.

"You, you, jackeen," she screamed at Brian Artur, "you'll either die on the gallows or of AIDS."

"That depends, madam," plagiarized the great one, "upon whether I embrace your principles or your husband."

HIS WAY

The room seemed as cold and sour as an abandoned diaper. Brian Artur tried vaguely to recall the evening's toping, failed, shrugged, and according to custom, took off his shoes and socks preparatory to retiring for the night. Mustn't wake the wife. He could do without her reproaches and imprecations until the morning. Concern for 'the little woman' flickered through his few remaining grey cells. He took off his shirt and simmet, removed his trousers and tiptoed up the stairs, discarding his drawers as he climbed, leaning heavily on the stair rail.

Eeeeeeeek! The voice didn't sound like the wife's dulcet tones. "Conductor! There's a madman up here!" Brian Artur slowly opened one bloodshot orb. Jesus Christ! He was on the top of the No. 76 double decker bus. "I knew it was going to be one of those nights," he mumbled as he groped for his knickers. "I thought it was a bit drafty."

As he slurred the words, the wind lethargically whipped his trousers off the platform as the bus careened around the corner and into Sandown Road. It was going to be one of those nights all right. The prophet had spoken truly.

Now, before any more mud is thrown, a few things should be made clear. It has been brought to this scribe's attention that some readers have felt that the writer is unduly 'soft' on his hero, Brian Artur, and 'hard' upon his long suffering wife, the lovely Hilda. Threatening phone calls HAVE been received and their wounding remarks noted. Obviously the writer has been misunderstood, due, no doubt to his own inability to succinctly express himself. Let him now, once and for all, make it quite clear that Brian Artur's wife, the 'Bean a Tighe', the lovely Hilda, was a wonderful person.

Indeed, many was the fellow human being who, upon encountering this blessed damsel referred to her as a 'breath of fresh air'. A description with which Brian Artur could only concur. After all, as he put it, she 'was forever getting up his fucking nose'.

Also, it is true that Brian Artur, the great one, did have certain flaws. For example, he was careless about his appearance – sometimes he didn't show up for days.

Nor should it be imagined that Brian Artur and the lovely Hilda did not co-exist in martial, nay even marital harmony. Had not Brian Artur once persuaded his lovely wife to do it 'doggie style' – true, as he put it, he had ended up begging and she rolled over and played dead. Nonetheless, this was, and still is, a marriage made in heaven. We humble mortals who have been privileged to witness some of their more touching moments together cannot forget the time, for example, when Brian Artur's poor wife once sent him out late at night for a packet of Tampax. Now, in chauvinist Ulcer there are not many self-styled macho men who will have enough unconcern for the sneers of their fellow males to venture out on such an errand of gallantry. But our hero did. Alas, the drink had fuddled his few remaining brain cells and he had returned with an LP by the Rolling Stones entitled 'Let It Bleed', but the point is, his heart was in the right place, even if his brain wasn't.

But he was not yet back in the blessed warmth of the domestic hearth. The chilly night air wafted itself around Brian Artur's nether regions. Hopping on one leg he attempted to put his trousers back on. "Evening, all." Stark terror gripped Brian Artur by the right testicle. It couldn't be! But yes, it was.

Hopping on the pavement he turned to see the leering porcine little eyes of Constable Ronnie McGonagle, the bane of every nationalist in town. Brian Artur's eyes watered like a blind beggar who'd just seen a bus token dropped in his tin mug. Was there no justice? Nope. "Indecent exposure. This'll look good on yer rap sheet, you Fenian scum," mouthed McGonagle. "Come quietly or it'll be the worse for ye."

"Fuck this for a jar of worms," muttered the great man. The indignity of it all. Better to say nothing. Sure wouldn't he only contaminate himself. Now he'd never get into the Felons Club. You had to have done time for Ireland to become a member and he was sure that six months for flashing wouldn't count. Sullenly he pulled up his mudstained trousers and accompanied a grinning guardian of the peace to the barracks. "Was it for this that the wild geese fled, was it for this that James Connolly bled?" he muttered to himself as he was stripped and pushed into the dank dark flowery dell.

See this whole sodding planet? A bloody vale of tears, that's all it was.

Was this the meaning of life? (Actually, a very wise old man in a Dublin pub had once sold Brian Artur the meaning of life for the cut rate price of two pints of Porter – a bargain, especially in those bygone days when a pint was less than a punt).

The oldtimer had also tried to sell him the third secret of Fatima which the little Portuguese girls had given to the Pope way back when, but our hero hadn't bought that one – everyone knew it already. [If you don't know the third secret of Fatima, send a used £5 note in a plain envelope to the author at Head-The-Ball Hall, Belfast, Our Wee Ulcer.] Still, although he now possessed the meaning of life it didn't do Brian Artur much good in his present predicament. Grunting, he rolled over and pulled the ragged blanket around his arse. Roll on the morning.

The sun, gazing fitfully between the bars, aroused him at the same time as the unforgettable smell of an RUC fried egg sarnie assailed his nostrils.

"Let's be having you, you Fenian bastards. His Honour doesn't like to be kept waiting." McGonagle was in good form this morning. Court duty would keep him off the street and Justice McDermott was always good for a laugh. He didn't even need to get his perjured testimony straight. The judge loved cops. It was something about the uniform.

"Silence. Be upstanding in Court." The bailiff shuffled his papers, McDermott slid onto the wellworn bench and signalled that the case of the People v. Grimshaw could commence. McGonagle took out his little black book and prepared to testify. He liked this part of it.

"And then your Honour, he resisted arrest and I had to restrain him." "Quite so, Constable. And the language. What did he say?" This was McDermott's favourite part. This was where he could polish his little gems of wit at the prisoner's expense. Anything for a cheap sycophantic laugh. Entering into his role with time honoured aplomb McGonagle played along. He shuffled his feet and consulted his swindle sheet. "The accused used a vile and opprobrious term referring to myself and the entire force, your Honour. A term that I'd rather not repeat." The judge gave a vulpine grin. "Come, come, Constable. You can't shock this court. We've heard it all before. Out with it man." McGonagle coughed. "Well, yer Honour," he said, pretending to consult his tattered notebook, "he called me a black bastard." McDermott was not pleased. This was tame stuff. He had been hoping for some picturesque phrase garnered from the underworld, the mean little back streets of Belfast.

Everyone called the cops black bastards. Really, it wasn't good enough. McGonagle wasn't playing his part at all well. He'd half a mind to let the prisoner off. Wasn't this the day that he was supposed to show some leniency – for after all, weren't the jails bulging at the seams? He was tired of being accused of being a bigot by the Fenian swine. He'd show them. He'd merely fine this croppie. A scowl crossed his face and he waved McGonagle off the witness stand and addressed himself to Brian Artur.

"Well, Mr. Grimshaw, you've heard the constable. Not a pretty story, is it. A man of your age. Drink taken, I imagine. The same old story. There's enough evil going round today that the constabulary shouldn't have to waste their and the court's time over drunken oafs like yourself. Have you slept it off yet?"

Still feeling distinctly queasy after the greasy sarnie, Brian Artur debated about whether to throw up or answer. Portia's quality of mercy speech came to mind but was rejected. That swine McDermott didn't like Jews any more than he did Catholics. He tried giving his Jimmy Carter smile until he remembered where his teeth were. Instead, he nodded towards the bench.

"Well, Sir, I'm going to take a chance with you. I'm going to allow you to apologize to this fine officer." Across the courtroom McGonagle smirked. "In the cold grey light of dawn, and now sober, are you prepared to recognize the error of your ways and apologize? I warn you, it will go ill with you if you don't."

This was really too much. Pulling himself together Brian Artur, a member of the legion of the beer guard, prepared to make his speech from the dock. Sure wouldn't the shade of Wolfe Tone and the Bold Robert Emmett be proud of him.

"Yes, your Honour," he said, loud and clear, "in the cold grey light of dawn I now see the error of my ways. It was dark last night. I apologize to the officer. Sure now in the court can't I see that he is not a black bastard – he's a bottlegreen bastard."

Back in his cell, nursing his bruises and contemplating the six months which lay ahead, Brian Artur thought of the meaning of life.

It was not much consolation, for as the old cadger had told him, "Son, when you come onto this mound of misery they throw water onto ye. When you get married, they throw rice at you. When you die, they throw dirt on ye. The secret of life, son, is that there's always some bastard throwing something at ye."

Aye, wasn't it the truth. Still, there was always one consolation. He had a real crack at getting into the Felons Club now. If he wasn't doing time for Ireland, who was? The tune of the old Frankie Snatters song came back to him, and tunelessly he began to whistle 'My Way'.

The Depth Charge Man

It was Brian Artur who pointed him out to me. We were sitting in the gloom of the 'Grotto' having a few pints for purely medicinal reasons when he came in and, I confess, like most people I didn't even notice him. The depth charge man. His real name, according to Brian Artur, who knew everyone who was nobody, was Francis McFall. We had gotten to talking about Belfast Street characters, like Buck Alec, the gunman who worked for Al Capone and ended up walking a toothless lion around Belfast's New Lodge road, and Stormy Weather and Silver McKee and their epic street fight and Connolly Quinn and the racehorse – but that's definitely another story! – and Brian Artur called up to old Steamer, who was propping up the bar on his usual stool, and he came over and, for the price of a pint, told us the depth charge man's story. And I think it's true.

He was about 65 and employed as a 'security man' at the bank next door to the 'Grotto'. He was thin, almost cadaverous, and his faded and dandruff-flecked uniform was two sizes too big for him. He used to come in, about six times a day, during banking hours, sink a depthcharge, pay, and nip back on duty next door. We used to time him, and it never took him longer than 90 seconds to 'depthcharge' the bottle of stout and the half 'un of whiskey, which Frank the barman set up for him automatically as he entered the door. Then he would turn on his heel and go back to work, without a word to anyone.

It happened in 1934, the hungry thirties. Being out of work like most of his peers on the Falls Road in Belfast, Francie McFall, then nineteen, was looking for a few shillings. Accordingly, he and another friend decided to rob a bank. In those far off days this took a certain degree of desperation.

Nowadays, when every eczema-pocked kid over the age of twelve is used to bopping into banks and stores and making withdrawals with imitation and not so imitation guns it's not regarded as a big deal. Why, the other morning on the Whiterock Road I saw them lining up in an orderly queue to take turns robbing the Post Office, but, as I say, things were different in those days. But Francie and his mate, who, ever since I heard the tale I've figured was old Steamer himself, were young, bold and foolish enough to take the risks. They didn't have a rod – a gun – which, of course, was a bit of a drawback for any would-be desperado, even in 1934. Over in the States, Machine Gun Kelly and Pretty Boy Floyd were carving out a name for themselves, but in depressed Belfast, things were a bit more complicated.

God, in his infinite wisdom, only sends us these little problems in order that we might solve them, however, and so, a week after the scheme had first been mooted, there was 'the mate' with a toy wooden pistol, half-inched from Woolworth's and Francie with a vicious looking Luger, carved out of a bar of soap, just like Dillinger had done it in the movie, standing outside the Bank of Ireland, nervously trying to adjust the handkerchiefs over their faces.

With a style and panache gleaned from countless evenings at the Alhambra Picture Palace, watching Messrs. Cagney and Raft, Francie burst open the swing door and strode into the office to cover the startled customers and staff with his bar of soap. Unfortunately he had been unnecessarily violent with the door, as a consequence of which his unnamed partner in crime received the backswing full in the face, dislodging a tooth, and knocking his Woolworth's artillery to the floor. Francie, a veteran of the movies, was only momentarily nonplussed.

"Freeze! This is a stick up! Everyone lie on the floor. You (this to the fresh-faced young cashier), fill this sack. This money is being commandeered by the Irish Republican Army."

"Certainly, Sir, how would you like it?"

Francie considered this for a moment. Then, deciding that the cashier wasn't taking the mickey, he waxed lyrical.

"I'd like it in a fuckin' bag in my fuckin' hand."

The teller smiled. "Certainly Sir, in a fuckin' bag in your fuckin' hand it shall be." Quickly and efficiently he filled the small sack and handed it over. As he reached for the loot Francie had a premonition, but it was too late. Despite a desperate grab, the handkerchief detached itself from his face and fluttered to the floor, leaving him staring right into the young teller's eyes. "Will that be all, Sir?"

Blindly, Francie turned, pushed his way past two startled customers who were stepping over 'the mate' who was still groping myopically on the floor for his toy gun, and rushed out into the street, up the road and into the first alleyway on the right. Within two minutes the ghetto had swallowed the pair of them up, and when the police arrived the scent was long cold.

Half an hour later the two desperados were sitting in McShane's public house, sipping a couple of wee Powers and downing foaming black pints of Porter. They had just about stopped shaking and were arguing about the shareout. Francie was claiming 75% because he had to do all the work, while 'the mate' asserted that the original 50-50 split arrangement stood. The 'take' had come to 680 pounds, more money than either of them had ever seen in their lives and so the 'discussion' was getting heated.

As a result, neither of them spotted 'Big Maxie' as he made his way over towards their table. This was a mistake. Everyone knew 'Big Maxie' and knew to stay out of his way. It was rumored that he was one of the 'bhoys', a real IRA man. And, remember, in 1934 there weren't too many of them.

"Francie, mind if I have a word with you outside?" It wasn't really a question. Silently Francie rose and made his way out into the entry. When he returned ten minutes later he was a wiser and poorer man. Six hundred and eighty pounds poorer, to be precise. Like Saul on the road to Damascus he had experienced a miraculous conversion. The blinding power of Maxie's logic that since Francie had claimed that the money was for the IRA it was only just and equitable that the IRA receive the money had convinced him. The parabellum pointed at his temple had had a certain logic of its own too. 'The mate' wasn't the best pleased either, but what could one do? Both accepted their loss with as much grace as they could summon up and sank into obscurity again. It seemed that fickle fame and fortune was not to be theirs. Not so.

While it had taken the IRA a mere half an hour to find out on the ghetto grapevine who had pulled the bank job in their name, it took the Royal Ulster Constabulary considerably longer. But, sooner rather than later, someone touted, squealed, informed, what have you. Francie was picked up and questioned.

True to the code of the movies he denied all involvement to the skeptical cops, took his beating, and then learned that he was to be put up in front of an identification parade. Inwardly Francie's heart sank. This was it. Goodbye Falls Road, hello Crumlin Jail. 'Fuck this for a game of darts', he thought to himself as he was ordered to line up with the seven members of the public who had been picked up for the line-up.

The door opened and in came the young bank clerk. He was

attired soberly and neatly and wore a somber expression upon his face as he walked down the line, slowing as he approached the spot where Francie stood resignedly. It was all up. There was no way that the teller wouldn't recognize him. And yet, amazingly, he appeared to do just that. He stared at Francie, shook his head slowly and passed on, similarly failing to identify any of the other men. Francie was in a state of shock. So too was the disgruntled police Sergeant, who, a few hours later was forced to release Francie, still dazed, onto the street.

Francie never was to find out that the teller, Aidan Andrews, just happened to have a cousin, one Artur Maxwell, known to the cognoscenti on the Falls Road as 'Big Maxie', nor that the fresh faced young teller was himself a member of B Company, Belfast Brigade, Irish Republican Army.

And that, by all rights, should have been the end of the story, but of course it wasn't. Francie drifted around. Went down to Dublin looking for work. Then, for excitement, he joined the International Brigade, fighting the fascists in Spain. Surviving that, he then fought in the Second World War, first in North Africa and then in Italy. Finally, in 1945, like so many others, he returned home to swell the dole queues. Eventually, after labouring in England he returned to his native Belfast in 1973, then in the throes of 'the troubles'.

Work was scarce, but there were always jobs going for 'security men' and preference was given to ex-soldiers, which was why Francie, now 58 years of age, found himself sitting nervously in the nice new ante room of the nice new Bank of Ireland in downtown Belfast waiting for an interview. The blonde secretary looked up at him as the buzzer sounded.

"You're next, Mr. McFall, please go right in."

The manager sat across the desk from him, smiling.

"Well, McFall, what qualifications do you have for this job?" Francie thought hard and then began to parrot out the fake curriculum vitae that he and his pals had cobbled up the night before in the pub. The manager let him ramble on. Finally Francie came to an embarrassed halt and sat there fingering his duncher. The manager leant forward.

"Do you still want the fuckin' money in a fuckin' bag in your fuckin' hand, Mr. McFall?" he asked, for Aidan Andrews had a good memory. Francie fainted and came round only when the manager poured a jug of water over him. "Get up, McFall, you're hired. Report tomorrow, and don't bother to bring any soap with you, we have plenty."

And that is how Francie got the job. A sinecure, really, that allowed him to nip next door into the 'Grotto' and sink depthcharges half a dozen times a day. I suppose there's a moral in it somewhere, but for the life of me I'm damned if I can find it.

Brian Artur claimed that it's all to do with the secret of life, but then, after a few dozen pints, he's been known to become a bit mystical. A very wise old man in a bar once told me the secret of life but I forgot it. Pity. It's probably a good thing to have. You never know when it might come in handy to be possessed of the secret of life.

The Baten Docket

For all you heathens out there I suppose I should explain that a 'baten docket' in the Irish vernacular is a failed priest. The family invest all their few pitiful shillings into getting the second or third son – for the eldest has to inherit, generally at age fifty, the wee piece of barren rock known as 'the family farm' – into the priesthood in order that their lifelong lives of dull drab misery on the diseased piece of carbon, the third rock from the big red one, may be rewarded by some kind of celestial Nashville or Disneyland, where Big Tom and the Mainliners play all day and God looks and talks like Father Ted.

But then, inevitably, because sure isn't it Murphy's Law, the wee gobshite ups and jumps over the seminary walls and goes off with some trollop of an ex-nun. And there goes your investment – a crumpled up slip, washed down Waterloo Street from Duffy's bookies. A beaten docket.

"Ah shure couldn't it be worse Maggie! Shure mightn't he have made the final ould vows and ended up a PRIEST. Ye know, Paedophile Ring in Every Small Town. Shure isn't it shocking – and what them poor Artane Boys had to put up with from them so called Christian Brothers."

"Aye, Fidelma, another scandal every week. If they're not one of them pederasts, they're alcoholic sanctimonious old financial pecculators."

"Maggie Daly, where did you ever get words like them from?"

"Ah! Padraig, the youngest, him with the green punk haircut and them funny tablets, sure he has me nerves shot. Didn't I have to go down to the centre and get an extra tube of them Valiums. And then didn't he go spare and start talking to me about some Amerikan called Patrick Henry who rode all around shouting 'Give me Liberty or give me death!'"

"Now Maggie, don't ye know, nowadays it's 'Give me Librium or give me meth!' Wasn't I just after scoring off me youngest. Didn't he come home with his pockets stuffed with Mars bars and packets of crisps and when I asked where the feck he'd got them didn't he say it was all you could get off the Far East for a blow job these days." ...

I swear to youse! I'm in a state of shock. Just back from the cesspit of decadence and dissolute depravity, San Bloody Francisco, after 17 years beyond the Ninth Wave and I find this kind of old chat going on in the Duds and Suds bleeding laundrette between two grannies who only a decade of the rosary ago would have been biting the altar rails and knitting little anti-macassars for the Bishop's Bentley. But, it must be true, for as the Gaelgoirs say 'Dúirt bean go dúirt bean leí' – 'a woman said to me that a woman said to her ...'

Still, I suppose a terrible beauty is better than no beauty at all! Needs must when the devil vomits in one's knickers. Ah! Mother Ireland, dead and gone – was it for this that the wild geese fled? Was it for this that James Connolly bled? But then, remember, this is our wee bleeding Ulcer – it's just blood under the bridge or money under the table. I must change my drugs!

Onward! Tonight's 'baten docket', as the blessed Gay Byrne himself might have said, is Paddy, the subject of this slight vignette or instructional manual. Paddy was a Derryman, a would be seminarian, who, as a result of getting caught in a compromising situation backstage of the parochial Bingo Hall with the young girl playing the Blessed Virgin Mary (or BVM as those of us who like to think we're on good terms with herself usually call her) had managed to get thrown out of the priesthood and had resolved to travel on the missions – all the way to Hong Kong to convert the heathen Chinee. A single minded saviour, he did not need the imprimatur of the senile delinquent in the Vatican, the Polish Papa, to validate him! He could stamp his own library card. And if the Far East failed him he figured he could always go down to Calcutta and join that Albanian conwoman Mother Theresa and her leper pals.

His evangelical ambitions lasted all of two days in the fleshpots of Kowloon* and were followed by seven years of oriental debauchery, after which he returned to work in England, in the belly of the beast, to earn some wherewithal and recuperate from the rare tropical, and extremely antisocial, diseases which he had speculatively accumulated in Honkers, as the Brit ex-Pats used so to call that piece of pestilence.

In John Bull land Paddy was regarded by his mates in the local pub as an intellectual. Mind you, to the average Brit an intellectual is someone who when he hears the 'William Tell Overture' thinks 'Rossini' instead of the 'Lone Ranger'. (You do all know that Clayton 'racoon' Moore's faithful sidekick was called 'Tonto' – Spanish for stupid? Of course you did, I must have told you so a dozen times.)

Caitlín ní Hooligan and Éire Nua beckoned however, and, tearing himself away from the 'delights' of warm beer that tasted like gnats' piss and the xenophobic banalities of the English, he arrived back in his native City. He was a qualified engineer, nurse, helicopter pilot, and sanitary engineer, and so, of course, he ended up on the dole. Eventually, however, he became a part-time plumber which is what this whole tale is all about.

Some of my more perceptive (and if they have been persistent enough, semi-brain dead) readers may immediately at this juncture assume that after opening with a few mildly anti-clerical remarks the author is, yet again going to engage in some adolescently arrested scatological or – to be pretentious, Rabelaisian soi-dit humour. The red flag being the word 'Plumber'. O ye of little faith! Nothing could be nearer to the truth!

We are sitting in a nameless hostelry in the Bogside. It is nameless because Paddy is boycotting it because of some complicated and bizarre slight which he figures they inflicted on him. Now, boycotting has changed a bit since the days of the absentee landlord – and perhaps the Invincibles saw to that.

So, anyway, we're sitting there having a clandestine pint because we're not really drinking here and Paddy starts to tell us about plumbing. And that's all right with me, for doesn't the Sprockett herself need a washing machine. Now don't get me wrong! It wasn't all talk of gaskets and mixers, faucets and fixtures, sewers and shit – although all did feature in the conversation. In between we found time to discuss the words of Lao Tzu, the 6 c. B.C. clever clogs.

> "The more laws there are, the more disorganized society will be. The more prisons are built, the more crime will increase; the more bureaucracy proliferates and experts are trained, the more social problems are aggravated; the more military power expands, the more conflicts occur and the more the threat of destruction looms larger."

Personally, I thought the old Chinaman had just about summed it all up. "*Nihil obstat* from me, mucker," I had said. As far as I was concerned Mo (or is it Mao?) Mowlam could have done with reading that.

"Shite!" exclaimed my cloacal companion.

A riposte was clearly called for but my words fell like faeces upon the ground.

But Paddy was up and running. "It was like Dante's Inferno all over again," he solemnly intoned. "Midway in my life's journey I went astray from the straight road and awoke to find myself in a dark wood." There were some in the company who yawned, but they were merely hangers-on, true scribes like mygoodself know a potential story when we hear one and prick up our ears.

'Is furasta codhladh ar chnea duine eile' – which my Gaelgoir comrades tell me can be loosely translated as 'it is easy to die on another man's wounds'.

Our narrator was about to continue his excremental (or incremental?) memoires when the TV was turned up, obviously to distract we few intellectuals in the corner of the shebeen. The news reader was pontificating hypocritically about my former beloved El Presidente 'Bubba' Clinton, he of Zippergate. The bar fell into a noisy exposition of the bizarre idiocies of Amerikkan politics. Foolishly I attempted to expostulate. "While it is true that the bould Bill has been going down as often as Arkansas University student scores, nonetheless he's never been more popular in the US of A." Silence. Time fell wanking to the floor. It seemed the entire bar was suffering from a major Prozac shortage.

The plumber saved the day (not for the first time in U.S. politics if Richard Nixon is to be believed, which, of course, he is not, nor ever has been). "I once installed a jobby wheaker for the Arkansas asshole." he adumbrated. He caught our attention. After all, it isn't every day that you get the inside scéal on a mass murderer's stools.

"Aye, it was only two years ago. Himself and all his henchpeople were over bringing peace to us benighted Paddies and he was up in Derry doing a gig in the Guildhall." Around the bar, heads nodded. I hadn't been there but they had. Some of them could even remember when the Yankee secret service had even ventured into the no-name bar and announced that 'the Milky Bars were on them' and all the punters had had free Guinness courtesy of the American taxpayer. While this may not have been politically correct it is only fair to point out that many of the punters had felt that Mother Nature's nipples had run a little dry and that therefore gift horses should not be ignored let alone have their few remaining fangs examined.

"So!" for Paddy would not be deterred, "I was sitting in this very bar when in comes the councillor, Armani suit and all, and slips up to me and offers me the job. No names, no packdrill. Fair play to him it was a nice little homer." It transpired that Clinton, the most powerful cigar afficionado in the world has something in common with our beloved Queen, in that neither of them go to the toilet, like us poor mortals, for the commode cometh to them.

At any rate, *mirabile dictu* Paddy's bid came in a few quid below the other putative contractors and he awoke, two days before the President of the United States and his entourage of want-to-be Clint Eastwoods and Tonton Macoutes descended upon the Maiden City – where most of the citizens would cheerfully have had no problem with giving Bubba their first born child, male or female, let alone a lousy blow job.

In short, as Paddy would say 'happy days'. All he needed to do was to attach a piece of stainless steel vacuum tube, known to those in the plumbing business as a 'jobbie wheaker' to the guest toilet in the Guildhall, half an hour's work at most and he would be some £7,000 richer. "And it's all due to that great and unappreciated Mr. Crapper," beamed Paddy. "Who he?" inquired a foolish punter at the bar. I tried to kick him but it was no use. He had enabled our honest, or not so honest, artisan to plumb the depths yet again.

"Ye don't know about Thomas Crapper?" Paddy bellowed. "They teach you nothing at school, ye omadaun." (Since most of his listeners had attended St. Columbs, the Derry school notorious for having produced not one but two Nobel prize winners and thousands of bampots, this question was fairly rhetorical).

"In the bad old days," intoned Paddy, "the dry closet, the outside privy, the weekly dung cart and shite shifters were all we knew. Toilets were operated on a tap and gravity principle before the bould Thomas, but in 1884 he invented a flush system – it was like magic. Just pull the chain and a small syphon inside the cistern and atmospheric pressure forced the water into the bowl. Sewage as we know it was made possible."

It was more than I or indeed most of the punters wanted to know about the internal workings of water closets but, as Paddy was in the chair and had just bought a round of drinks, it would have been a churlish member of the company who would have tried to curtail the flow of his rhetoric. No churls here.

"I had it all worked out. I got a second hand jobbie wheaker from a mate of mine, big Hughie, ye mind him well." The company nodded. 'Big Hughie' was apparently locally known as 'the Merchant of Menace' and it had nothing to do with the Bard. As a recent returnee to the Maiden City I hit the old memory bank. "He's the one who used to trail his knuckles along the cobblestones?"

Paddy interrupted. "That was in the old days. Now he's like a hamster whose exercise wheel is fucked up." A strange simile, but then, it's a strange wee city. "As I was saying, I cleaned up the jobbie wheaker and ..." "What the fuck is a jobbie wheaker?" This from Dominic, who'd just been laid off from the rapidly down-sizing Fruit of the Loom (or is it Fruit of the Doom?) factory – anyway, everyone knew the writing was on the T-shirt ever since they opened to get the big tax free grants and Dominic had joined us merry band of 'job seekers' as the unemployement or 'bru' now call us.

The plumber was incensed. You could never get finishing a yarn with all these ignorami butting in. "A jobbie wheaker, my ould son is a piece of stainless steel with a high pressure sprocket rammed up inside it and inserted at the trap in the toilet. When the toilet is flushed the turds are syphoned off into a cunningly designed plastic receptacle where they can be stored for posterity or posterior. And before any of yese come up with stupid questions why anyone would want to collect shite unless it was for their rosebushes, let me tell you that in the intelligence business it is a big deal. In the old days the Greeks and the Druids and all them pagans used to foretell the future or auguries by inspecting the entrails of sacrificed animals, today the spook chemists collect the crap of the rich and verminous so that they can diagnose their state of their health. Why back in the eighties the Yanks were able to forecast to within days how long yer man Brezhnev had for the land of the living by analysing his keek. And the Pentagon has no intention of letting the Rooskies or anyone else find out about ould Bubba's little prostate problems. Hence, whenever the Zipper is in a foreign town they need the services of a skilled jobbie wheaker installer such as my good self."

"So what was the prognosis?" asked Declan, who fancied himself as a bit of a medical expert though as far as I was aware his pharmacological skills only ran to doping greyhounds.

Paddy snorted. "I don't get to examine it, ye eejit, I just hand it over to the men in the grey suits. But here's what I'm trying to tell yese. I arrive at the Guildhall in me motorcycle jacket and crash helmet and march up to the door four hours before El Presidente is to helicopter in, present me clearance papers and ask for the chief of security. And they show me in and escort me up to the Councillor's throne room. Ye want to see the state of it! All done up like a dog's dinner and it must have taken three cleaners with a gallon of Mr. Muscle to get it that clean, and there's this goon there who looked as if he was straight out of Quantico or Napalm Colorado or wherever and he starts to give me the third degree while I'm just trying to install the wheaker and get the fuck offside. And then he orders me to take off the crash helmet. And I ask why and he says I could be a fucking terrorist. And he seems like a decent enough fella, although thick as two short planks, so I explain to him that since I'm doing the double, a wee nixer, I don't want to be identified by the tout from the Social Security who sits up on Derry's Walls noting down every unemployed punter who might be working on the side.

Paddy leant back and suddenly began laughing. The rest of us did not, feeling that our time had been wasted enough with this banal tale.

"Hey, Paddy," asked Declan, "did you ever see the yellow brick road?"

Paddy, annoyed at being interrupted, scowled. "Yeah, of course, we have to watch it every Christmas, along with bloody 'Mary Poppins' and 'Gone with the Wind', so what?"

"Well, do you reckon the yellow brick road was that colour before Toto pissed all over it?"

"No, but I reckon that the Garvaghy Road will have to soon be renamed the Orange Prick road! Now let me finish. So I'm trying to keep the helmet on and the Yank asks who are these people?"

"They're the 'bru', the bureau," I explain, because you have to make it simple for these head-the-balls, and then the light dawns on the spook and he leans over and says to me, I swear to God, 'Ah you don't need to bother about that son, we're the CIA, not the Bureau. They wouldn't let the Hoover men anywhere near a sensitive operation like this.'"

What can I say, comedy is after all only tragedy plus time.

* The author's reasons for disliking Hong Kong, a pearl in the Orient, are adequately explained in his short epic 'Hong Kong Horror Hotel' which is included in this slim volume.

The Pilgrimage

The rain was coming down in stair rods when the van slid to a halt in the dung spackled main, indeed the only, street in the village of Ballinamuck. We were on our way to Sligo to attend a failed bank robbers reunion but Sean, our driver, had insisted that we stop in the armpit of county Roscommon to meet 'a true hero of the revolution', none other than Captain Bovril.

Sean parked the minivan in front of the only pub in the village – the Arm Alight Inn, which took its name from a notorious Falls Road shebeen. We splashed through the muck and Sean hammered on the flaking mud splattered door. For what seemed like an eternity there was no response and the rest of us were cursing Sean and preparing to motor on to Sligo when the door creaked open and a dirt encrusted gnomish visage peered out, muttering "Fuck off! We're closed!"

Ignoring this ungracious welcome, Sean pushed the dwarf back, dragged us inside and followed, closing the door in a vain attempt to keep the rain out. Through the gloom I took in the bar. Even through the miasma I could discern that beer crates provided the only 'stools' and 'tables' which sat sullenly in front of a smouldering turf fire. The battered wooden counter had a filthy strip of plastic stretched along it which had seen better days. On the sagging shelf behind leant a couple of bottles of whiskey and vodka. A couple of crates of Guinness seemed to comprise the rest of the stock. On the walls there were a few tattered Guinness posters, vintage circa World War II and a reasonably new poster of Glasgow Celtic. There were more flies than at the crucifixion. Squalor seeped through the very walls.

Throughout my adult life I have been assiduously engaged in a noble quest. A search for the Grail. I have sought to find the worst bar in all the Emerald Isle. One that even Bord Fáilte would warn tourists off from. I exaggerate not when I affirm that the Ballinamuck Arm Alight Inn is definitely on the shortlist.

"I told yese, we're closed!"

It was the poisoned dwarf again.

"Owen, it's me, Sean – from West Belfast. The White Fort Celtic Supporters Club!"

"Jesus, Sean, is it really you?" The dwarf squinted and rubbed a rheumy eye.

"Sure yer welcome. Céad míle fáilte. Sit down. Sit down. I was just clearing up. Here, have a drop of the cratur." He reached under the bar and pulled out a Lucozade bottle and poured us all two large shots of poitín. "What's the scéal from Belfast?"

For Owen Harrington, the poisoned dwarf, was a refugee. An exile from his native West Belfast, forced by the exigencies of fate to rot in Ballinamuck 'running' the pub a long lost uncle had left him. He couldn't sell it since no one would buy it. He hadn't the wherewithal to get out of town. His life was over. Life by misadventure.

Owen threw a scrap of turf on and attempted to get some heat from the fire. Outside it poured down. Inside the walls were covered in damp sweat. But there was poitín and there was craic. 'So this is the legendary Captain Bovril', I thought, as our host poured out another couple of large slugs of *uisge beatha*. 'Tell it not in Gath nor whisper it in the streets of Askelon. How are the mighty fallen. Lo, all our pomp of yesterday is one with Nineveh and Tyre!' My gloomy philosophical musings were curtailed by Sean who playfully kicked the beer crate from under me.

"Wake up, you dozy bastard. You're here to interview the Captain."

I had heard of the Captain of course. Indeed, who in all of Andersonstown had not, but I had always secretly thought that he was some kind of mythical figure whose heroic actions had been blown out of all proportion. What a foolish cynic I was.

"Pleased to meet you Captain, Sean's told me a lot about you." I attempted to ingratiate myself. "Lies, all lies!" The dwarf bristled. "Sean Morris wouldn't know the truth if it bit him in the arse." Sean casually reached behind the counter and produced another bottle of moonshine. "Glasgow, March 12th 1982," he intoned solemnly. "Some of us still remember." Owen's one good eye appeared to mist over. "Glasgow '82, aye, that was a day and a half. But you've heard the story a dozen times – hell, Sean, you were there." "This man," Sean indicated my goodself, "has travelled half way round the world to hear the story from your own lips Captain. He is the People's Archivist. You owe it to posterity to let him record it." Owen spat into the smoldering fire. "Fuck posterity! What did it ever do for me," but the flattery was clearly working. I eased out my tiny recorder and switched it on. And so I was to hear the infamous story from the horse's mouth.

1982. Was it really so long ago. Sean, Owen and 18 other stalwarts from the West Belfast Celtic Supporters Club (White Fort branch) had hired Mickey Marley's clapped out minibus and made the hazardous trip to stab city for the 'Old Firm' game. Rangers v. Celtic. This time the game was to be played at Ibrox Park, Rangers HQ. The lions' den.

The plan was a simple one and therefore, by definition, doomed to failure. They would march together to the game and after it retire to the Gorbals for an evening of sportsmanlike bigotry and party songs in the Brazen Head.

Alas, the fickle finger of fortune was to intervene. Owen became separated from his comrades when he stopped to get a pastie supper and a haggis sarnie. He made it to the ground all right but due to his inherent myopia and the consumption of six pints of 'heavy' that morning, to say nothing of the previous night's carousal on the Larne-Stranraer cattle boat, Owen committed the cardinal sin. The one for which there is no forgiveness. He inadvertently entered Ibrox from the wrong end and found himself surrounded by a sea of blue scarves and banners. Hastily he tucked his Celtic scarf down inside his donkey jacket and gazed glumly across the pitch to the other end of the ground where the 'bhoys' of Celtic swayed and sang. The crowd was so dense that he couldn't get out and anyway, he hadn't enough money to purchase another ticket. He had to grin and bear it. Surrounded by bluenoses.

And then, after 15 minutes the unbelievable happened. Celtic scored. The far end erupted into a frenzy of green and white. The chants started up. 'Ten men dead but not forgotten! We got 18 and Mountbatten!' As Macaulay put it 'Even the ranks of Tuscany could scarce forbear a cheer'. Owenie's position was somewhat different. Surrounded as he was on all sides by specimens of humanity which would have given Darwin at least three major new tomes on evolution, he scrunched his scarf down even more and attempted to give a soundless whoop of joy. To no avail. He positively smelt of fear.

There was a tap on his left shoulder. His huge neanderthal neighbour stared down at him. "Hey, Jimmie, go get me a cup of Bovril." It was an order that brooked no resistance. "O, and Jimmie, just in case you get any ideas, leave me your left shoo." It was the infamous Big Sammy, a man well-known for his propensity for causing

GBH. Particularly on Catholics. Owen limped through the crowd and up to what was laughingly called the 'refreshment counter'.

But I must divaricate. I have told this tale in several countries and, inevitably, I am asked 'What is Bovril?' This sterling product, it seems, is not available in alien climes. Its fame has not spread to far off Colombia nor even Cologne. So for those amongst you who have never undergone 'the Bovril experience' a short explanation is in order. Bovril is, quite simply, a vile non-alcoholic hot beef drink found only at Scottish football matches. Jars of it do appear from time to time on supermarket shelves but no one has actually been observed purchasing or stealing one. But on cold days on the terraces in Scottish football grounds a vague form of insanity seems to descend and infect hitherto reasonably normal individuals with a craving for this evil potation.

Owen limped back to his place on the terrace and proffered the cup of Bovril to the large Rangers supporter. "Thanks, Jimmie, there's your shoo. Put it on!" Ah no! Surely not, but, yes, there it was. A big steaming jobbie in his shoe. "I said put it on!" Big Sammy's tone became threatening. Squelch. Ah Jesus. At least he got a bit of elbow room as some of the crowd edged away from the odiferous Owen, forming a temporary cordon sanitaire. And then, of course, for despite all the propaganda God is not always good, Celtic scored again. A lovely cross from the right and the centre forward soared high to nod it into the old onion bag. 2-0! It was unheard of. As the far end of the ground erupted in delirious frenzy, with a sagging heart Owen felt the tap on his other shoulder. Big Sammy was not alone. His friend Big Mervyn was there too, his knuckles trailing the terrace floor. His brawny biceps were striated with worn and ill-drawn tattoos. His breath reeked of stale beer.

"You're going tae get me a cup of Bovril too, aren't ye!" Does the Trojan Horse have a wooden dick! "Aye." Sullenly Owen turned towards canteen. "And leave your aither shoo." Sammy guffawed. Obviously he and big Mervyn shared a similar sense of sophisticated humour.

Just as Owen returned with the boiling cup of hot Bovril Celtic scored again. "Put it on." Big Mervyn's tone of voice allowed for no demurral. Ah Jesus! Another steaming jobbie. Christ, can these Orange bastards shit at will! He couldn't take it any more. He oozed his way through the crowd which parted like the Red Sea on one of Moses' good days. Offensive remarks vis-à-vis his personal hygiene washed off him. Oblivious to Hunnish taunts he slurped out of the ground and into the car park. The gate slammed behind him.

As if it had happened yesterday the little gnome shuddered at the memory. He reached for the poitín and absent-mindedly filled our glasses. Just then the front door crashed open. From the tinnient torrent which was still lashing down two shivering figures forced their way in. A man and a woman. They looked like tourists. Wet tourists. Lost tourists. Moneyed tourists. As Owen pulled himself out of his reverie and prepared to throw the intruders out Sean interposed himself.

"Come in, come in. You must be foundered. Here, take a seat at the fire," he indicated the few lumps of smoldering turf. "Owen, what are you thinking. Get our guests a drink." Owen was too drunk to quibble and lurched round behind the counter. "What are ye having?" he mouthed.

They weren't too hard to figure out. Yanks. Over here looking for their 'roots'. Obviously disillusioned with the hostile climate I guessed. Rightly so. A retired cop from New York and his wife. The guy was all right. The rain had become so incessant that he had been forced to stop in this Godforsaken hole. And he wanted a drink, Whiskey. Owen provided him with a shot, charging him tourist rates   not that he got many tourists but even he knew that tourist rate was three times the local rate. "And what'll you be having, Missus."

Wrinkling her proboscis in distaste Maureen, for such it transpired was her name, averred that she might be able to handle a 'G & T'. This one baffled Owen, stuck as he had been for the past ten years in this rustic hell. "Ye what?"

Effortlessly, Sean took charge. "Sorry missus, but we don't run to that. Guinness or whiskey." "I suppose that a hot whiskey is out of the question?" "You suppose right," snorted Owen pouring her a dram into an unwashed tea cup.

They sat shivering and sipping their drinks as we quaffed our poitín. Owen thawed slightly as Benny, who was indeed an ex-cop from New Jersey, handed over a wad of notes and asked him to 'take what he needed'. Benny had to try the poitín of course and to try and negotiate the sale of a bottle to bring back Stateside. Maureen however was not so easily cajoled.

"Where's the restroom?" she asked looking around with distaste. "What's that?" asked Owen, "Owen, it's the bogs, the jacks, the shithouse." Not for nothing had I lived in the belly of the beast. "Oh, why didn't you say. It's out back," he gestured at the back door. Maureen rose and circumnavigated the beer crates. She pushed open the door and disappeared into the murk.

Acting instinctively to his wife's departure Benny ordered a double whiskey and started asking Sean about fly fishing in the locality. The fact that Sean had never held a fishing rod in his hand in his life did not deter him from giving detailed advice. But Benny appeared to be so glad to be out of the rain that he'd put up with any bullshit. Sure what is a stranger but a friend you've never met. Suddenly, the back door swung open and Maureen stood there, dripping onto the floor. One of her high heels hung awkwardly from her mud splattered shoes and her emerald coloured dress had clearly seen better days. She was in a state of shock. "Benny, do something!"

"What's up, honey?"

"What's up! What's up! Is that all you can say. Look at my dress, it's ruined."

"And you won't believe what's out there. The yard is like a pig sty. There's no light, no seat on the toilet, and no toilet paper in the privy. There's not even a lock on the door!"

Owen roused himself. These Yanks might be a financial gold mine but they had no right to demean his bar. "A lock on the door, is it Missus!" he roared. "Why would we need that. I've been here ten years and during that time divil a bit of shite's been stolen."

Wailing like a banshee Maureen dragged an apologetic Benny, who was only starting to enjoy himself, out the front door and into the storm. Foolishly he left a wad of notes on the counter. "Good riddance," muttered Owen, "Bloody Yanks!" pocketing the money.

Personally, I concurred with this view. I mean to say, why do they call it 'tourist season' if we're not allowed to shoot them. "Get back to the story," I exhorted. My batteries were running out. Seanie decorated the mahogany (or, in this case, plastic) and Owen took another sip.

"Where was I?"

He was in the car park outside Ibrox. He could hear the roar of the crowd. His beloved Celtic were winning and he'd never been more miserable. He stood there morosely. Suddenly his reverie was interrupted by a tweed capped bespectacled English radio reporter, his microphone in hand, in search of yet another vox pop.

"Excuse me Sir – Jesus Christ, what's that smell" – he ploughed on manfully. "I'm interviewing Scottish football fans to see if we can get some answers to the question why is there so much trouble at Rangers v. Celtic games? Our listeners in London would be most interested if you could share your thoughts on this matter with them. What is the cause of this insensate violence?"

Drawing himself up to his full 5 foot 1 inch Owen did his best to muster some dignity. "Listen, you stupid pratt! There will always be violence at Rangers v. Celtic games so long as they shit in our shoes and we piss in their Bovril!"

He had been reunited with his comrades after the game which had been a Celtic 4-1 rout. He had to get rid of the boots and socks but the lads piled him into the back of the van and got him back home. By the time he hit Andytown he was so pissed that he was certain that he'd seen the whole game. But his interview had been aired. Word spread in the ghetto. He came a hero. Kilwee Kash and Karry even presented him with a new pair of boots.

His fame, of course, was only fleeting, as Andy Warhol had predicted. But there had been a little peripeteia, a sudden reversal of fortune. A little matter of misinterpretation. There was a bank job and an argument about whether it had been an official job or a homer. He'd had to leave town and hide out in his uncle's shebeen. And he'd been there ever since. A long forgotten hero.

O tempora, O mores!
Do threascair an soal is shéid an ghaoth mar smál
Alastrann, Caesar, 's an méid sin a bhí 'na bpáirt;
Tá an Teamhair 'na féar, is féach an Traoi mar tá,
Is na Sasanaigh féin do b'féidir go bhfaighidís bás!

(The wind of time has blown away like so much dust,
Alexander and Caesar and the rest of them.
Tara is under grass; what remains now of Troy?
Even the English will meet their death in time)

THE GRAPES OF WRATH

"How are they hanging?" I brightly inquired as I walked up to the bar in the Trinity Lodge and greeted my old chum B.A. Grimshaw himself. A mistake. An inadvertent mistake but a bad one nonetheless. And I hadn't even brought him any grapes.

The great one swivelled, apparently painfully, on his bar stool and fixed me with a baleful eye. "By the bloody haemorrhoids of Martin Luther (*molimina excretoria*)! I could expect nothing better from the likes of a Protestant gobshite such as yourself. Pity – sympathy even – yer black heart doesn't know the meaning of the word."

I hastily purchased two pints but essayed a riposte. "Brian, sure it was only the wee snip and it's been almost a week now since you had it." Wincing, Brian Artur raised himself from the stool and bellowed. "They only jest at scars, who never felt the wounds!"

"Look, mucker, I feel for your pain, but sure it was the right thing to do. You can't afford any more kids. You've already done your bit for Ireland in the 'outbreed the Prods Handicap Stakes'. You outnumber me four to one – and mine's a fucking peacewanker (peacewankers, in my experience, suffer from 'Donne's Syndrome' – you know, 'no man's an island so you have to weep or gnash your few remaining National Health fangs about some train crash in Bangladesh or Paddington or some famine in Fiji – to say nothing about all those little unborn foetuses [or foeti] flushed down the tubes even before they can join the great game of screwing up the planet), whereas two of yours are already fine Irish gombeenmen."

He was not mollified (though secretly no doubt pleased that I appreciated the sacrifices he and the blessed Hilda had made to raise a future generation of bloodsuckers), but settled, albeit gingerly, back down on his seat. "Do ye want to hear about it?" Noddingly I lied. He shuddered and began the graphic masochistic tale of his vasectomy. By the time he got to the part where he'd had to shave his own pubic hairs and was then confronted by the surgeon who was a be-turbaned Sikh, armed, at least according to B.A. and who are we poor mortals to contradict the great one, with a kukri knife – and you know what they say about the Gurkhas – once unsheathed the sacred kukri must shed blood ere it can be resheathed – I had started to drift off into one of my meditative states. You know the kind. Where you quietly ponder the great mysteries of life. Like, how did a fool and his money get together in the first place? What was the best thing before sliced bread? Before they invented drawing boards, what did they go back to? If God dropped acid, would he see people? You know, those kinda questions. Go on, admit it, you think about crap like this everyday, don't you? (If not, why not!)

The clip on the ear alerted me to the fact that the maestro had stopped, temporarily at least, from giving an account of his dong's trials and fibulations at the hands of Dr. Singh and required more liquid refreshment. Suitably chastised I divvied up. Needs must when the devil drives as my dear old Dad used to say. No one understood what the fuck he was talking about, but then, he was a Freemason and it didn't do to inquire too closely into the words of wisdom of they who know what to do with goats at the back of the Martyrs Memorial Hall in Drumcree.

"Ye weren't in on Thursday!" It was said in an accusatory tone. I bridled. It's not often one gets the opportunity to bridle so when you do, make sure its a good bridle. "I was at Jack the Whack's funeral. Why weren't you there. He was a comrade and a lumberjack. And he outranked you. And don't play the old soldier with me. It was only from St. Theresa's down to Milltown – and we got to stop off with the coffin at the Felons on the way. Even your poor squirreled nuts could have done it." I was irate. In high dudgeon. (Has anyone ever been in low dudgeon? Don't go there, it's a miserable place. Ask Jeffrey – but that's another story.)

"I'm sorry I missed it." He sounded apologetic. *Mirabile dictu!* "It's just the mban á ti wanted to have a wee check up to see if it was still functioning." My data retrieval brain/brian cells reached out and plucked the only apology that we have been able to record coming from Grimshaw's lips and stashed it in the memory bank. Maybe it is worth staying around the vale of tears for a few more years.

"How was it? Were there enough old comrades to carry the kid up the road?" I nodded. "Aye, not as many as should have been, but enough. He was only 47 you know. And he was one of our kids." Thankfully, before I could get maudlin, Brian Artur began to wax lyrical. "D'ye remember Dun Laoghaire?" Aye, I do. You tell it, Brian Artur and we'll sit here and drink to Jack the Whack, for remember, amnesia is the handmaiden of hypocrisy, and we may be rightfully accused of many things, but hypocrisy is not one of them.

A Story of Jack The Whack (as told by B.A. Grimshaw) Or 'Life by Misadventure'

"It was you introduced him to me. He'd been one of your students before he'd been interned and had to go on the run and he'd ended up in Dublin with some of your other disreputable anarchist bampots. He and another of your ould Proddy anarchists – Robin." (Grimshaw, atheist though he was, stolidly believed that Catholic anarchists were better than Protestant anarchists. Speaking as the survivor of the trio I think I can truthfully say that neither 'Catholic' Jackie nor 'Prod' Robin gave a monkey's.)

"So I arrived down to teach yese all how to do a decent bank job. And devil the bit of thanks did I get for it. There were the lot of you, associating with some boyos whose names I don't know to this day and don't want to, smoking that mary weany all night and planning next days 'big one'. Big one, me arse!"

I ordered two whiskeys and tried to cast my mind back to Dun Laoghaire days. Memory lane seems to be covered in cow shit these days but there had been some good times. Stores looted, people stampeded, cattle raped. A typical night in South Dublin.

"Jackie always had a vision, I'll have to give him that," mused Grimshaw. In my experience, having studied the likes of Joan of Arc for my history courses, having visions can only mean two things: either you're touched by God or you're as barking as a shithouse rat. Jack the Whack was never touched by God.

"D'ye not remember some of his get rich quick schemes?" asked Grimshaw. I shuddered. Dimly I recalled some of Jackie's would be scams. "He advertised a penis enlarger for sale for £50 and sent two poor mugs a magnifying glass each, didn't he?" Grimshaw perked up and shifted his not inconsiderable girth on his bar stool of misery. "Aye, there was that one, but how about the time he advertised '50 cigarette lighters for £10' and sent punters a box of matches." Yes, that had been a good one. But it had not kept the polecat from the portals.

We took another swallow and ordered a couple of pints and chasers. "You still writing them crap articles?" asked Grimshaw, wiping the froth from his lambent lips. Ah! Criticism! The venom from contented rattlesnakes. "Journalism is but the harridan of history," I smirked. "The hoor, more like," muttered the great one. "Still, I suppose I'd better let you record the kid's finest moment for posterity. You weren't here when it happened. You were off defending foreign criminals instead of being here at home defending our own." This was true, so I had to pay for my guilt with another round.

"I taught Jackie how to do a solo bank job." Grimshaw was not to be distracted. "Sure them boys who he was with were useless. Not a decent getaway man amongst them and they couldn't even hot wire a cripple car! No, I taught him the joys of the Dublin bus schedule."

And so it was that back in the bad old days of 1983 Jackie had walked into the Allied Irish Bank on Dun Laoghaire's main street on his Todd Sloan and queued up with the other customers in line for the till counter. When he had finally reached the counter he had poked the muzzle of the barrel of his imitation pistol, purloined not half an hour ago from the local Woolworth's from out of the tattered copy of the *Daily Mirror* and told the teller "to fill up a bag of money and not to make any funny moves." The teller, a decent working class Dubliner had not batted an eyelid. "Certainly Sir, won't be a minute." Jackie had been edgy. "Don't go pushing any alarm buttons!" he had whispered as menacingly as he could. The teller smiled. "Certainly not, sure the customer's always right."

The line of customers behind Jackie were apparently oblivious to the somewhat irregular banking transaction which was going on. The teller, a nondescript fifty-something pushed over a sack of money. Jackie reached for it. The teller withdrew it. "I've just remembered, there's more in this other drawer." The sweat broke out on Jackie's face. "I told ye, no tricks, hurry up and don't touch that alarm bell for five minutes, I've a backup gang outside who'll plug anyone who tries to follow me."

The teller smiled at this blatant farrago of nonsense and handed over a second sack. "Thank you Sir, come again." Jackie walked quickly out the door into the bustle of Dun Laoghaire's busy main street and hopped onto a number 38 green bus. By the time the Guardians of Peace had arrived and set up their perimeters around the peaceful suburb he was long gone and sitting drinking with his mentor in a bar in Dublin's North side. The first sack contained £2,500, the second one over £6,000. No exploding green dyes, no bugs or transmitters, just used twenty pound notes. Happy days! By nightfall he and Brian Artur were back in the fair city of Lurgan.

Jackie had always wondered about the wee teller and why he hadn't pressed the alarm, and, normally, that's all he could have done – wonder and thank his lucky stars. But life, as those clever old Greeks knew, is strewn with the odd bit of Peripeteia (a sudden reversal of fortune for the koineically challenged amongst my ever decreasing readership). And so it was with the Whack.

Six months later he was picked up in Dublin with his former would-be John Dillingers on suspicion of being involved in a string of bank jobs, most of which he had had no part in. He was put up on a couple of identity parades. The usual thing. Jackie hadn't been too worried – on the other jobs he'd done he'd either worn a mask or been the getaway driver, but of course on the Allied Irish solo op he had been stockingless in Gaza, and so his heart sank when the door opened and the little teller from the bank was ushered in by a brawny garda from County Kerry. He had a laugh like a goat walking on a tin roof. Fear gripped Jackie by the scrotum. There was no way that the teller could fail to recognize and finger him. He looked like the guy in the horror movie who is the first to see the Creature. Fear is a good chief but a poor Indian. Jackie prepared to meet his doom.

The teller appeared to take his work seriously. He walked up and down the line up twice. The other punters in the line-up, drawn as they were from Dublin's finest, were all well over six foot. Jackie was 5ft 6". They all had short hair. Jackie's was shoulder length. 'Eli, Eli, lama sabachthani!' Just as Jackie was about to utter the immortal words, so beloved by policemen testifying 'it's a fair cop, Guv', the teller straightened up and spoke to the Sergeant. "No, the man who robbed me isn't here." He smiled and walked out of the line-up hall. Outside Jackie could hear the Sergeant cursing and excoriating the poor man. "It was number 4, I'm telling you! That Northern bastard."

After half an hour Jackie was released. In a state of euphoric stupor he joined Brian Artur in the Legal Eagle, the lawyers' bar down the street to celebrate his escape. They had finished their first pint and Brian, for once, went up to the bar to order another couple of celebratory tinctures when who should he bump into but the little teller, standing there with a pint in his hand. He looked at Brian Artur. "You're a friend of your man there, aren't ye?" he asked, nodding over to the corner where Jackie was sitting.

Cautiously, Brian Artur affirmed that he might be. Cautious Brian Artur might be, but curiosity got the better of him. "Will you take a pint and join us?"

Jackie blanched when he saw Brian Artur's new companion. He

gulped nervously at his pint. The wee teller smiled. "Don't worry, son, you're all right with me. You obviously don't know much about banks here do ye?"

Jackie gulped. He was grateful to this new found friend but he wasn't about to admit that he'd robbed half a dozen of such establishments in the past year.

"Sure it's like this," explained the teller who had introduced himself as Frankie. "These bloody Kapitalists sweat you for thirty years for miserable wages while they send all the money off to off shore accounts and line their pockets and those of the TDs and property developers. And they then have the gall to expect the likes of a poor wage slave like me to protect their filthy ill-gotten gains." He proceeded to launch into a diatribe of which Jimmy Connolly would have been proud. Pausing to wipe the foam off his lips he proceeded, over embarrassed objections to buy a round.

"Sure this one's on me son. The bank had to pay me £50 danger money and because of the shock and stress your disruption caused to my daily drudgery I got two months off on the sick – nervous debility they call it. And on top of that, they even have to pay for me to come down to the pig sty today to look at line-ups. You know where I work. Come again anytime." He winked, stood up and shuffled off into the Dublin gloom. When Brian Artur and Jackie stumbled out several hours later the moon was a smirk on the face of heaven.

Brian Artur finished his tale and belched sonorously. "Quite restores your faith in human nature, doesn't it." Yes, Brian, it does.

Crapulous by now we repaired to Jim McCorry's Mexican Taqueria and Tequila house, formerly the Cous Cous kitchen, across the way from the heavily fortified Andytown barracks. We needed to eat and I had a Whack story of my own for the would-be omniscient Grimshaw.

The Tale Of The Rover's Return

It was 1977. The Whack and I were part of the annual Celtic Supporters Club outing to Glasgow. This one was really organized, we even had a teetotal driver, and that was a first. The game had been a stirring victory for the bhoys over the Hearts huns, and, having braved the sectarian chants of the bluenoses our gallant team had succeeded in gaining entrance to the Brazen Head, the Mecca of all West Belfast pilgrims. A night of ferocious drinking and good natured sectarian bigotry and banter was guaranteed. Rebel songs were sung. Great Celtic victories recalled. Absent friends toasted. Jackie, fresh out of Long Kesh was in fine form. It had been several years since he had been on a Celtic cultural outing and he was making up for lost time. The minibus with sober driver had been ordered for 4 a.m. in order to get us to the Stranraer boat and home to darkest Turf Lodge by breakfast. Sleep was out of the question. It was an obvious all-nighter.

At three thirty in the morning the survivors took stock as the Brazen Head staff began the business of cleaning up. Four of our numbers had passed out but the rest of us, Jackie included, were still in reasonable fettle. The van driver appeared and began to help us load the troops in. Being of a responsible nature deep down Jackie went to check out the toilets to see if we had missed anyone.

The toilet was not a pretty sight. To be fair, few Glasgow toilets are. The single light bulb was smashed but lying passed out in the blood and vomit on the tiled floor was a wee man wearing a Celtic scarf. Jackie rolled him over with his foot and called me in. "I recognise this guy. He's Liam Begley. He lives in the Turf somewhere. Give us a hand. We can't leave him here." Blessed are the good Samaritans.

Between us we were able to drag the unconscious punter out into the bar and bundle him into the back of the minivan. He slumbered on as did we, awaking only as the van was driven onto the boat in order to drink the last of the cans of heavy as we crossed the Irish Sea. Begley was still out of it as the cold grey light of dawn proffered its roseate fingers over West Belfast and our driver started dropping off the punters who were groggily waking up and half heartedly trying to cobble up some explanation for their wives and weans as to their absence for the past two days. The Whack and I were not so beset by such mundane family concerns. We would gain brownie points in heaven by delivering Begley back to the bosom of his grieving family, repair to the Whack's billet for a black and evil triple by-pass traditional Irish breakfast and then trundle down to the Felons to get up to date on the latest lies and disinformation, quaff a few pints and shoot some mean pool. Well, at least we had a plan. Of course, having just returned from fair Caledonia we should have known that the best laid plans aft gang aglae – or fuck up, at least according to Rabbie Burns and as a noted tosser he surely knew a thing or two about screw ups.

Our driver, the sober Francis Moriarty, known by those in the local sodality as 'St. Francis of Assisi' because of his apparent love of God's little creatures, but vulgarly referred to as 'Frankie the pig fucker' by our fellow felons, wheeled into the Turf Lodge estate. Jack, apparently compos mentis asserted that he knew exactly where 'yer man' lived. The ever tolerant Frankie screeched to a halt outside a small terraced house. Like its neighbours it had seen better days, but it had a tiny front 'garden' into which we dragged the still unconscious Begley and rang the doorbell, prepared to immediately run away as soon as Mrs. Begley manifested herself. Frankie, no fool he, had already driven off.

There was no reply but almost at once the inevitable nosy woman next door, the local Gauleiter, appeared from over the fence and confronted us. "What do yese want?"

Jackie drew himself up and prepared for the good neighbour award which he obviously expected to receive. "We seek Mrs Begley," he declared. "We have returned her beloved to the bosom of his family."

"She's no here," quoth the neighbour, "sure didn't she and that useless wino of a husband of hers and the weans go over yesterday for a week's holiday in Scotland. She'll not be back until Saturday. Who's that corpse anyway?" She pointed at the recumbent form of comrade Begley.

We fled the scene. Well, it sounds better than 'the two drunks staggered offside'. An hour later in the PDF – for we had decided to give the Felons a miss for a few weeks in case questions were asked, Jackie raised a pint and said to me, "By and large we did OK McG?" I choked. "Yes, Jack, we kidnapped a tourist from Glasgow and deposited him back in Belfast leaving his wife and weans, probably penniless, in Scotland." Jackie smiled and supped his pint. "Aye, like I say, we didn't do too bad."

I turned to comrade Grimshaw. My Jackie story was at least as good as his I thought. I turned sentimental. "His name was Jackie Crawford. He was a comrade, a volunteer, an anarchist and a lumberjack. Death – life's hooded hangman and time's earnest executioner has taken him from us. Rest in peace, Eric the half a bee (his favorite song – don't ask why, you really don't want to know!)."

Brian Artur snorted.

"Death is but a poultice to the pain of life," he pontificated.

"Anyway, I thought you wanted to hear about my vasectomy! Do you know that my pubes and arse look like that burning map they always used to start 'Bonanza'?"

No, Brian I didn't really want to know that, but, still:

'What a vas deferens a day makes!'

THE MAN WHO SHOT D. I. SWANZEY

I only met him the once. In a bar in a particularly uninspiring village in County Tyrone. I was sitting chatting to Brian Artur when he came in, glanced around and shot over to join our company. Brian Artur introduced him to me as 'The uncle'; he had a swift half pint of Guinness, excused himself and darted off again back to the shop. A small man, pushing seventy, with what appeared to be a perpetually worried expression.

"What's up with the uncle?" I inquired of Brian Artur when he came back with the pints. He grinned. "Henpecked, me ould son. A walking warning to the rest of us. A living advertisement for not getting married. He did, after he got out in 1924 and he hasn't had a happy day since. Forty-nine years of nagging hell. Why, coming in here to see you was probably the most courageous thing he's done in the last decade. I'd lent him your last book you see, and he'd never seen a real live author."

I tried not to look flattered, failing dismally. "What do you mean 'after he got out'? Surely that old kiddie never did time?" Brian Artur smiled, took a sip of his pint and savoured the moment. "Little did you but know it, my son, but you were drinking with the man who shot D.I. Swanzey."

To most people it would have made more sense if he had said 'Liberty Vallance'. I mean to say, everyone knows John Wayne did for him and let Jimmy Stewart take the credit. After all, Swanzey was shot down on the steps of the chapel in Lisburn way back in August, 1920, and few but the historically minded Republicans or Loyalists would recognize his name today. Or maybe not. Ulster is a small place, filled with, some would say, though not I for I value my patellae, small minded people whose motto is "Never Forget, Never Forgive."

As it was however, I had just written a book on the history of Internment in Ireland and was well aware of the late and unlamented District Inspector Swanzey, the man who had been named by a Cork jury as the Inspector who led the police murder gang who had killed Tomas MacCurtain, then Lord Mayor of Cork, at his home on March 20th, 1920. The jury had returned a verdict of guilty against the British Premier Lloyd George, the Lord Lieutenant, Lord French, the Chief Secretary for Ireland, Ian McPherson, three Inspectors of the R.I.C. including Swanzey and other unknown members of the force. It had been a cause célèbre at the time, even in those dark days when the Black and Tans and the Auxies had been running amok, with British governmental approval, burning, looting and murdering at will.

After the murder Swanzey had been transferred up North, to Loyalist Lisburn, where, it was felt, he would be safer, but Michael Collins had vowed vengeance for his dead friend the Lord Mayor, and, presently, he had got it; five unknown assailants had gunned Swanzey down as he emerged from Mass one Sunday morning. According to the history books no one was ever made 'amenable for the crime', and now, here I was, sitting with an old friend and being told, quite seriously, that the mild-mannered henpecked pensioner who had just left our company had been the man who had pulled the trigger which had ended the inglorious career of Swanzey. It had done more than that too. The night Swanzey bought his, the Loyal citizenry of Lisburn had burned every Catholic family in the town out of their homes, while their equally loyal comrades in the UVF had instituted what at best could be called a mini-pogrom in Belfast which, two months later had left 2,000 Catholics homeless, 80 dead, and over 10,000 out of work. Such was, and alas is, the power of Irish history.

Brian Artur told me the rest of the story. There wasn't all that much to it. The local police had had a fair idea which of the 'bhoys' were responsible and had arrested the uncle and a few of his sidekicks a couple of days later. They had been held and interrogated for a week but had said nothing. In those days the Royal Irish Constabulary did not have the sophistication which their Ulster counterparts have today in such torture centers as Castlereagh, and so, as the next best thing, they had interned them, without charge or trial, on the Argenta, a prison hulk moored off Larne. They had remained there, and in Derry jail for four years and then been released. The uncle had married almost right away to a big country woman called Fidelma, who had visited him in jail. She had set him up in a wee corner grocery shop and forbidden him to so much as speak to any of his former comrades, let alone have anything to do with politics. And there he had remained. A frightened, dominated little man until his death in 1975.

He had only once talked of Swanzey in that entire time, 53 years. That was to Brian Artur and another nephew at a particularly drunken wake which he had attended while Fidelma was away nursing a sick relative. All those years he had been frightened. Frightened that the Loyalists would find out that he had been the hit man and come to his shop and kill him, but frightened even more that the wife would find out what he had done before he met her.

She'd known all along, of course. She said as much to Brian Artur at the uncle's funeral. "He was a hardworking wee man," she had said, as she poured out the tea and brushed aside Brian Artur's ritual condolences, "and he was heart scared of me, which is how it should be. Sure didn't I have to put up with living with an ex-gunman all those years. It wouldn't have been right if I'd let him enjoy himself. Sure aren't we put upon this earth to be punished in some way or other."

She was a hard woman. And a hardworking woman. Dour and devout. An Ulster woman. I better end now, I think I hear the wife coming in. Still and all, when I read in the papers about some assassination and the brutal beady-eyed psychopathic killers, I occasionally think back to that old pensioner in the bar. Republican folklore has it that Swanzey was shot with MacCurtain's own personal gun which had been sent up from Cork. I wonder where it is now?

POPULAR PETROL-USERS' SLOGAN

NORMAN II

Years ago I wrote a poignant tale entitled 'Norman' about the dimmest Intelligence Officer the Republican movement ever had in the fair city of Derry. Some of my few faithful stalwart fans have since accused me, ever so politely, of having invented Norman, their reasoning being that no one could be that stupid. I have always rather resented that but there was little or nothing I could do about it until I finally made the move and relocated from Sodom and Begorrah beside the Bay to the former oak grove known as Doire or Derry. Last month I arrived there with my esteemed translator CK, who also happened to be a Norman sceptic.

For those of you who have bothered to follow the events in our wee Ulcer for the past few years it will come as no surprise to learn that the war is over and the good guys lost. Changed, changed, a terrible ugliness is born as Yeats might have put it if he hadn't been wrapped up in his Celtic fascist little dreams. Now it's Brit supermarkets and garish nightclubs and crapulous Techno blaring from every shop, apartment and Walkman with its cacophonous repetitive malign zombifying malice stupefying the punters. It has been long established – right back as far as the Romans, that if you can't give the deprived punters bread you give them circuses – and the circuses resemble Duffys rather than Barnum and Bailey or Ringling Brothers. But of course, as usual, I digress.

Some things never change however, and, a mere half an hour after hitting the Maiden City – so called because in 1689 the gallant Apprentice boys slammed the City gates to prevent the mad Papishes from ravaging their fair city – for which we are still grateful, for do we not burn Lundy in effigy in the main square every year? Do we loyal sons of Ulster not march down the Garvaghy road in the spirit of Drumcree every year – oh dear! not this year – we were in the Bogside.

Anyway, no sooner had I, with my faithful Teutonic witness, entered the dim fastness of the Dungloe bar than I recognized two of Derry's finest unsung heroes, Thomas and Seamus, the source of my Norman stories. They were older now, though surely no wiser. They had fought the good fight for the revolution and lost – as had we all. It was four years since I had seen them but it was as if t'wer only yesterday.

"Where have you been you fat bastard! You owe us two pints." It was good to be back. Nonetheless there was a pall of gloom over what was normally a happy and convivial crowd. "What's the craic?" I ventured, old journalistic habits dying hard.

"You mean you haven't heard?" sneered Thomas. "I thought you reporters knew everything." "Ah shure he's been away in Amerikay," said Seamus, surreptitiously signalling for two more pints. "He can't be expected to have heard the scéal." "What scéal?" I asked, as naive as ever.

"About PUGI! Sure hasn't he gone and got anal syphilis." At this stage I suppose I should explain that PUGI was our friendly acronym for Phil the Unemployed Greek Idler aka Chuckie Enba aka His Royal Highness Prince Phillip our wee Elizabrit's old man, though judging by the look of herself it would be a fair bet that Phil hasn't been slipping her any for at least forty years – still, wasn't she herself artificially conceived because her Da Georgie VI couldn't get it up way back then.

Anal syphilis! Some of the punters unconsciously and surreptitiously groped at their few remaining and shrunken testicles or scratched their bums. "I bet that hurts worse than haemorrhoids," vouchsafed Paddy who knew all about Preparation H and the uses to which it could be put. "Serves the bastard right for swanning around with all those sailors," sneered Joe, a dyed in the wool anti-monarchist, the man who had sent Prince Chuckie, old big ears himself, a jigsaw puzzle of his uncle Lord Mountbatten after that terrible day in Mullaghmore.

Gloom descended upon the congregation. My intrepid Kraut partner who had been attempting to follow this arcane conversation with some difficulty was not to be sidetracked however. The company did not intimidate her though they still scared the shit out of me at times, for I could remember the days not too long in the past when it was easier to get a gun than a drink in Belfast and in the fair city of Derry these middle aged men had been only kids with Kalashnikovs, guarding the barricades of Free Derry and driving round in hi-jacked Staff Cars. "Can you confirm for me that this bastard has been lying all these years about someone called Norman who allegedly used to operate with you terrorists." There was a brief silence while some of the punters appeared to think over whether they objected to being called terrorists or even former terrorists by some German Sprocket. Thomas, who, in his time probably had as much blood on his hands as many a Nobel peace prize winner, appeared to be about to take umbrage but Seamus, ever the pragmatist, summoned two more pints, at our expense and turned his pointilliste bloodshot little eyes on my Kraut Kompanion. "What are you blethering about Fräulein, sure isn't that the boul Norman sitting over there in the corner." I peered through the haze of nicotine, which seemed also to have the odd odor of reefer about it – Ah, changed times in the Dungloe, where are ye Hookie now that we need ye? Sure enough, unless my beady little orbs deceived me – and, to be fair they were known to do that on the odd occasion, there at the very end of the bar he sat. Norman Morrison. Norman the bampot. Former, albeit briefly, Intelligence Officer of the nameless but feared.

Proudly I steered my companion down to the end of the grimy bar and made an attempt to introduce myself. Norman looked up from his pint. "Sure don't I know ye'. You're that Belfast bastard who said all them cruel things about me. Lies, a pack of lies. And after all I done for the cause. There's just no honour left." He supped his Guinness morosely. "Sure a prophet is without honour in his own country." Down the other end of the bar Joe and the boys snickered. We rejoined them hastily.

"Get the whiskeys in, McGuffin, and we'll tell you some real Norman stories." And so they did.

For those of you who did not have the pleasure or misfortune to read the first book of Norman some brief introduction is necessary.

First, it must be said, Norman was a Prod. A tame Prod. A wannabe bona fide Irish Republican Revolutionary. An amalgam of Wolfe Tone and Che Guevara. And amongst the Loyal Brethren with whom he grew up on the Waterside this was not a realistic ambition. The average UDA hit man in one of the little streets where the kerbside is painted red, white and blue to cheer up the visually challenged amongst them, if asked, would probably assert that Wolfe Tone sold ice-cream and that Che had just been signed for Chelsea.

As Jack Butler has said, work was invented to channel drudgery, to put all the shit in one place and keep it away from the fun stuff. To give people something tangible to blame the boredom on. That's why the people you work with are idiots and dipshits so you can go home and live with nice people. Of course a lot of people are unclear on this concept and go home and live with idiots and dipshits. This was Norman's situation. And so, one day in the 1970s he had quit his mundane job in the meat packing factory, walked out of the family home with its red, white and blue kerbside and its limp butcher's apron fluttering from the telegraph pole and joined the great Diaspora. For most Catholics – or taigs as Norman's lovely siblings would have, and still do, call them, this would entail a trek to the building site in Birmingham or, if you had a long lost cousin in the Bronx, a cheapo Aer Cunninglingus plane ride to the Big Apple. For Norman it was a bit easier. All he had to do was walk over the Craigavon Bridge and find a disused slum in which to squat in the Bogside. And that was how his long night of the soul began.

In those days the Provos were not too keen to recruit a hun from the Waterside but other opportunities were at hand, for in the heady days of 'Free Derry' (with every six pack of Guinness) there existed the NBF – the nameless but feared, an intrepid band of fervent left wing revolutionaries who had evolved out of the DYH – Derry Young Hooligans. It was they and the dispossessed lumpenproletariat who had kept the RUC rioters out of the Bogside and set up and manned the barricades armed only with sticks and stones and the peoples' weapon for which they daily and dutifully thanked the late Comrade Molotov. By the time Norman took his big trip on the road to Damascus, or at least the Creggan, the days of 'throw well, throw Shell' were almost history. The bhoys now had real guns and real explosives. This was pre-Semtex of course but the narrow little streets of Derry reverberated daily and nightly to the sounds of urban renewal in the form of five hundred pounders demolishing the commercial centre and robbing the fair maiden city of her innocence. To the NBF the acquisition of a tame Prod was a matter of some kudos. Belfast had its Ronnie Bunting Junior, a Prod who had joined the Republican movement. Now the Derry NBF had Norman.

This, of course, as Thomas was to point out to me years later, was a two edged weapon, for although Norman was keen and dedicated to the cause he was an incorrigible head-the-ball.

"Did you get those whiskeys in yet, you miserable Belfast bastard?" queried Seamus. It was a rhetorical question. The bartender had already set the company up and was hovering over me for payment. "Did I ever tell you about Norman and the thermos?"

It had been a long week for the leadership of the NBF. They were awaiting supplies of gear from Donegal and planning the next ops but every day a zealous Norman was pestering them for some action. It was then that Thomas hit upon the plan. They would make Norman the I/O – Intelligence Officer. Give him a staff car and send him to patrol around the sanctum of Free Derry to 'suss out targets' and locate spies and report on anything suspicious. This had a double advantage, it would keep Norman off their backs and give the Britz on the City walls with their infra red binoculars and hi-tech surveillance equipment something to look at and record.

And so it came to pass. Three of the younger recruits from the DYH, fearless street fighters in their own right but even dimmer than Norman were instructed to hi-jack a 'staff car' and, at 11 a.m. pick up the new I/O and drive him around the Bogside every morning. Young Spider was the driver and Malachy and Aidan sat in the back seat, fingering an ancient parabellum and a modern Walther, formerly the property of Constable Sammy Campbell RUC, RIP. As Jerusalem Slim aka Our Blessed Lord used to say 'I come not to bring peace but with a piece'. Something like that – I think it's in the new trendy revised edition but probably not the Douai version.

Aidan jumped out of the car and rang the doorbell of the shabby flat in Clarendon Street where Norman was squatting. Norman emerged into the drizzling rain of a typical Derry day. He was immaculately attired in a pinstripe suit, stolen from the local haberdasher – and this was long before days of Gerry Adams and Chucky Armani – and sporting a British Army regimental tie, purchased at a bring and buy sale. A pair of steel rimmed glasses glinted from his nose. He carefully carried a thermos flask. He nodded politely to the bhoys and stepped into the front passenger seat. "Where to?" asked Spider, the driver. "Let's just start by going up to Rosemount and then maybe taking a run out to Shantallow." Norman spoke laconically but authoritatively. He knew it was important to establish his hierarchical status with these young volunteers.

"Your word is my command, Oh learned one," muttered Spider as he edged the brand new Cortina up the street towards the Northland Road. The drive proceeded uneventfully at first. There weren't too many people about. The bars and bookies weren't open yet and most punters didn't have to sign on the dole until the early afternoon. Norman wedged the thermos between his thighs and took cryptic notes in a Woolworth's diary. In the back Malachy and Aidan were bored but at least they were dry. Suddenly Malachy nudged Aidan. Every time the Cortina went over a ramp or had to skirt a burnt out car, Norman would clutch his thermos flask. Malachy's mind was beginning to work overtime. He'd never trusted Norman – he was from the Waterside wasn't he, and no matter what the Socialist Revolutionary leadership might say that still made him a bluenose. Suddenly it all became clear. They were on a suicide mission. This mad Prod was carrying the nitro. He flashed back to that old movie which he'd seen on the box the other night. What was it called? 'The Wages of Fear!' That was it. These loonies bouncing around South American roads with a cargo of bleeding and weeping gelly. And what about those camel jockeys in Beirut. Suicide bombers the lot of them.

He and Aidan began to pay more attention to Norman. A lot more attention. Spider swung down around Foyle Springs and prepared to head for the Buncrana road. The rain started to come down in torrents. As Spider wiped the windscreen, ahead of them loomed the impossible. It looked like a Brit roadblock. That wasn't in the script. The Britz never ventured as close to the Bog as this. Spider attempted a U-turn but the Cortina slithered in the mud and stalled. Malachy and Aidan hastily tried to stuff their weapons under the back seat but it was a new car and they'd neglected to slit the seat lining. Spider spun the wheels in a frantic effort to get off side. Norman beamed cherubically and picked up the thermos flask. As he began to unscrew the top Malachy collapsed in a babbling heap and Aidan shit himself.

"Cup of tea, anyone?" asked Norman blithely pouring out the Earl Grey into the thermos top. The Brit roadblock turned out to be three rain sodden cows but it was the last time any of the volunteers travelled with Norman. Or used the odiferous staff car.

Seamus seized the time to order another round of nippy sweeties at my expense. From the shadows came a sepulchral voice. It had an accent more redolent of the Ganges than the Foyle. It was Ahmad, Derry's very own Pakistani. "You think Norman is funny?" he asked. "Norman not funny, he bloody dangerous." "Is it yourself, Ahmad?" queried Thomas, peering through the gloom. "I know it's been a few years but don't you owe us something for that wee job we did for youse a while back?" "I no owe you anything Thomas, you promised me your best operator and you gave me that bampot." He pointed down the bar towards Norman who sat there oblivious of being the subject of our reminiscences. "He nearly kill me." Thomas pondered this indignant protest and, fair man that he was and is, agreed that on balance Ahmad was all square with the NBF. It was only after their erstwhile Pakki chum had downed his pint and shuffled off that Paddy told me the story. It's a touching story really, of hands across the sea and international co-operation. But it's Ahmad's story and it's Norman's story. Of course.

Ahmad had come to Derry back in the early 1970s. The ne'er-do-well son of a wealthy merchant he had been banished to Derry to expand the burgeoning family empire. To that endeavour he had opened Derry's first nightclub – 'The Pride of Pakistan' on the Strand Road. 'Nightclub' was perhaps a little too pretentious a title for the premises and I doubt that James Bond or the glitterati would have deemed it such had they ever had occasion to set foot in it, but in Derry it masqueraded as a nightclub because, after the necessary palm greasing Ahmad had convinced the City Council and the Royal Ulster Constabulary to grant him an extended liquor license. In those far bygone days bars had to close at 11 p.m. Sure there were shebeens where men desperate for a gargle after hours could congregate with little fear of being raided by the cowardly RUC but all too often these not so illustrious establishments were prone to being visited by the bold Martin McGuinness and his Pioneer pals who frowned on alcohol at the best of times let alone three o'clock in the morning on the Lecky Road, and who were known to make their displeasure felt in no uncertain terms.

And so the Pride of Pakistan, for a short time at least, provided an alternative for those upon who the great thirst descended after midnight. It had the advantage of being near the RUC barracks and therefore less likely to receive a visit from Armalite toting Provos. And the RUC had been bought off. For almost two years the P of P, if not flourishing at least made a small profit from the hookers and insomniac alcoholics who frequented it. Ahmad the neer-do-well of course squandered any profit on the whores, the horses and the gargle as any stranger in a strange land would do and inevitably the telegram had arrived from Ahmad Senior that the venture was to be shut down and sold for whatever Junior could get for the kip.

Property values were not of course exactly cresting in those days as the 'urban renewal' hitherto referred to continued to rock the town. Nowadays MCP stands for male chauvinist pig, in those days it stood for 'make car parks'. But Ahmad was ambitious. He would show Pater that this Pakki was made of sterner stuff than to easily capitulate to the market forces. 'Jewish lightning' immediately came to mind. Ahmad however was no torch. Arson was beyond his ken and explosives as mysterious as the Derry dialect.

Shrewd, or not so shrewd businessman that he was he did the obvious thing. He contacted Thomas and the NBF. "How much would a good torch job cost?" The insurance wouldn't be much but the good old Brit taxpayer could be relied on to fork out a hefty bit of compo. Nae bother to the NBF who always needed the odd readies to refurbish the old arsenal. "I'll put my best men on it," Thomas had promised. And Thomas had really meant to, or so he told me many years later. But on the night in question some emergency had come up, as they have an annoying habit of doing and Thomas and the A team had had to go over the border on a run. That left Norman and young Dekesey.

The Pride of Pakistan closed early that night and ten minutes after the last punter had drifted off into the mean streets the battered red door on the ground floor burst open and a masked Norman and Dekesey entered waving a short at Ahmad. Ahmad took control. "All right, tie me up and make a good job of it," he ordered. "Did you bring the petrol?" "Shit!" exclaimed Dekesey, "I knew we'd forgotten something." "Never mind," snapped Norman, "you go and get some gas (Norman had been reading too many American crime novels) and I'll tie this heathen up." The original plan had been that Ahmad would be loosely bound, petrol scattered and set alight and Ahmad would free himself and emerge from the soon to be engulfed in flames building and present himself down the road at the RUC station as yet another innocent victim of the men of violence.

Mentally thumbing through the pages of his memory banks which related to knot tying as a boy scout amongst the late Lord Baden Powell's proud band of pederasts, Norman trussed the unprotesting Ahmad to a chair and exited down the street to a bar which shall be nameless since it yet stands and actually still is prepared to serve your honourable scribe.

He settled down with a pint and awaited Dekesey. Ten minutes later he arrived, sat himself down and demanded a pint to wash away the taste of the recently syphoned petrol. "Alles in Ordnung?" inquired Norman, the aspiring linguist. "Ye what?" replied the Bogside man. "Did ye do the job?" queried Norman, looking out the darkened window up the street at the corner of the P of P where as yet no mighty conflagration was making its presence felt.

"Sure," replied Dekesey swilling down another Guinness. This arson was thirsty work. "Didn't I slosh a whole gallon around the floor." Norman was thinking ahead. "You did remember to throw a match on it, didn't you?" he asked accusingly. Norman may have been accused of being a head-the-ball but he knew that Dekesey was an even dimmer lightbulb. "Wha? Nah! That was supposed to be your job," was the insubordinate response.

Never send a boy on a man's errand! Getting up as inconspicuously as possible Norman prepared to make an unobtrusive exit. Unfortunately he drew some attention to himself by tripping over Derek the Blinky's guide dog which bit him savagely on the left ankle. Muttering the odd Biblical imprecation Norman hobbled into the night. Blending into the shadows he hirpled down to the corner. A passing car light transfixed him in its glare and he froze. The car passed by and Norman, deciding that time was of the essence hastily pushed open the door of the P of P and tossed in a box of lighted Swan Vestas. He was rewarded by a gratifying 'whump'. He sat over his third pint down the road, insisting that Dekesey pay since it had been his fuck up in the first place, then he joined the spectators as they watched the Fire Brigade futilely trying to extinguish the inferno. (I had originally written 'holocaust' here but was reluctantly persuaded by my horrified German comrades to change it.)

Suddenly there was a stir in the bar. Although fire(s) were nothing new to them it wasn't every night that you see a screaming Pakistani tightly bound to a smouldering chair, lurching into your local hostelry.

Ahmad, for it was indeed the Pride of Pakistan himself, tripped over the guide dog, showering sparks all around him. The bar owner threw a jug of water over him, extinguishing the flames. "What the fuck do you think you're doing Ahmad! Nobody here ordered a shish kebab let alone a döner."

"I knew we'd forgotten something," muttered Dekesey. "It's all your fault, Norman. Some fucking I/O you are." When the A team returned from deeds of derring-do and Thomas learned that the singed Pakistani was not too keen on paying the agreed upon fee Thomas had no option but to sack Norman. For a time Norman was as welcome as a fart in an astronaut's suit, but time heals all wounds and indeed wounds all heels. Ahmad finally got the compo and opened another 'nightclub' in Protestant Coleraine. It was called 'Bhutto's revenge'.

It was the late lamented (or demented) Arthur Schopenhauer who said (on the Gay Byrne Late Late Show if I'm not mistaken but I probably am):

'Jede Nation lacht über die anderen – und sie haben recht' – or for those of you not as familiar with the Teutonic tongue 'every nation laughs at the other nation – and they are right'.

Poor Ahmad. Poor Norman. May the senile delinquent have mercy on us all whether we deserve it or not.

We left the Dungloe in a haze of alcohol and nostalgia. I had attempted once more to introduce my Sprockett partner to Norman but he had merely cast a baleful eye on me and spat out – "I know ye, McGuffin, you're just another failed tame Prod like meself." Fair play, Norman. Fair play.

I do so hope that PUGI didn't give any of that old anal syphilis to Her Majesty – or indeed, the Corgis. It sounds nasty.

GLOSSARY

As a service for the linguistically challenged we present this brief glossary

Bampot	An idiot
Bangers	Nerves ('Bangor Reserves' – also nickname of Danny Morrison)
Barking	Raving mad
Bash	Drinking binge
Bint	Woman
Black Hack	Falls Road taxi
Bluenose	Protestant
Cúchulainn	Former heroic champion of Ulster
Cumann	(Ir) Irish society
Croppies	Rebellious Catholics
Dig (w/wrong foot)	Belong to inappropriate religious faith
Doddle	Easy
Doodle Bug	Peoples' weapon. Molotov cocktail
Dole	Unemployment money
Double dunt	Two weeks unemployment money
Eaksie peaksie	(Fake Ulster 'Gailans') see 'Wee buns'
Eejit	see bampot
Emmett	Robert. Irish patriot, executed 1804
Everton	Suburb of Liverpool full of Orange bigots and pigs

Far East	Priest
Fash	(Scot) Concern, worry
Fenian	see Croppies
Fianna	(Ir) Youth movement of IRA
Flowery Dell	Prison Cell
Garda(í)	Irish police
Gargle	Drink
Gauger	Customs inspector
Get	Progeny – abusive
Gombeen	Money grubbing Irish Kapitalist and loan shark
Half-Inched	Pinched, stolen
Head-the-ball	see bampot
Hirple	Limp
Homer	Moonlighting job
Hood	Petty criminal
I/O	Intelligence Officer
Jobbie	A turd
Jobbie-wheaker	An instrument to remove jobbies
Jumper	Bus inspector
Kafflik	Catholic
Kathleen ni Houlihan	Mother Ireland
Kneecapping	Restorative Justice
Long Kesh	Brit concentration camp near Lisburn
Malacca	Wanker
Melt	The spleen of a slaughtered animal
Mitch	Play truant
Molucate	Massacre
Moonlight flit	Abscond without paying rent
Mucker	(Derry) Friend
Mundies	Cheap South African red wine, used by winos (especially for armed combat)
Nixers	see homers

O/C	Officer in command (IRA)
Omadaun	(Ir) see bampot
Pallatic	see stocious
Pioneers	Irish temperance organization
Poitín	Illegal moonshine whiskey
Porter	Guinness
Punt	To gamble, also an Irish pound
Sarnie	Sandwich
Scéal	(Ir) Gossip, rumour
Scratcher	Bed
Sediki	(Arabic) 'my friend', i.e. illegal alcohol
Segocia	(Ir) see mucker
Shebeen	Illegal drinking den
Sheugh	Ditch
Simmet	Vest
Slats	Ribs
Sodality	Pious religious Catholic group
Stale Bun	Nun
Stocious	Steaming, pallatic, full as a sheugh
Supergrass	tout
Taig/Teague	see croppie
Teac Ban	(Ir) literally 'White House'
Táin Bó	Legendary white bull of Ulster, stolen by Maeve's men
Tirconnel	Donegal
Tube	Television or bampot
Twalf/Twelfth July	Triumphalist Orange march day
Uncle Robert	Bob Hope = dope = marihuana
Uxters	Armpits
Weans	Young children
Wee Buns	Easy
Wellies	Rubber boots much favored by the Royal family when shooting grice and the SAS when shagging sheep
Whitehouse, Mary	Puritanical Brit television censor

Also by the author:

Internment, Anvil Books, Tralee 1973

The Guineapigs, Penguin, London 1974

In Praise of Poitín, Appletree Press, Belfast 1978, 1988, 1999

Tales from the Barricades, McNally&Loftin, Santa Barbara 1990

Der Hund, Edition Nautilus, Hamburg 1990

Der Mann, der mit Chuck Berry getanzt hat, Edition Nautilus, Hamburg 1992

Der Fette Bastard, Edition Nautilus, Hamburg 1996

IRISH RESISTANCE BOOKS

Irish Resistance Books will publish the books that the straight publishers won't. We intend to publish books on Irish history, primarily from a Republican and Socialist standpoint. In addition we hope to publish books on local history, prison memoirs, new Irish fiction, subversive texts, rants, the Irish Diaspora, and whatever is progressive and can't find a 'commercial' publisher. Immodestly we see ourselves as one of the very few groups out there who are attempting to write and assemble a true people's history of 'the troubles'. We won't publish any politicians' ghost written memoirs. We will record the working class' history, warts and all, and we will continue to name and shame the enemies of freedom.

We also want to produce and sell CDs of 'alternative' music – songs which have been censored for years, artists who aren't 'acceptable' to the main stream. Additionally, we hope to publish art work, murals, cartoons, video documentaries and posters. We unashamedly nail our colours to the mast.

That shameless old lexicographer Dr. Johnson castigated 'patrons' as 'wretches who support with insolence and are paid with flattery' (that didn't stop the old hypocrite from accepting a healthy pension from mad old King George III for 20 years). We however are not recipients of monarchical, governmental or indeed any largesse and welcome esteemed patrons such as perhaps your good selves. And if you have a book which you think we might be interested in and no one else will publish, contact us.

We take our philosophy from the 'Father of All Historians' the great Herodotus. In the 5th century BC he succinctly laid down the historian's function.

> 'Very few things happen at the right time, and the rest do not happen at all; the conscientious historian will correct these defects.'

And, it must be said – 'amnesia is the handmaiden of hypocrisy' – which is basically what George Santayana meant when he wrote: 'Progress, far from consisting in change, depends on retentiveness. Those who cannot remember the past are doomed to fulfil it.'
Irish Resistance Books concurs and will attempt to encapsulate these views.

The Skibbereen Eagle is Alive and Well and Nests in Derry